Echoes in the Storm

by

Debra Jupe

The Echo Series, Book 2

Echoes in the Storm

Cover Art by *Diana Carlile*

The Wild Rose Press, Inc.
PO Box 708
Adams Basin, NY 14410-0708
Visit us at www.thewildrosepress.com

Publishing History
First Crimson Rose Edition, 2020
Print ISBN 978-1-5092-2853-9
Digital ISBN 978-1-5092-2854-6

The Echo Series, Book 2
Published in the United States of America

"Doesn't matter what we do at this point. The bottom line is you didn't confide in me on something that really mattered to you until you were ready to burst." His manner calmed. "Or make the reason clear as to why you felt the need to move forward at this particular time. So, I didn't get a chance to tell you."

"Tell me what?"

"I may not've been ready to move to where you were in that moment, but I wasn't going anywhere. I was working toward it, because I wanted forever with you."

Their gazes locked. Darla's mind froze. The air thickened as the diminutive cabin shrank. For a second, a familiar glint brightened in his eyes. The sexy tease he used to taunt her, right before he kissed her. His look ignited a deep-seated hunger inside her.

"I wanted forever with you, too," she softly confessed. "I guess I was ahead of you."

He broke their visual link. "I guess." His inflection reverted back to its harshness, demolishing their tender moment. "You shouldn't have waited until this problem consumed you. It made you impulsive and dump me in an all-out brawl."

"Terminating our relationship wasn't pre-determined. It happened in the heat of the moment."

"Really? I think it was stashed somewhere in the back of your mind."

"It was not."

"Okay, how about this? You just accused me of disrespecting you and what we had. You did too. You didn't believe in me or us."

Dedication

Margaritas and desserts always taste better with your bestie! This book is dedicated to my sister from another mother, Linda.

I'm not sure how I was lucky enough to have such a dedicated, supportive friend in my life. I'm so grateful for the 40+ years of fun, friendship, and fabulous sisterhood.

This one's for you, dear sister. Many thanks for the past years and the many great ones ahead.

Other Wild Rose Press Titles by Debra Jupe:

Echoes in the Wind
Tomorrow Doesn't Matter Tonight
Toxic
Afraid to Breathe

Chapter 1

"I'm getting married today," Darla's best friend, Stephanie screeched when she entered the dressing room. Stephanie's hands swayed in the air as she awkwardly scuttled toward Darla.

"Can you believe it?" Arms wrapped around Darla's shoulders and squeezed, binding her into a stifling hug. "Today's my wedding day."

Darla returned Stephanie's embrace. She flashed a semi-grin, trying to ignore the fact she was five-foot seven and dressed like an ambulatory blueberry, and still be happy for her friend. "Yep, Steph. You and Blaine are tying the knot in about thirty minutes." Her smile widened. "I can't wait."

A ripple of melancholy swept through her the moment the words left her mouth. She *was* excited for them. Darla loved them both, she really did. Thanks to Blaine's busy schedule, the engaged duo put an eighteen month hold on their nuptials. They were more than ready to become husband and wife. But she didn't lie when she said she couldn't wait. She couldn't wait until the evening ended. Her gaze trailed Stephanie, who pattered to a full-length mirror and swished her poufy, white gown side to side.

For many reasons.

Stephanie stared into the glass. Her animated expression grew concerned. "You're okay, aren't you,

Dar?"

Darla forced a brave laugh and smoothed the ruffles on her dress, straining not to make a face. She paced to a nearby loveseat and lowered to sit. "I'm fine. I'm super-excited for you. You're about to become Mrs. Blaine Stewart, wife of mega-band Spiraling UP's bass guitarist, slash co-songwriter, while *I* get to stay at a lush, Tluq Cay Island Resort a whole week and frolic with the rich and fabulous." She twisted a wayward curl around her forefinger. "All expenses paid."

Stephanie elevated her gown's hem and toddled to Darla, her high heels hammering into the floor tiles.

She sank onto a cushion beside her. "You're positive you aren't too miserable? Your breakup happened just three months ago, and your wounds are still fresh. You're a little blue, aren't you?"

"More than you realize, but today's about you, not me. You're my closest friend. I'm overjoyed you and Blaine are formally committing to each other. I'm also thrilled you included me in your special day."

"I'm glad you're delighted, but you may not stay so pleased. I have to tell you something." Corners of Steph's mouth tensed. "A teeny, tiny, ever so slight glitch might've come up."

"Might've or did?"

"Did. Definitely did."

"Okaaay, spill."

"Blaine's brother fell off a horse this past Thursday. He was knocked unconscious and fractured his leg in two places. The leg injury required emergency surgery. He's okay now, but obviously, he's unable to travel, nor can he perform his best man duties."

"Wow, too bad." Darla didn't quite grasp Steph's dramatics, but whatever. "No worries. I can do the precession unescorted."

Anxiety flickered across her friend's face. "Um…no. You won't walk alone. Blaine chose a substitute. He made arrangements as soon as he received word."

"Made arrangements with who?"

Stephanie's discomfort increased. She seemed opposed to revealing more.

An ominous stitch caught in Darla's chest. "Steph? Who did Blaine select to replace his brother?"

"Eric," she mumbled. "Eric's agreed to step in."

"No. Eric can't come. He has a prior commitment."

"Had a prior commitment. He's worked hard to find a way around his contract since he discovered promoters scheduled the Rockers Running for Autism benefit the same day we planned to marry."

"How can he back out when he's an event founder?"

"He took care of details up until today and found a replacement to finish his co-chairman obligations. He hopped a plane this morning." She paused uneasily. "It landed earlier, around noon."

Darla didn't respond. A tidal wave of tension surged. A spontaneous reunion with her ex-boyfriend, Eric Boyd, stirred her—the wrong way. His missing the Stewart-Duckworth nuptials had troubled everyone involved. Except her.

She felt downright giddy he couldn't come.

Now, not only had her reprieve suffered an equine malfunction, she and Eric would be required to stand five feet apart and feign graciousness during and after the ceremony.

"Dar? You're cool about this, aren't you?"

No, she didn't find a morsel of coolness regarding this situation, which Stephanie already knew. But today was her day, and Darla wouldn't spoil it.

She inhaled to summon the maturity she didn't feel. "Yes, Stephanie, I'm an adult. I can act normal a few hours." Her fingertips grazed her forehead to wipe away an imaginary line of perspiration. "I'm sure Eric can too."

Stephanie's mouth contorted. "I'm not so sure about Eric."

"He knows I'm in the bridal party, right?"

"Yes, but he doesn't realize we scaled our attendants down to one. You're my only, and he's Blaine's. Blaine didn't give him the head's up since we assumed he couldn't come."

"And Blaine hasn't corrected his assumption now that he can?"

Stephanie shook her head, having the decency to look guilty.

"You're sure that's a wise idea? He's a lot more hotheaded than me. He may storm off if we're the only two standing up front."

"He might. Unless…" Stephanie studied the massive diamond donning her third, left finger. "You still love him, don't you?"

Darla hedged, debating if she should give an honest answer or duck the question. Then again, Stephanie knew her, maybe too well. She was Darla's rock after Eric, and she split. She was attentive to all the gory details, no sense dodging her now.

"Of course, I do, but I'm royally pissed at him."

"No doubt your royally pissed sentiment is reciprocated." Stephanie looked optimistic. "Have you considered extending the proverbial olive branch to attempt a friendship—or possibly reconcile romantically?"

"Ummm, no. I didn't start this."

"This is behaving like a grownup? Not so much. Seriously, you can't say you don't have regrets."

Darla groaned, hating to admit her desire to relive the day they broke up and handle things differently, happened hourly. "I do. To a point. He erupted when I tried to have a reasonable conversation. His blow up caused me to get a little miffed."

"More than a little."

"Okay, I snapped." Relentless unhappiness she strived to leave behind crept front and center, settling deep into her gut. "Blame's mutual."

"As is compromise. Both of you are stubborn. You especially don't like to give in once your mind is made, even when you're wrong."

"You sound like Eric. You're supposed to be on my side."

"I am. Except you two wrecked an amazing relationship due to a stupid argument. You both walked away, and didn't consider the foundation you built, or the powerful love you share. In my opinion, you messed up." Her brows raised as she eyed Darla. "One of you ought to fix this."

"Not your decision."

"I'm aware. And I respect yours." Stephanie sighed and relaxed. "Despite gloomy statistics, I intend to marry just once. I don't expect today to be perfect, but I'd like everything to go as smooth as possible."

"I won't intentionally ruin anything," Darla hurried, a bit indignant. "If you think I will, I'll bow out and go as a guest."

"No, I want you to stand up for me." She adjusted her veil." Unless you don't want to?"

"Are you kidding? Of course, I want to. You're getting married, maid of honor is all I have."

"Crap. I'm acting like a bridezilla, aren't I?"

Darla repositioned Stephanie's headpiece to its original spot. "You're a typical, anxious bride."

"Just prepare yourself, and there won't be any surprises."

"I swear. I won't look at Eric during the service. I get we have to walk together at the end, but rules don't state we must touch. It's not necessary he lend me his arm." A panicky giggle slipped. "I can assure you we'll duck each other at the reception."

"I'm sure you'll avoid him." Stephanie faltered as she shot Darla a concerned look. "He brought two dates."

Darla's brow wrinkled. "Two?"

"Yes, he invited a pair of women as his guests."

This news shouldn't shock her. Since they separated, the popular Scottish band's lead guitarist, Eric Boyd's cheery photographs had been splashed on every major and minor media outlet. Most displayed his wild partying and womanizing ways, a lifestyle he'd resumed since he and Darla ended their relationship.

Photos of him attached to sexy actresses, gorgeous models, or spicy female singers who were practically salivating, draping themselves over him. He and the women were paraded across the entertainment markets. Stephanie constantly reminded her how these flashy, demonstrative females were quite opposite of Darla, a studious geologist, who earned her PhD a year ago.

"Apparently, he hooked up with them on his flight over."

"Classy."

"No, it's not." Stephanie shook her head and included a tsk. "It just shows how sad he is."

"Right. A double to one ratio date screams sadness. And you're suggesting I try to reconcile."

Stephanie flung a hand. "Those women are nobodies. He'd drop them in a heartbeat and come running back if you merely hinted you still wanted him."

"Come running back?" Darla cackled sarcastically. "You must be referring to another Eric Boyd. The one I know would never stoop to running to anyone."

"Fine, he'd have to be dragged kicking and screaming. But in the end, he'd be happy about it." Stephanie looked at her expectantly. "I'm not trying to make you feel awful, but Eric's hurt, and he's lonely. He tends to behave childish when he's upset. I'm worried how he'll act this evening."

"His inner four-year-old does emerge when he's angry. Still, he cares for you and thinks of Blaine as a brother. I might've insinuated otherwise, but I can't imagine him ruining your ceremony on purpose."

"You haven't been around him lately. Eric's a powder keg, and a raging fire is heading right at him. One rogue spark," Stephanie's arms circled above her head, "and KaBOOM." Her hands divided and dropped. "I'm petrified you'll inadvertently misstep, causing him to lose it."

"Perhaps Blaine should reconsider using him as his

best man."

"Blaine was extremely disappointed when Eric couldn't come, and then he went to such great lengths, so he could make it—Blaine's sorry over his brother's accident, but he's excited Eric's here. He preferred Eric as his best man, all along."

"I figured. I'll do what I can to *not* give him a reason to explode." Darla scooted off the couch to stand. "We should ditch this negativity." She offered a hand to Stephanie and tugged her to her feet. "Let's do one last check to make sure you're ready to become Mrs. Stewart."

Stephanie's semi-bland expression revived. "How's my make-up? Am I wearing enough blusher?"

"You're stunning."

Stephanie wandered back to the mirror and abruptly stopped. Again, she seemed apprehensive. "There's one more issue you may oughta worry about."

"A second problem?"

"Maybe. I'm not sure." She hesitated. "Morgan texted me today."

Another hitch jabbed into Darla. Only this catch was different, more incensed than apprehension. "My ex Morgan?"

Stephanie nodded.

"A little odd, I guess. But you were friends when we were going out. Kinda."

"Not so much after the jerk so harshly dumped you."

"Distant past. Why did he text you, and why may this be an issue?"

"I sort of phoned him first."

"Stephanie?"

"Let me clarify. I contacted his company. I want a big firework show before Blaine and I leave the reception. Morgan's business does pyrotechnics and the surrounding islands use his company a lot. I assumed he would send a representative to do the actual show only…" Stephanie's mouth twisted in the mirrored reflection, "he's personally handling the exhibition."

Darla inhaled as she silently deliberated, then blew out a thin stream of air. "I don't anticipate a problem. He works behind the scenes. Besides, a lot of people are invited to your wedding. Even if he makes an appearance, I doubt we'll run into each other."

"I'm not so sure. His text this morning was to congratulate Blaine and me. He also added he and his wife have divorced." She turned to Darla and scowled. "I mean, who does that? Why would anyone put they've ended their marriage in a wedding congrats? Seriously, what a downer."

"I'm assuming you didn't know about the split before you contacted him?"

"Of course, I didn't. Did you?"

"I don't keep up with Morgan. Hopefully, he'll do his job and leave. I'd hate to have to dodge him the entire week."

"I'm afraid he's hanging around a while," Stephanie revealed, worriedly. "Like I said, he frequently organizes displays on neighboring islands. The positive? He's not staying on Tluq Cay. The not so positive is he's on site tonight."

Flabbergasted, Darla searched her brain for a response. "Hmmm. I've got nothing."

"You might want to find something. I believe he clued me in on his deficient marital status because he's interested."

Darla's tongue skimmed her lips. "Interested in what?"

"Not what, who. You and Eric split…he and his wife split…" Stephanie's shoulder raised, "he's free, you're free. Do the math."

Darla and Morgan Wilmington III were a couple for four years. After he unofficially proposed, and their relationship pointed toward forever, his well-to-do parents intervened, insisting he wed a woman whose blood-lines matched closer to his lineages. The catch was if he disregarded their wishes, the substantial trust fund slated to appear on his thirtieth birthday would vanish.

For sake of maintaining the Wilmington dynasty, Morgan didn't give his parental stipulations a second thought, much less a first. He complied immediately, caving to his family's demands, and deserted Darla, barely bidding her a meager goodbye. Dust didn't get a chance to reconcile the crushing sendoff before he married his pre-chosen socialite six weeks later. The same night she met Eric.

Morgan didn't matter. Darla was long since done and indifferent to potential appearances, other than she would rather avoid him.

"His divorce doesn't surprise me," Darla declared. "He's served his time and has his cash. He doesn't need a socially prominent wife."

"Or he's fed-up, annoyed, and sprouted a backbone. Which is where you come in."

Darla grunted.

"Fine. But beware. The guy's sights are aimed on you."

"Seriously. Not a smidgen curious."

Stephanie's wedding coordinator stuck her head into the cozy space. "Close to show time, ladies. Maid of honor. You're on in five."

Darla grinned, giving a suddenly nervous Stephanie a quick squeeze. "Everything will be perfect." She scooped her spring bouquet off an entryway table and walked toward the door.

"The ring? You have Blaine's ring, don't you, Dar?"

She extended a thumb to disclose a silver circle surrounding her digit. "Never left my hand." She spun to leave. "See you at the altar."

Shoulders squared, she inhaled deep, exited outdoors, strolling to the venue's rear, until she took her place. Waiting for her prompt, she skimmed the lovely scenery in front of her.

White chairs faced a flowered archway, decorated in tropical blends. The pleasing, floral aroma drifted amidst the calm wafts, spreading sweet fragrances across the setting.

Beyond the arch, a sheer, turquoise ocean wavered effortlessly above coral sands. A subtle breeze glided off the water, enough to drive away the day's heat, while the brilliant orange sun descended beneath the skyline, and completed a flawless picture.

Music started to play. On cue, Darla sauntered across a silky, jade path, scanning the audience. Numerous rock and roll monarchs and music powerhouses sat speckled among relatives and friends. Finn O'Conner, a former bandmate of Eric and Blaine's, was seated near the podium, performing enchanted Celtic melodies on a set of pipes.

In front, standing by the minister, handsome and carefree, was Eric Boyd. The love of Darla's life. A familiar lump molded inside her throat and stole her breath. In mere moments, she broke her promise to Stephanie, and her view segregated to focus only on him. Layers of his dark hair tossed in the gentle winds. The deep blue in his eyes matched the sky and darted in every direction but hers.

Her heart sank as she advanced toward him. Regardless of Stephanie's bleak analysis, he gave the impression he was doing just fine without her. Careful not to expose her sorrow, she kept her pasted smile in hold as her fists choked the flower stems in a trembling clutch. She pivoted left, nodded at the cleric, and braved a final glance Eric's way.

Disinterested, he didn't engage and stared straight ahead.

The livelier Celtic tunes modified to a subdued bridal march. Invitees turned in their seats waiting for Blaine's parents to escort him in. Finn played through the complete track. The walkway remained vacant. Stretching, he peered across the grassy grounds and replayed the song.

Nothing.

Finn's composition carried into a third set. The reverend shifted from one foot then to the other, his mouth pressed into a distressed frown. Darla dared another glimpse in Eric's direction. He abandoned his nonchalant bravado and frantically scoured the site.

A subtle chatter rumbled among the attendees. Guests' heads cranked further as Darla combed through the sea of people again. No one was marching down the aisle to get married. Something was wrong.

A sudden shrill erupted from the rear. Everyone quieted.

"Nooo," came a succeeding high-pitched scream.

Finn stopped his performance and bolted off his perch. He overextended his neck to catch a glimpse of what was happening.

Blaine's father burst past the cabana's opening and jogged across the passage. The guests' murmurs escalated. Mr. Stewart halted in front. He stood silent several seconds, and stared at nothing, his shocked expression hard to miss. Finally, he raised his arms and waved overhead.

The noise subsided.

"Thank-you for coming." He flipped a handkerchief out of his lapel pocket and mopped his beaded temples. "Can't say anything...a setback's developed...the marriage is..." He cleared his throat and straightened. "I'm sorry to announce, the wedding...the wedding has been cancelled."

Chapter 2

Stephanie and Blaine called off their wedding? This had to be a prank or a bad joke. Possibly a family member's lame attempt at humor?

Darla studied Blaine's dad. His sorrowful expression didn't reveal a hint of hilarity. Nor were any of the guests in on the gag. Stunned faces conveyed this was no stunt, but the real deal. Blaine and Stephanie were done.

Except, they loved each other. Either of them cancelling seemed insane and breaking up on their wedding day amplified the lunacy. Something unimaginable must have happened. Blaine's father swayed his arms above his head. The rowdiness quietened. "Both families are aware you spent your time and money on a trip to visit the Turquoise Archipelago to witness Blaine and Stephanie's union take place, which regrettably won't happen.

"A reception and meal are scheduled. A band's been booked to perform, and a dance floor is provided. As a way of thanking you, we invite everyone to stay and enjoy the festivities."

The hotel manager appeared at Mr. Stewart's side and whispered something in his ear. Blaine's dad's appearance became more alarmed. He pointed to a bar. "Liquor's on the house. Help yourself."

Swiftly, he and the other man disappeared.

The crowd scattered. Volume levels erupted. Many were enthusiastic to accept the invite to imbibe and rushed to guzzle unlimited amounts of alcohol.

Others hustled to a lavish buffet spread and loaded their plates. A few scurried to the dessert table, primed to consume a slice of custom-made, six-foot-tall cake, donned with buds and blooms, harvested from the islet's botanical wilderness.

Darla chose none of the above. Stephanie would need her. Even if she had called off the wedding, not marrying Blaine would devastate her.

She spun toward the rear, eager to rush back to the dressing room. But she didn't sprint across the venue as she anticipated. A swarm of warm bodies blocked every route leading to the bridal quarters, converting her hurry up mode into inoperative.

She left the dais, anyway, and barged ahead, invading the mass. Regardless of the constant roadblocks, she had to get to Steph.

As suspected, her progression was sluggish. She ducked, zigzagged, and stopped many times until reaching halfway. The massive crowd at the bar waylaid her. The area was jammed, stagnated by people lined around the counter, packed in multiple rows.

Darla rose to her tiptoes to locate an alternate course, then lowered to her feet. Too much gray matter obstructed her view. She half-turned to look in another direction and froze.

Eric strolled into her peripheral. Her heart exploded. Rhythmed beats pounded inside her ears and drowned out the noisiness around her.

Then a willowed, over-processed blonde, and a curvy, bottled redhead joined him. Blondie blew him constant air kisses, and red had superglued her fingers around his upper arm. Eric divided a sexy smile between them as both beamed brighter than the afternoon sunshine.

Jealousy pounced and dug its steely claws into Darla's gut. Of course, those two women were excited. They'd hit the rock and roll jackpot and nabbed a primo rock star for a weekend. Never mind they had to share.

Darla inhaled to calm herself. She loathed her inability to control her resentment, but there it was. Nothing would stop it. Detesting her envy, she veered away so not to see.

But she ought to do more than visually avoid the scene. She should leave. Depart. Exit. Vamoose. Prevent a public meltdown and avoid placing her heart on the chopping block.

Instead, she realigned and glided her chin across her shoulder. The green talons burrowed in deeper.

Eric had curled an arm around each woman's waist, and tugged them close, their foreheads drawn together. Moments later, they separated, wearing broad grins, intermingled among sly glimpses.

The muscles in Darla's face tightened. Observing his antics in photographs was awful enough, but awful enough didn't compare to witnessing him operate live and in person.

Unable to stand this nauseating coziness any longer, Darla swung around and shrank into the unruly mob encasing the bar. Leers and whistles emitted as she fought her way through. The inebriated behavior might be shameful, but struggling among a collection of smelly, raunchy drunkards was a step up from witnessing Eric arranging an intimate evening for three.

She shoved past the congestion, omitting conventional niceties, her elbow jamming into an iconic guitarist's ribs as he accidentally back stepped in front of her. She barely acknowledged the miscalculation and continued to propel her way through tangles of guests as her incense soared.

How could he act cheerful when she felt so miserable? How was he able to move on so quickly and worry free without her? Like their two years meant nothing. Too bad she couldn't reduce her emotions to equal his detached way of thinking.

Finally, she surged passed the human maze and into the open. Liberated from the fermented crowd, she inhaled actual air, and then exhaled, releasing a joyous whoop. An empty path lay before her.

Cerebrally, she thrust Eric and his deplorable conduct aside to contemplate later. Bundling her long skirt, she accelerated, dashing across the thick grass, or as swift as one could run clad in three-inch heels. Racing inside, she slowed to trek the same hallway she strolled thirty minutes before.

A strange silence encompassed the space.

Darla slackened her stride, straining to catch a noise, but only intense stillness lingered. Had Stephanie left? Darla wouldn't blame her. Seclusion after a traumatic experience was a natural response.

A loud thump came from the dressing area, followed by a second. It sounded like something hit the wall. Rounding a slight bend, Darla paused to angle across the entrance, and peered into the room.

A pair of sparkling, super-spiked Louboutin's lay near the doorway. Soggy, wadded tissue littered the floor and furniture. Flowers and ribbon were scattered from a ripped up bridal bouquet.

Stephanie sat, wilted on the sofa, her full-length gown tucked underneath her curled legs. Mascara mixed with tears streamed across her spray-tanned cheeks. Her veil dangled sideways as if she sought to rip the vintage birdcage off her head, forgetting to unpin it first, then conceded, and let the netted material flop.

Darla tore past the doorway and crouched by her knees. "Steph?" She ditched her bouquet and stretched to a near empty tissue box, fluffing the last wipes. She dabbed Stephanie's face to swab away the flowing inky black stains. "I don't get it. What happened?"

"I don't know," Stephanie wailed, pushing Darla's efforts aside. "Blaine's dad met my parents and me when we walked outside. They can't find Blaine."

"Can't find…they've looked everywhere?"

"His father and uncle searched the grounds. There's no sign of him. Relatives are checking the island. He won't answer his phone. They think he's left."

"Why would they assume such a thing?"

"Figured he changed his mind."

"Changed his mind? As in not marrying you? No way."

"His family disagrees. Mrs. Stewart's contacting all airlines to find out if he's on any passenger list." She sniffed. "Mr. Stewart's online corroborating outbound flights. His uncle's cruising the docks and harbors for boat departures, in case he boarded a ship. They're supposed to keep me updated."

"Steph, I'm…shocked."

"Me too. And his parents. They're so disappointed,

Dar. Disgusted their son acted like," Stephanie straightened and hissed, "a selfish coward."

"What about a note. Did he at least leave a note or message explaining why he left?"

Stephanie slumped into the couch. An uncorked champagne bottle sat within arm's reach. A half-filled tumbler rested in her grip. She swiped a tissue across her nose, then downed the liquid. "Nope. He just opted to not show up at *our wedding*."

"Has anybody checked his room or the cabana he used to change into his wedding suit? See if he's packed or is his stuff still there?"

"I hope he left his clothes." Stephanie snickered through tears. "I'll use them to build a bonfire. I'll throw a party and roast hotdogs and s'mores with his charred socks and underwear."

"Appetizing." Darla's lips twitched. "Maybe he had an accident on his way. Or something unexpected happened." She motioned at Steph's cell phone lying on a table nearby. "He might not answer his parents' calls, but surely he phoned you. Did you check?"

Stephanie's wet eyes stared, lost in obscurity.

"Steph?" Darla fluttered her fingers ahead of her face. "Stephanie."

"Hmmm?"

"Did Blaine call you or send a text?"

Stephanie snatched her cell and previewed the screen. She thrust the device under Darla's nose and emitted a derogatory noise. "Nothing."

"Did you call him?"

She gulped another mouthful of champagne, shaking her head. "Don't want to talk to him."

"You should. He owes you an explanation."

"Negatory. My goal is to sit, sip my champagne until I forget the previous two years."

"Seriously Steph, go easy on the alcohol. You're not a big drinker."

"I wasn't, you mean." She replenished her glass, filling it with the fizzy liquid. "But I am now."

Darla opened her mouth to argue but decided against it. Stephanie was already half soused, which made her unreasonable. She wouldn't win her case.

She looked around the room. "Why are you alone? Where's your family?"

"Gone. A minor disagreement developed, and we required a cooling off period." Stephanie continued to explain, sans a prompt. "They concocted a brilliant plan and intend to take me home tomorrow."

"Back to California? Where you and Blaine live?"

"No. Much better. Montana." She tasted her bubbly and smacked her lips as she swallowed. "According to them, I'm not rational, and I'm unable to manage my life decisions."

"Not an awful suggestion."

She discharged a harrumph beneath her breath. "I declined."

"What are you planning to do?"

"It's pretty here. I'm thinking of hanging around a while."

"Stay in the honeymoon suite? Solo? A room you were supposed to share with your new husband, who was a no-show at your wedding? And sleep in the same bed? Stephanie, no, not a great idea."

"It's a perfect idea. Blaine, my *love*, paid in advance and gave me a free ten-day vacation. I plan to relish every second." Her teary eyes sparkled in defiance. "The place has two bedrooms if you're interested. I could use a partner. You can move your stuff and stay with me."

"How are you not dying to hunt him down and demand a reason why he did this? I'd insist on answers."

"I don't need answers, because I don't care. I've officially voted him off the island."

"Consensus says he did that himself."

She hoisted her glass. "It'll be the final thing we agree on."

"I can't believe he just left, Steph. More's going on."

"Obviously." Stephanie placed her wineglass to the side, wiggled her engagement ring off her finger, and hurled it across the room. "His feet are frozen, and he doesn't have the *cojones* to man up and say so." A soft ting echoed against the tiles. "Asshole."

"Cold feet aren't the problem, Steph. Blaine can't wait to marry you. Another reason must—"

"Excuse me?" The same resort proprietor who spoke to Blaine's father earlier, poked his head inside the dressing room. His knock followed. "Ms. Duckworth? A moment of your time?"

Stephanie glowered and flung a hand. "Ms. Duckworth's busy."

"This is important," the man insisted.

She bent forward to retrieve her drink. "Go away."

"Ms. Duckworth, I realize you're distraught—"

"I'm not disanything. I'm extremely happy." She raised her glass to study the rising bubbles. "Or I will be soon, and I'm disinclined to interrupt my road to euphoria. Tell your story to someone who cares. They can tell me when I'm ready to hear it." Her lips puckered. "*If* I'm ever ready to hear it."

Darla slanted nearer. "Stephanie, you should reconsider. He might have information concerning Blaine."

Her tongue darted past her lips and she blew. Darla's face contorted, recoiling to avoid the spray of spit.

"Blaine Stewart's nothing but a sorry ass deserter. I *despise* him." Stephanie nodded toward the manager. "I bet *he* expects compensation on some idiotic surcharge he's invented now Blaine's missing. Probably stuck it in the fine print on our contract." She straightened and raised a fist, sending an ominous glare toward their newest arrival. "You can forget it. I won't shell out one cent for a venue I didn't use."

Darla laid a palm on Steph's upper arm, easing her back. "I'm sure he's not so coldhearted. Listen to what he has to say."

"Not interested."

"But—"

"You go talk to him."

Darla's hand slapped her chest. "Me? He asked to speak to you."

"And I explained, my calendar is full. Since you deem his news important, you can find out what's so damn urgent. If I need to know, inform me later." She seized the champagne bottle. "After I'm unconscious."

Darla eyed Stephanie as she topped off her flute. She was broken. In time, she would recover, but Darla doubted she could handle any additional tragic updates tonight, if that's what the manager intended to deliver.

He continued to linger near the entry. "Ms.

Duckworth?"

"Go, Dar."

A reluctant Darla rose, hating to abandon her. "Will your family return soon?"

A careless shoulder lifted. "Lots of kinfolk flew in. I'm sure they're busy socializing. They might swing by later."

"You're fine on your own, then?"

Once again, she elevated her full goblet. "I'm great."

"I'm around the corner. Yell if you need anything."

The man gazed at Darla as she approached. "We must speak in private. We'll go to my office."

Without a word, he led her outside and headed to a building designed to fit into the surrounding bungalow cabins. Darla shadowed him across a concrete walkway to a set of glassed double doors.

He punched a random set of numbers on a keypad to unlock the entryway, and held one side ajar, signaling for her to enter. She stepped across the entrance and waited on him. Once inside, he walked around her and led her down a dimly lit corridor, bypassing an array of unlit units, toward a harsh fluorescent light emitting near the hall's end.

His personal office and their destination.

She walked to the threshold and stopped. Her hands gripped the doorframe, saving her from an embarrassing collapse onto the carpet.

Eric sat inside, in front of a massive desk. Finn was seated next to him.

She loitered in the doorway, preferring not to enter. She wasn't ready for this initial face to face encounter. Besides, Eric may get up and walk out if she went in.

Maybe she ought to go back to Stephanie and forgo creating a possible scene.

The cozy image of him and his two girlfriends flashed through her mind.

Or she could say to hell with her ex-boyfriend and determine the root of this mysterious summons.

The director stood behind his desk. His brows inflated across his bare forehead as he watched her. He indicated for her to sit next to Eric.

Her bottom lip slipped beneath her teeth as she willed her feet to go further and minced to the offered seat. Eric noticeably stiffened when she sank into the empty chair. Her gaze fell to his hands. Deft fingers coiled around the attached wooden support as his fury radiated from his seat.

Her own rage skyrocketed. Why was he mad? He was clearly over her.

"My name is Alexis Dugas." The gentleman eyed them, drawing her attention away from her ex's ire, and yanking her to the present. "I am the administrator of this facility. You are here to discuss Mr. Blaine Stewart. Mr. Boyd and Mr. O'Conner are liaisons, in lieu of Mr. Stewart's parents, who were called away on an emergency. Ms. Hennessy is present because Ms. Duckworth is—incapacitated." He waited. "Now, formalities are clarified. The reason I asked you to join me, is to review Mr. Stewart's ill-fated circumstances."

Eric's familiar sarcastic chuckle filled the room. Darla's stomach lurched at the sound of his laughter.

"How's Blaine runnin' out on his bride ill fated?" he questioned in his thick Scottish brogue.

"Blaine Stewart isn't considered a runaway groom, Mr. Boyd."

"Meaning?"

The man's face turned graver. He stared at Eric. "Meaning, Mr. Stewart didn't leave on his own accord."

"I'm not following."

"He was taken off the premises against his will."

Hesitancy arose as a charge of shock arced throughout the room. Darla peeked at the men next to her. Their bewilderment appeared identical to her own.

Eric edged toward the desk. His brow dipped. "Just what are ya' sayin', Mr. Dugas. What's 'appened to m' friend."

"Your friend, Mr. Boyd, was kidnapped."

Eric scowled. His expression turned suspicious. "Kidnapped?"

Skeptical, Darla twisted Blaine's wedding band, still around her thumb. "Why would anyone take Blaine?"

"Not just anyone. Pirates."

"Let me get this straight. Y'r saying, Blaine's been kidnapped," a cynical smile crept across Eric's face, "by pirates?"

"Yo ho ho. Guess we'll go search for 'im in Neverland." Finn snorted. "What kind of bullshit are you tryin' to sell us?"

"I assure you this is not a hoax. I suggest you take the issue seriously." Dugas whipped out a postcard sized picture and held it to them. The photo displayed a vivid, red star sector embedded on a black background.

Eric accepted the card to inspect. "What's this?"

"It's their calling card. Their mark. This was located among Mr. Stewart's possessions."

"Should you have taken that?" Darla gestured at

the card. "Won't investigators need to lift fingerprints or keep it as evidence in their files if Blaine was abducted?"

"Sadly, this is not the first abduction on our island. Authorities have many of these in their possession, Ms. Hennessy. I guarantee, it is fingerprint free, like all the others." He pointed toward the photo in Eric's hands. "Total payment demand is found on the reversed side."

Eric flipped it over and exploded out of his seat. "The amount's fucking huge."

Darla stretched to peek at the sum, and gasped.

"Holy shit," Finn yelled as he looked at the card. "How are we gonna find that much dough? Siphon blood and sell it?"

"Says we have ten days to pay." Eric returned to his chair. He flicked the postcard forward and backward. "Bastards didn't leave directions on how to send it." He slid the card back onto the desk. "Guess they expect us to get it to 'em by telepathy."

"They will find you."

Eric's scowl intensified. "If what you say is true and pirates kidnapped Blaine, how does this fun game play out?"

"Wait until you receive word. Obey every instruction and prepare to forfeit the amount of funds requested. Do not attempt to deviate, try alternative methods of rescue, or trick these men."

Eric's brows rose. "And if we do?"

"Simple. Mr. Stewart will die."

Chapter 3

Darla squirmed and nestled into her spot. The ground beneath her was lopsided and lumpy, yet somehow perfect. She raised to straighten her towel she used as a barrier between her and the gritty sand.

A stout, balmy breeze floated off the sea and tossed a tangle of unruly curls clipped atop her head into her eyes. Hair brushed aside, she lengthened her body and breathed in, prompting her senses to embrace the elements. Warm sunshine, rumbling waves, and fresh, misty ocean scents lured her into a peaceful calm.

A drawn-out groan erupted beside her. Darla sighed. If only she could find harmony to complement her serenity.

She twisted toward the noise. Stephanie lay next to her. Her body was rigid, and her face was buried in her circled arms. Any movement elicited a painful moan or sorrowful exhalation, results from either a massive hangover or Blaine's plight. Darla couldn't tell which, since she tended to jump from one to the other.

"I feel so guilty," Stephanie droned in a muffled whine. "I shouldn't just lounge around on the beach. I need to go look for Blaine."

"We will. You said Eric's talking to local police now, and he'll speak to island ministries afterward. Once the detectives inside Blaine's bungalow are finished gathering evidence and reach a conclusion, we'll know the authority's intention and what we have to do. Till then, we wait."

Darla yawned and sank onto her beach towel. Last night was uber-long. By the time she returned to the bungalow, Stephanie had drunk herself into a full bender and collapsed from the stupor.

If Darla understood correctly, a second argument regarding Stephanie's refusal to accompany her family to Montana had ensued and accelerated her champagne blowout.

Darla roused her and tried to explain Blaine's situation, but inebriation hindered her comprehension. After Darla forced her to down six cups of coffee, Stephanie gained enough coherence to fathom Blaine didn't run away, but was kidnapped, and they had to pay a massive ransom to get him back.

Trips to the bathroom followed. Many, many trips. At four in the morning, Stephanie crumbled, and wept until she drifted into a semi-contented sleep.

Darla wasn't as lucky. She managed to steal a few winks, but too much occupied her mind. Blaine topped her worry list, but she and Eric's interaction also kept her reflective.

Correction.

Non-interaction. Eric hadn't spoken a word to her during their meeting. He managed a series of angry looks her way, which spoke volumes, but death glares wasn't the same as verbal communication.

Stephanie elevated her torso and patted until she tapped a minor bulge underneath her towel. Flapping a corner over, she removed a pair of sunglasses, caked with sand.

She held the lenses face-high, pursed her lips, and

blew. "How many days do we have before Blaine's time is up?"

"I think it's ten."

"Does yesterday count?" She found her cover-up, rubbed the cloth across her lenses, blew again, and slid them onto her face. "They took him in the evening, around sunset. That shouldn't be seen as a day, right?"

"I wouldn't include it, but I'm not a kidnapper."

"I don't get why they took Blaine." She snatched a bottle of water from their cooler, rubbed it across her face until she reached her forehead, and held it steady. "Pirates are supposed to sail the high seas and hijack ships. Not come onto dry land and abduct people."

"According to Mr. Dugas, this particular band, Les Brigand is different. Researchers keep documentation and track them. Records reveal years of pursuits on land and sea. Lately, they increased their terrestrial corruption. They discovered additional revenue is available in abductions of wealthier island tourists."

"Blaine's financially okay, but he's not wealthy by today's standards."

"I thought Spiraling UP was doing well. Or they were when Eric and I split. Are there new money problems I'm unaware of?"

"Not really. They've suffered a minor set-back because they haven't toured as much this year, but they expected a slight loss. You know the music industry's fickle."

"I get it, out of sight, out of mind."

"They're writing, putting down tracks, and they plan to spend the next few months finishing their latest recordings, which you already knew. They also intend to do a few live dates to test their new stuff. Once they're back on the road, they figure their sales will pick back up."

"I hate how hard they have to work to keep the public interested."

"Me too. If Dugan Holt hadn't embezzled nearly every penny during their teen idol duration, they wouldn't be forced to put in near as much effort. Which again makes me wonder why the pirates chose Blaine. They ought to know he's not mega-rich."

"Dugan's stealing Raising Impulses' earnings isn't a secret, but it's hardly common knowledge. I imagine pirates aren't informed and assume his finances are heftier."

Stephanie crisscrossed her legs and examined the aqua-blue water ahead. She sat quiet for a long minute. "I should be on my honeymoon."

Darla shifted from sunning herself to sitting up. She stretched across a tiny gap and grasped Stephanie's clenched hands. "Don't do this."

"I said horrible things." Her voice cracked. "Wished horrible things. If I realized, I wouldn't…"

"But you didn't know. You believed the worst."

"I didn't have a clue, did I? This is the worst."

"Stephanie?" A baritone voice hovered amid the gentle winds.

Darla and Stephanie exchanged a glance, frowned, and rotated toward the sound. Beams of sunshine blocked the newcomer's identity. Only his approaching silhouette was distinct.

Darla didn't require a clearer picture. She recognized the casual gait. Slipping her sunglasses to the top of her head, she squinted against the bright sun. Her forefinger captured a strand of hair and twisted.

Stephanie flattened a palm across her forehead. "Is that…?"

"Yep." Darla inhaled. A lump developed inside her throat. It tasted coarse and pungent as if she ingested a morsel of a sour melon and it refused to advance down her windpipe. She grabbed her tunic and tugged it over her bikini. "Morgan."

Morgan Wilmington III, her ex-boyfriend. She completely forgot about him working nearby.

Hands stuffed into chino pockets, his tall form ambled easily across the seashore. His features became recognizable as he strolled beyond the sun's blinding rays. Styled, blond hair defied the sturdy draught, and he was impeccably dressed, as always. He slowed to stop, waiting a safe distance from them.

He watched them with a hint of caution. "Hey, Steph. Darla. Nice to see you."

"Morgan," they murmured, simultaneously. Just uttering his name strained Darla's vocal cords.

He directed his attention to Stephanie and nodded at the white stucco buildings looming behind them. "I left your wedding gift at the check-in desk, yesterday."

He hesitated. "What happened? I spoke to your wedding planner to firm up the time to start the display. She said the wedding had been cancelled."

"Yes, Blaine is…" Stephanie's bottom lip trembled. She removed her glasses to swipe away a fresh attack of tears.

"Look what you did. You made her cry." Darla's eyes bored into him. "We came to the beach to help her relax. She'd just begun to unwind."

Morgan scraped an unmarred Sperry across the silt. "I wasn't trying to upset her. I wanted to make sure she is okay."

"You can see she isn't," Darla snapped, not bothering to contain the spiteful edge in her tone.

"Dar. I understand you're mad at me, but I meant no harm."

He sounded patronizing, which ticked her off more. His arrogance, believing it was fine to show up was enough to ignite her temper, but she wouldn't tolerate his additional condescendence.

"Mad at you? You're ego's a bit inflated. You're not even a blip on my anger radar."

He chuckled. "Nice to see you've kept your edge. I'm glad. I worried that rocker guy might've broken your spirit when you split." He allowed his words to linger a moment. "Your temper's still intact, too."

"I'm not mad."

"I'm calling you on this one. Hiding your feelings isn't one of your strengths. Your show of anger is comparable to a neon sign. Facial expressions, body language…in your speech."

Her frown deepened.

His lips curved. "You're tense too." A finger air circled. "You were twirling your hair when I walked up. Your go-to anxious tell."

"As much as I'm enjoying this rehash of my nervous tics, I suggest we table this conversation and focus on what really matters."

"Table the conversation? Sure. But I'm curious to know why. How come you're uncomfortable I remember your quirky mannerisms or that I still find them charming? You say you're not angry, but I disagree. You're extremely agitated."

She paused a moment. She'd way overreacted at

his appearance, and he'd gotten the wrong idea. "I am stressed. The last few hours have been the lowest. My closest friend had her world turned upside down, and no one knows how to fix it. I'm tired, scared, and drained, so don't flatter yourself and believe my irritation escalated due to your arrival."

An eyebrow arched. "Not even a little?"

"Not even." Her frame braced, and she spun the other way. "You brought your present and checked on Stephanie. Time to go back to your rosy world where all is right if there's a preceding dollar sign."

"Glad you're not bitter." He advanced closer and squatted next to her. "You don't want to talk to me, hear me, or see me. I get it. What I did to you was terrible, wrong, and just plain stupid. I spent countless nights loathing myself because of my behavior."

"Makes two of us," she mumbled.

He ignored her dig and continued. "I didn't appreciate you or the happiness you brought into my life." A fingertip slipped underneath her chin and prodded, so her gaze linked with his. "You don't owe me a damn thing, but I'm begging for a chance to make amends, or at least tell you how sorry I am."

Darla's body stiffened. She was rendered speechless by his remarks. The massive bonfire inside her extinguished. Precise words she longed to hear. Declarations she dreamed of receiving.

Only not from him.

She truly was over him and just incensed at everything else in her life. She swallowed past the blockage in her throat to control her sobs. Unable to bear him physically near, she drew away to break the connection. She caught Stephanie in her peripheral, who hadn't budged since Morgan's arrival.

Darla returned to Morgan. "I accept your apology."

"Really? You forgive me? That easy?"

"Actually, I forgave you a long time ago. Recent tragedies have me upset, but I moved on from you. Us. I'm satisfied with my choices."

"Are you? You and your rock star boyfriend recently parted."

"Amicably."

Stephanie hiccupped. Darla sent a silent warning glance in her friend's direction.

"Hmmm. You're pleased he hit the party circuit so soon after you split? It doesn't disturb you a little?"

"We're not together. His behavior isn't my concern."

"I read a recent interview in a rock magazine the other day. He says he's happier than he's been in a while. That doesn't ruffle you."

"Morgan, seriously. Stop."

"Don't go all huffy. Guy's a jerk. You don't deserve his negative inferences splashed across every media channel."

"True. If he made those comments. Our time as a couple familiarized me with reporters' tactics. Some are masters at word twists. I'm never sure if what I read is a direct quote or an interviewer's spin."

"You're defending him?"

"Why are we discussing this?"

"I'm trying to gage you. I don't want to step on any toes."

"You're attempting to learn if my toes are squished. They're not. I'm fine. You requested forgiveness, and you're absolved. You can sleep now."

"Can we be friends?"

"Like on Facebook? Sure. Send me a request."

"Wow. Social media alliances. Giant step." Morgan laughed quietly. "That'll work. But since the islands we're staying at are within a mile's distance, why not join me later." His lips lifted into an appealing grin, yet his words challenged. "We can have a drink and catch up."

Stephanie's knee bumped Darla's sending an I *told you so* message. Darla's lips tightened as she slightly nodded to convey the implication was recognized.

"Not a terrific suggestion."

"Why? You're worried over, what? Our past before I was an idiot? It's in the history books, Dar. Can't go back, can't change it. We can only go forward."

She looked at him, her expression pained.

"Cliché, but true. Honestly, what's the harm in two future Facebook friends sharing one drink?"

Darla scooped up a handful of smooth sand. She despised the position he was putting her in. They were both single now, so there was no harm in meeting him. Except she preferred not to.

"Mayday, Dar," Stephanie whispered. She leaped to her feet, wriggled into her cover-up, and sprinted across the shore.

"Where are you—?"

Movement behind caught her eye. Darla dropped the granules and peered up. Her heart broke into a gallop.

Eric and Finn had appeared in the distance and walked in their direction. Stephanie darted to them, throwing herself into Eric's arms when they met.

Darla's chest constricted at their embrace. Misery

shimmied through her. Eric comforting a friend wasn't the issue. Since they parted, he merely sucked in the same air as another woman and green swallowed her whole.

When they were together the story was different. Women hitting on him didn't trouble her. He was a good-looking guy, and a musician in a popular rock band, which doubled his desirability. His profession put him in a position where ladies attempted to entice him in numerous ways.

Some were remarkably creative.

He always made a point to excuse himself when conditions intensified. If advancers became too aggressive, he'd smile and firmly tell them he was taken. He made sure the world knew he had a girlfriend, and he was deeply in love.

Unfortunately, nowadays were different, and her friends weren't excluded from jealousy's wrath. Struggling to find perspective, she tamped her resentment and rose to stand as the trio approached.

Morgan also stood. He wandered nearer and placed his mouth close to her ear. "This situation is about to get very interesting."

This situation was about to explode. Darla resisted the urge to run. Both were exes, yet she didn't anticipate a meeting between the pair to turn out well.

Eric caught sight of her. His jaw clenched, and the rest of his expression hardened. The arm resting across Stephanie's shoulders slid off as he back stepped, prepared to abandon the scene. Then he paused.

His gaze centered on Morgan. He separated from the others and stormed toward them, taking long, deliberate strides as if he were a predator stalking his prey.

"Your ex isn't a happy camper." Morgan eased around her. Walking straight and tall, he strolled to intercept Eric before Darla realized his intentions. He extended a palm. "Morgan. Morgan Wilmington."

Eric halted, disregarding Morgan's greeting. Both froze to size the other up.

"I know who you are." Eric's raspy voice sounded sharper than shards of broken glass. "What I don't know, is why the fuck you're here."

"I need a reason to visit friends?" Morgan withdrew his offered handshake and half-turned to flash a smile at Darla.

Crimson seeped from underneath Eric's tanned skin as Darla held back a scream.

"If you insist on an explanation, I brought a wedding gift for the happy couple, but I suppose the point is moot." Morgan faltered. "Shame how last night ended."

Eric's fists tightened. "You're an invited guest?"

"Why does it matter?" Morgan's timbre lightened, yet his attitude took on a hostile overtone. "Why does anything I do matter. To you?"

Eric leaned inward, close enough that their noses nearly touched. His pinned gaze raked over Morgan as icy contempt covered his face. "We're dealing with a crisis, and I don't want outsiders fucking up what's already fucked up." His rough tone lowered to equal Morgan's. "Get it?"

"Oh, I got it."

"Good. Then excuse y'rself and let us handle our business."

"I'll leave when I'm ready. Not when you tell me."

"Wanna bet?" Eric flicked a surprised possessive gaze Darla's way.

Darla stared helplessly as Stephanie and Finn merged into the group. Stephanie smacked Finn's shoulder and signaled for him to intercept. Violently shaking his head, Finn's arms crossed over his chest in defiance. Darla gestured at Finn, amplifying her motions to indicate he get into the middle of the two bulls and stop the escalating clash.

Finn set his shoulders and snapped a sharp salute. He stuffed his hands into his pockets, rolled his eyes, and huffed, wandering to the standoff. He stood next to Eric.

"Man. We don't have time to do this whole who's got the bigger drill bit routine. Refocus. Blaine's time's limited."

Eric didn't flinch. Blistering rage between the two men persisted as their gazes remained locked.

"Fine. If you won't stop this idiocy, I will." Finn positioned his elbow, forcefully poked Eric's ribs, and shouldered between the pair. He easily wrangled in the center. He faced Eric, placed his palms onto his shoulders, and shoved.

Without taking his eyes off Morgan, a much bigger Eric leaned forward and braced his legs to counteract Finn's push. The lanky Finn couldn't make him budge.

Frustration covered Finn's face. He slipped from the middle and ambled back to Eric's side. "Any other time, this macho impasse would end in a landslide, in your favor. I'd place m' bet on you." He glanced at Morgan. "'Cept this guy's your size, maybe bulkier. Not sure you'll win, man."

"Then it's a good thing you're broke."

Finn's energies were hopeless. Darla stared at Stephanie and silently begged, mouthing, "Do something."

Stephanie nodded and quickly moved to Eric's side. She grasped his upper arm and gave it a rough shake. "Eric, this is unnecessary. Listen to Finn. Blaine doesn't have a lot of time. We need to be prepared when the pirate's call comes, and your help is crucial. You spoke to the police. What did they tell you?"

Eric's harsh expression softened. "Sorry." He pivoted so his back faced Morgan. "They said Tluq Cay law enforcement services are undersized, and brigands outnumber their men. They don't possess enough manpower required to challenge 'em. They can't help."

Stephanie's face paled.

Darla relocated to her side and looped an arm through hers. "You're joking."

Eric's expression turned to stone. "Y' don't hear me laughin'. Regional cops are useless. Pirates seize unsuspecting guests and hold 'em until they're paid. Turquoise Archipelago officials can do nothing to stop them."

"Get this." Finn snapped to unfold a sightseeing pamphlet. "Don't mention anything 'bout pirates in their brochures. Misleading, that's what it is."

Darla grimaced and shook her head. "I doubt they advertise pirate invasions, Finn."

"Wait." Morgan infiltrated the circle. "Stephanie didn't marry because her fiancé was taken by pirates?"

Eric's glare speared into Morgan. "Not your business."

Even though she agreed, Darla was already tired of Eric's heavy handedness, and his attitude toward her.

She ignored his outburst. "Yes, Morgan. He was abducted as he dressed for the ceremony."

"Les Brigand's got him?" Morgan appeared troubled. "No, you won't find support around here."

An agitated Stephanie gnawed a fake thumbnail. "You're familiar with them?"

"Representatives warn people who come here often." Morgan's expression stayed grim. "Bunch's bad news. They grabbed an associate of mine last year."

Stephanie repositioned to stand closer to Morgan. "Did they hurt him?"

"We never saw him again. Authorities suspect he's dead. We couldn't locate his remains. They probably tossed his body in the ocean."

Stephanie gasped and covered her mouth.

Eric's eyes tapered as his chin jutted toward Morgan. "Happy?"

"She asked, and I answered. I won't lie to make her feel better."

"You're making the situation worse."

"How? By telling the truth? I'm not the enemy. I'll help if I can, but you should be aware of who you're dealing with, and what they will do." Morgan planted his fists on his hips. "What's happened up to this point? Where's the rest of his family?"

"We're keeping his parents updated," Stephanie replied. "They're distressed over Blaine's abduction. Unfortunately, they experienced another setback with their other son, Bennett. He had surgery after a freak accident. Medications triggered an allergic reaction, and he's in a coma. His parents flew to Scotland last night. Prior to leaving, they appointed Eric as liaison. Communications will go through him. His dad hopes to fly back within a week and take over."

Morgan nodded sympathetically. "That's tough."

"Morgan. Representatives notify you relating to hostage activity when you're visiting the Turquoise Archipelago, correct?" Darla was unsure how this news made a difference, except none of them were warned.

"Yes. They post alerts to those at risk."

"By risk," Finn's brows sank, "you mean because you're loaded, bureaucrats believe your chances of getting nabbed are upped?"

"Exactly what he means," Eric responded dryly.

Darla continued to pump Morgan to gain information. "Do you know how many victims have been kidnapped?"

"Last count…eleven are on record. That may've changed, though."

"All are tourists?"

"Seems so. Natives are safe. Even the wealthier residents are immune."

"Eleven people." Eric whistled. "Quite a few. And those in charge sit on their asses and twiddle their thumbs. Gotta wonder if something fishy's stirring." He nudged Finn. "Maybe we ought to go rescue Blaine ourselves."

"Sounds like we're his best chance."

"All we gotta do is find out where—"

"This is not a situation where playing hero's an option," Darla cut in. "You heard Mr. Dugas. This is Blaine's life. Yours too, if you do something irrational like attempt a rescue, yourselves."

Frosty blue eyes locked onto hers. "Your professional opinion isn't required, Dr. Hennessy."

"Too bad." Hot, bitter anger flared. "You just got

it. When the call comes, follow instructions. Don't try to be supermen. You're not."

Eric's jaw defiantly tensed as he closed in on her. Warm breath wafted over her skin as he challenged her stare. Darla's heart fluttered, which annoyed her. She didn't want to be thrilled because he stood close.

"Watch it, luv." His lips arched, displaying an icy scorn. "I might start believing you still care."

"Me care?" Her tone mocked his. "Seriously?"

"Then it shouldn't be a problem if I live or die."

"Um…it is…you're being an ass."

"I'm a charter member of BAS. Belligerent Asshole Society." His mouth transformed, displaying a sarcastic smile. "Got my membership pin to prove it."

Finn jumped in and maneuvered between them. "Stop the crazy. Y' gotta put your personal shit aside. This is about Blaine."

"Detectives?" Stephanie blurted as if the thought just occurred. "Eric, when you texted earlier, detectives were in Blaine's dressing room. Did they find anything beneficial?"

"Almost forgot." He fished into his pocket and brought out a folded printout. A soft crackle sounded in the wind as he unfolded the paper. "They didn't find anything, but they did give me names of bounty hunters who may help rescue him."

Stephanie took the list and studied it, releasing a forlorn moan. "They'll expect payment for their services, and their fees are probably as much as the ransom. Either way, my bank account isn't huge, but I'm willing to empty it for Blaine. Even if it won't be enough."

Darla moved and slid a comforting arm around

Stephanie's shoulders. "We'll figure something out. Even if we have to hock everything we own, we'll get him back."

Stephanie spread her fingers to exhibit her engagement ring. "I can sell this."

"No, you won't. We'll find money someplace else. Blaine'll kick *my* ass if you pawn your ring." Eric spun to Morgan. "You're full of information." He sounded civil, though his face looked as if he'd eaten a bowl of lemons to accomplish the feat. "What are their rules?"

"Kidnappers should open communication lines soon. They'll maintain contact until the funds are dispensed or their timeline ends. Relatives are phoned and given sixty seconds to speak to their loved one."

Eric exhaled noisily. "What next? We deliver money and they deliver Blaine?"

"You can hope. They're pirates and not necessarily men of their word."

"What are you saying, Morgan?" Stephanie's speech trembled. "If we pay, they'll return Blaine, won't they?"

"I'm sorry, Stephanie. Every abduction ended the same as my friend's. They disappeared and have yet to be found, whether ransom was paid or not. They're all assumed dead."

Chapter 4

"We can't let pirates kill my Blaine," wailed Stephanie. Darla stood close by, protectively clutching Stephanie's arm. "We have to save him. What can we do, Morgan?"

Already sick of Darla and Stephanie treating Morgan Wilmington like he invented chocolate, Eric's brows jerked together. He snapped a scowl toward his new nemesis, fighting the urge to boot him off this island and send him back to his way too rich ass mummy and daddy.

What right did he have to waltz in and assume control? Because his *family* had tons of money? Or his friend happened to've gotten snatched by the same group holding Blaine. Didn't everyone realize, *those same pirates killed his buddy*?

Darla's hopeful gaze zoomed in on Morgan. "You researched this bunch after they took your associate. Did you discover anything that might help us?"

"My team put together a task force when we learned of Hugh's abduction. Plans were to organize a rescue. Unfortunately, we were too late."

"Would it be possible to regroup and help Blaine?"

A hand slipped into his back pocket to retrieve his cell. "I can't say. I'll call the project's lead and speak to him about missions he's coordinated since. See if he can assist." Morgan swiped the icon on his phone and furthered himself from the crowd. "I heard he recently used successful methods in similar situations," he finished, placing the phone to his ear.

"He wasn't so successful saving his friend," Eric muttered.

Darla left Stephanie's side and glided to him. A serious glower spread over her face. She jabbed her forefinger into his chest. "Try and pretend to be grateful, even if you aren't. Morgan might be Blaine's only chance, and he's doing what he can to help get him out of this mess. He doesn't have to, you know." She whipped around and hurried back to Stephanie.

Finn leaned in and lowered his voice. "Yeah, he does have to help, if he intends to get Darla into—"

"Shut it, Finn."

While mindful of Wilmington's intentions, Eric preferred to forgo any verbal recreations and avoid mental pictures. He didn't need that now. He was pissed enough Darla treated Morgan as if he was the latest Avenger.

Yet, when he insinuated that he and Finn should orchestrate a release, she spoke to him like a parent scolding their child who forgot to do their homework.

So, he didn't own a superhero cape. Did she not remember their week-long grueling episode when they first met? Or how he took a bullet, and was left for dead, *but survived*?

What aggravated him the most, if Blaine had been taken three months ago, and he chose to go after the bad guys, she wouldn't have just encouraged him. She would've seized her 9mm and insisted on fighting by his side.

Eric spared her a final glimpse, feeling his face

turn crimson. He jammed his hands into his pockets, and spun toward the water, no longer able to stomach her gooey, doe-eyed gawks at Wonder Wilmington.

"Man." Finn tapped Eric's shoulder. "Sorry 'bout what I said back there. Didn't mean to upset you."

"I'm not upset," Eric lied. "I know what he's tryin' to do. I just don't require the added visuals."

"You gonna stop him?"

"Stop him from what?"

"Seeing Darla."

"What can I do? She's free to pick who she dates." Eric touched his shirt, and then thrust his hand back into his pants pocket. He quit smoking two years ago, but circumstances had him ready to kill for a whiff of nicotine. "Honestly, I don't care what she does."

"Your lack of caring's obvious." Finn's tone was laced with mockery.

Eric's frowned deepened.

"Dude, you practically started a war cuz the guy stood next to her. It took you fifteen minutes to back off. Anyone sportin' a pair of eyeballs can tell you're riled she's giving him attention." Finn chuckled. "Classic *not* caring."

Eric's jaw tightened to the point of discomfort. He was ready to leave. He didn't need this shit.

Morgan rejoined the women and looked at Stephanie. "Got the info." Eric and Finn gradually integrated themselves into the group. "My guy says they're swamped in assignments. They're unavailable to help Blaine. Sorry."

Stephanie groaned. "I guess we sift through bounty hunters."

"Be careful who you choose." Morgan's lips

pressed into a thin line. "There's as many shysters as there are legits. It takes a while to weed them out, too. Plus, you'll need to watch your timeline. Pirates will."

"Did he give you any advice on how we should proceed?" Darla inquired.

"He did. His suggestion sounds radical, but he swears it worked in other instances."

Stephanie bounced on her toes. "Extreme or whatever, I'm willing to try anything. What's his recommendation?"

"He says you propose to pay the total amount and tell them once Blaine is returned unharmed, you'll make a second payment equal to the first. It's risky and expensive, but Blaine may have a shot at freedom if they buy into it."

"Why not just do the same with the original deal?" Eric interjected. "Half in advance and half after Blaine's delivered."

"Pirates won't consent. They stipulated they have the full amount prior to handing Blaine to you. If you attempt to negotiate their current terms, they'll cut off communications and kill him."

"According to you he dies either way. Why bother to pay 'm at all?"

Stephanie winced. Horror spread across her face, signaling she was primed for another meltdown.

"Eric." Darla patted Stephanie's shoulder. "We have to try."

His mouth snapped shut, not bothering to respond, since his every suggestion was wrong.

"They're greedy," Morgan explained further. "Sweetening the pot may work to Blaine's advantage. Whatever you do, you better act fast. Ten days will shrivel away quick."

"Then we have to get started. The sooner we get things in order, the sooner we get Blaine back." Darla looked at Stephanie and grinned. "And get you two married."

"One tiny hitch." Eric's features turned more severe. "How are we gonna find twice as much money if we don't have enough for the initial payoff?"

Morgan appeared confused. "You're in a band. A well-known one and by today's standards, lucrative. You spent years as a teen idol in a boyband, too. I know you were popular. My kid sister and her friends listened to your music constantly. They had posters, t-shirts, and, " he scratched his head, "if I remember correctly, underwear with your pictures on them. Panties freaked out my dad."

Eric managed to meet his gaze without wincing. "Undies weren't my idea."

"You don't come off as a rock and roll cliché who squandered your money away." Morgan hesitated. "What happened to the income you netted?"

Eric's temper flared as his fist balled. He ought to leave or the impulse to whack Morgan Wilmington solid enough to bury him would overpower his resistance.

"Morgan." Darla glanced Eric's way. "Eric's finances are his business."

"I'm aware, Dar, but he brought up the subject."

"They made money." Stephanie's voice wobbled. "Raging Impulse made tons of money. Except their manager embezzled it all and then he vanished. They still can't locate him. Attorneys are involved, and they've rerouted royalties, and merchandizing disbursements back to band members or their families two years ago. But they've barely recouped their losses.

"Blaine and Eric created Spiraling UP after Impulse dissolved. They fiscally back themselves to maintain control of their music. But most of their earnings that clears sustains and promotes Spiraling UP."

Eric longed to dig a deep hole and crawl inside. First, Darla defends him, then Stephanie spills his cash flow history.

"Tough break."

"We're okay." Eric hated the sound of his weakened tone. "We're just not in a position where we can pay so much at one time."

Morgan swept a gaze across the group. "Maybe I can help. Let me speak to my accountants and make sure I'm flush enough to withdraw the asking price. You'll have to find surpluses if you choose to bargain for an increase."

Stephanie squealed and clapped her hands. "You'll give us the ransom money?"

"Not give. This is a loan. We'll arrange reimbursements once the conditions are calmer. Repayment is not an option. I insist on you paying me back whether Blaine lives or not."

"Hang on." Eric patted the air with his palms. "Let's think b'fore we storm in and agree. That's a hell of a lot of cash to pay back, plus we still will have to find more. I'm sure Wilmington will incorporate accrued interest in the deal. I prefer a total breakdown and have an idea of what my payments will be b'fore signing dotted lines."

"I normally add interest to any loans I make."

Morgan gave Darla a quick wink. "In this case I won't."

An emotion resembling jealousy ignited Eric's blood, setting his plasma ablaze. Heat rose and burned his skin. He inhaled to reel in his feelings so he could speak. "Still, we shouldn't jump and accept any monetary transactions without checking other options and determine what fits our budget."

"What other options?" Darla argued. "We don't have time to shop loans, even if we could get one. I mean, has anyone heard of a financial institution approving a loan to pay off a ransom?"

Unwilling to concede, Eric angrily disputed her logical reasoning. "Blaine's dad put me in charge. I say we postpone one day and do more research."

"We're in a time crunch. If we go with Morgan's suggestion, we'll only need to find the second half. If we reject Morgan, then we'll have to hunt for double or hope Blaine survives if we can get the amount of the original ransom. I say we accept Morgan's offer, and if the pirates agree, then we work to locate the rest."

Finn tilted nearer to Eric. "Hate to say it, but your lady's got a point."

"She always does."

Darla met his gaze sans a trace of emotion. "Mr. Stewart handed you the responsibilities, but Stephanie is Blaine's fiancée. You should hear her opinion before you decide anything."

Eric's mouth opened to disagree. Blaine's dad passed the reins to him since Stephanie was too overwrought to make sound decisions, but she should have a say.

Morgan's hands raised in a form of surrender. "You all can figure this out and text me once you're done." Not trying to hide his satisfied smirk, he pivoted toward the resort's back entrance. "I'll stay on the island a few hours, and we can meet later if you decide you require my assistance."

"Meet where?" Stephanie yelled as he strolled away.

"Tequila Sunset. It's a tavern located in the town square. You can't miss it."

"Great bar." Finn grinned. "Visited twice."

Eric's brows dropped. "Shit, Finn, we only arrived yesterday."

"I know, right? The place is great. They stock an impressive collection of imported beers. Prices are reasonable, too."

"You made two trips to a bar in less than twenty-four hours for cheap foo foo pints?"

"Bartenders are cool." His smile widened. "One's a chick. A very hot chick."

"There you go."

"Eric." Stephanie approached him. "You're not a fan of Morgan's, I get that."

"I don't trust him." He flicked a glance Darla's way. "S'all."

"I disagree that's your only problem, but we'll save the debate for later. Regarding Morgan's offer. Final verdict is yours, but I assume you'll consider my feelings when determining a decision."

"Blaine would ream my butt if I didn't."

"And you understand what I want."

Eric didn't respond immediately. While he could dispute the issues, he couldn't overlook the problem and automatically refuse Morgan's generosity. Regardless of having to deal with a guy who made him feel like he bathed in pig slop or the sensation that the loan included additional strings down the way. "Send Wilmington a text so he can start the motions. Since Finn's a regular, he can lead me to the pub, and we'll talk details."

"Wait." Stephanie ran to her towel lying twisted across the shoreline, along with a mountain of scattered necessities. She bent to gather the spread, cramming various items into an oversized bag. "I'm coming too."

Eric grumbled. He rather she stayed on the beach, but if she chose to accompany them, he wouldn't stop her. She had a legitimate investment in Blaine's recovery.

Arms loaded, she rushed to where he stood next to Finn. "Come on, Darla," she hollered across her shoulder. "Pack up."

Eric pointed to Darla. "No, no, no. You're not invited."

Darla had stooped to snag her possessions. She dropped her sunblock and lengthened to full height. "And why not?"

"You broke up with me, and I don't want to spend any more time with you than necessary."

"Ouch." Finn chafed his arms. "So cold, I need m' jacket."

"Whatever." She lowered onto her towel. "Just so you know, I'm the reason he's supporting us."

Unhappiness flooded through Eric. "Only too well."

Stephanie planted her hands on her hips. "Quit being an ass. I want my best friend along for support. Like it or not, she's included, so get over it." She motioned to Darla. "Come on. Let's go rescue Blaine."

Chapter 5

Two days later...

Eric lay supine in bed, staring at the rotating ceiling fan above. A comfortable breeze rustled past his raised window, lifting the curtains into a graceful billow, and fragranced his room with a fresh, clean smell.

Just beyond his hut, roars of surf pounded the shores. Waves splashing provided a soothing rhythm. On normal nights those sounds would lull him into a comfortable doze. Tonight, however, every noise irritated the crap out of him and frayed his already ragged nerves.

He kept his focus on the whirling fan stirring the air. The slow methodic spin didn't budge an inch, which reminded him how their efforts to free Blaine hadn't progressed a millimeter.

Stressed and on the verge of detonation, he flipped to his abdomen, kicked the covers off his legs, and shoved his head beneath his pillow. He rested in the position mere seconds, then he boosted a corner of the pillow to check his cell phone's readout once more. Bright numbers gleamed back at him as if to mock.

Three a.m.

Three hours late and no missed calls.

Worries cluttered his mind.

Wilmington made a money transfer after their meeting two days ago. Per pirate demands, he also arranged to convert the sum into cash and smaller bills, which was no minor feat. It took forty-eight hours to complete the process. They got word funds were ready to collect earlier today.

Eric flopped to his back, checking his bedside. A suitcase packed with a shitload of loot was placed on the floor. His Glock 19 rested on the nightstand next to him. Raising up, he jammed his fist into the pillow and shoved it behind his neck, laying stiff-backed upon the mattress.

What happened to the midnight call that was supposed to come? More importantly, what the hell had happened to Blaine?

Snapping on a lamp, he sat again. This time he rose to his feet and wandered to his suitcase and dug inside until locating a notebook and pen. Then he went to his acoustic guitar and gently picked it up by the neck.

He'd had a difficult time penning tunes since he and Darla split, but tonight, lyrics and music were bursting to escape.

He sat down on the edge of his bed and began to play, stopping to jot down the notes and words flowing from his mind into his fingertips. Taking a quick break, he reread the chorus, making sure it jived with the song's content.

A light tap drummed on his bedroom door. Eric spun toward the rap and frowned. Kidnappers wouldn't knock, would they?

A click resonated, followed by the scrape of his door sliding ajar. He stretched to the nightstand and snatched his gun. Using a thumb, he cocked the striker toward him as the entrance's slit slowly widened. A vague shadow scurried past the gap.

"Eric?"

Replacing his weapon, Eric didn't respond.

Finn wandered farther inside without an invitation. He leaned against the wall and eyed Eric, his expression suspicious. "You're still here."

"You noticed that too." He re-settled on the bed, positioning his guitar onto his lap.

An insomniac and prone to nightly visits, Eric never enjoyed rooming with Finn during Impulse's primitive days when traveling from one small town to another. Back then, they'd been forced to double up and share motel rooms due to limited resources.

He and Finn didn't stay together often, because their turbulent relationship was filled full of hostility and metaphorical head-butting. While recent mutual events evoked a shaky truce, they were hardly close.

Since Eric delayed in accepting his wedding RSVP, island suites, bungalows, and hotel rooms were booked. Their latest stabs to make nice had Finn volunteer a spare bedroom in his bungalow, which Eric gratefully accepted. Except he had to endure Finn's demand to share his sleepless tendencies.

"Have you delivered the money and now you're back?"

Eric scratched his side and yawned. "They never called."

"Huh. Wonder why?"

"S'all I've done since midnight, Finn."

"Hope this isn't a bad sign."

"Me too." He rubbed his eyes and then froze.

"What kind of bad sign?"

Finn strolled to the opened window and gazed into the night. "Not sure. Call it a feelin'. A dark one. I don't mind tellin' ya, the stuff that's been happening worries me. Been more afraid as each hour passes."

"Afraid of what?"

His shoulder lifted. "Dunno. Island's got scary vibes."

Eric never knew Finn experienced clairvoyance, but this new creepiness wreaked havoc on his own growing concerns. Then again, Finn lived in his own little world, so his formidable sensations were probably equally as farfetched.

"I didn't realize you were psychic, Finn."

"First time it's occurred." He continued to dawdle at the window. "You think Blaine's captors blew us off?"

"Crossed my mind. 'Cept I assume they want their cash."

"Speaking of cash, that song you're working on will bring y' a lot when y' finish it. Even though it's a ballad, the refrain's catchy." Finn stopped a moment to sing the words Eric recently wrote.

Confused, Eric wondered where this sudden shift in conversation was leading. "That's great, Finn. Don't go stealing my work."

"Won't. Just a reminder, I can play bass, too. If it comes to a point where you have to replace Blaine."

Eric was silent, uncertain how to react. Did Finn seriously suggest he take Blaine's job in their band? A bit above the norm, even in Finnworld.

"Can't even begin to think about it, Finn. It's kinda inappropriate."

"I shouldn't't've mentioned it." He visibly shivered. "But I just got a horrific premonition."

Eric studied his former cohort. This was a side of Finn he hadn't seen. He did act frightened or maybe he was weirder than Eric imagined, and he'd begun to further expose his eccentricities.

Or it could be something else?

"Are you worried since Blaine was kidnapped, same'll happen to you?"

Finn looked uneasy. "Gives me jitters when incidents strike Impulse members. Two years ago, Drake was murdered. So was my brother. Killer mistook both, thinkin' they were me. I should be dead, not them. Haunts my dreams."

"Mine too, although probably not in the same way as yours."

Eric shifted, surprised Drake and Richard's deaths affected Finn so much, but he understood. None of those associated with the horrible crimes discussed them often. The memories were too disturbing.

"You should head home, Finn. Go back to the states or visit your mum."

"What? You serious?"

"You're spooked and it's got you sayin' crazy shit. You can't help much if you're too busy checking behind you."

Relief flooded Finn's face. He tilted his head to one side to consider Eric's suggestion. "Leavin's never crossed my mind, but since you mentioned it, I'll book the next flight. Probably 'll fly out in the morning." He scuttled to exit, suddenly in a hurry to go. He slowed when he reached the doorway. "Um, I'm a bit short on cash."

"Credit card's on the dresser."

Finn swiped Eric's card off the surface and tucked it into his jeans. "I'll reimburse you the cost for my plane ticket after our next residual check arrives."

"Take your time."

Eric figured giving Finn permission to pay the balance off when he could was nothing short of a formality, since Eric would probably never see a dime.

A gentle click ricocheted, and Finn disappeared. Eric put aside his guitar and notebook, then fumbled with the lamp switch, turning off the light. He flung his body onto the mattress as his head began to pound like someone played a bass drum inside his brain.

Too much to deal with, and he was too tired to deal with anything. His eyelids grew heavy, and within seconds he drifted into a peaceful, but dreamless doze. A peculiar thud awakened him seemingly only minutes later.

He sat up straight and peeked at his phone. The display on the clock read four a.m. Darkness blanketed his room. He peered through the window to look outside. Murky clouds blotted the moon's glow, covering the entire island in blackness.

Eric sat still and listened. Nothing. Yet, he sensed he wasn't alone. Somebody invaded his space. Or somebodies. Either way, company called. An arm extended to retrieve his gun as he simultaneously placed a foot onto the floor. Clutching his weapon, he slowly rose.

His crown rammed into a stagnant roadblock. "Holy fuck."

His limbs thrashed as gravity dragged him backward, and his firearm flew from his grasp.

Fortunately, the bed deterred his fall. He lay motionless several seconds, then sluggishly pushed to sit.

He made it part way up. A giant claw grabbed a clump of hair and yanked. Pain ripped through him as Eric leaped backwards, but the grip fastened to his follicles didn't allow him to move far. The intruder whipped him around to face forward, preventing him to get a clear description of his assailant.

Muscular arms coiled around his upper torso to pin him into a large chest. Eric's feet left the ground, drawn into the mass of power. A forceful clutch encased his neck and tightened. Sturdy fingers dug into his larynx.

Air abandoned his lungs, and his surroundings faded to black. An image of Darla flashed inside his mind before darkness took over. The chokehold slackened moments before he surrendered to obscurity. His throat muscles relaxed. He heaved deeply, gradually releasing a flow of coveted air.

Only his tormentor didn't let him go. Arms were repositioned, embracing Eric's waist, and placed his fists underneath Eric's diaphragm, and yanked upward. A knifelike sting stabbed as Eric's rib snapped, followed by a second.

Eric stiffened, unable to move. Agony tore through him. Raw groans erupted, scorching his throat. Without a moment to inhale, the bastard hauled and wrenched the other side. A third and fourth rib cracked, causing his interiors to scream.

He was dropped to the floor. He collapsed farther into the tiles. His lungs burned. He choked, straining to inhale. Curling his body into a ball, he hugged his core and gasped. The briefcase full of the ransom's first installment sat within reach, next to his pistol. A shaky palm extended. His fingertips grazed the firearm's cool metal.

Long, deft fingers snatched his shoulder and dragged him upright and stood him on his feet before he could grab his weapon.

"Son of a bitch," he shrieked, between coughs and sputters.

"Keep quiet. Just givin' you an example of what can happen if you don't behave. Y' understand my message?"

"Kinda hard not to."

His new friend jerked his wrists behind his back and fastened them with what felt like plastic strips. Tape was placed across his eyes to seal his lids shut. A lightweight fabric hood was roughly pulled over his head to shield his face.

Eric stood still and prayed not to faint.

A shin kick urged him forward. Dizzy, Eric buckled and tumbled, falling headfirst, crashing toward the floor. A rough hand snagged him in mid-fall and straightened him.

"Not a word," the mysterious voice instructed. "Now walk."

Eric had no choice other than be navigated through the cottage. A brief thought of Finn's whereabouts flitted across his mind. He wondered if his roommate had left for the airport, or did he possibly suffer an equal assault, or even worse?

He was brought to an abrupt halt. A door squeaked. A cool draft blew inside, whipping across his bare arms. His abductor seized his secured wrists, and slung him, slamming him into an unforgiving hardness, possibly a wall.

He sank his teeth into his bottom lip to refrain from making any more noises, although an "oomph," managed to escape when he was smashed.

The large hand clutched his hair again and shoved him past the opening.

"You're doin' fine, mate. I expect ya to keep on or we'll have to stop for another refresher. Only snapped four of your ribs, 'member, ya got twenty more. I got no problem breaking 'em one at a time." His capturer chortled. "Or I can always make it easy on m'self and pop your neck. Your choice."

Cold steel wedged underneath his burning ribs and nudged him to go. Two years had passed since someone aimed a firearm at him, but the memory hadn't gone away nor was the experience less terrifying.

"Where you takin' me?"

"We're goin' where we're goin'. All you need ta' know." Another malicious chuckle followed as his abductor pinched his elbow to guide him. "What the hell. Y' been such an accommodating hostage, I'll *shoot* ye a hint on what's gonna 'appen to ya." He laughed again. "Didya catch ma' clue?"

"Hard to miss. Gonna have a bang-up time, 'eh?"

"You're a fucking comedian, ain't cha?"

"I'm here all night."

"Maybe, maybe not."

"Now who's funny?"

Eric labored to mentally control his throbbing ribcage and commit his senses to memory in case he managed to getaway. Waves rumbled nearby. A crisp scent floated amid the light winds. Big surprise. They stayed on an island, so they were by water.

But this shoreline didn't feel the same as the

beaches near the resort. This pathway was littered with seaweed, slimy crap, and jutted objects, which tripped him and shredded the bottoms of his feet. His ribs jarred as his aches exploded. Each stumble worsened his agony, yet he forged onward, not emitting a sound.

After a lengthy hike, the texture under his soles changed. The gritty, polluted sands altered into a wooden surface. Breakers below sprayed and dampened his bare feet. Sensing a narrow width ahead, Eric carefully walked, alert to his vulnerability. One push or misstep, and he'd topple over the edge, and be a goner.

"Wait here," he was ordered.

Noises generated around him. Someone caught his forearm and backed him into a cold, wet, pipe-like bar. Probably a banister, since it felt like he stood near an edge, possibly stairs.

Eric also detected a change of guard.

Whoever steered didn't possess near the strength of the man who'd escorted him here. He listened, trying to hear over the breakers' rumble to determine how many deviants participated in this fun game of torture. He thought he caught the low sound of a second voice when they moved, but the beating he'd taken earlier had fucked up his mind. He couldn't distinguish reality from imagination.

"Okay, now step," commanded his previous leader.

He edged down a staircase, snatching the rail behind him, and used it to pilot to the base.

Once he reached the bottom, a large palm covered his head. His chin was rammed into his chest, hard enough to cause his teeth to clench.

"One more step and you're there."

Eric's leg extended and planted a foot. He stepped

into air and quickly spiraled downward. He crashed onto a rigid exterior. Laughter dwindled overhead, followed by a muffled thump.

With his body broken, he could hardly move. His resolve to survive weakened. Every muscle throbbed. Consciousness waned in and out until he relented and allowed insentience to overcome.

****

A featherlike stroke caressed his open palm. Eric stirred as he lay curled against a merciless surface underneath him. Raw pain seared from every pore, and the insides of his mouth tasted like the entrails of a garbage can.

He moaned and shifted his knees to his chest, shrinking into a human ball. Outbursts bashed around him and smacked the exteriors of whatever he lay in. The room tipped to one side, then the other, inciting waves of nausea to accompany his other ailments.

His eyelids cracked open into tiny slits. Remnants of a weakened dawn—or was it dusk? seeped in past a tiny round porthole.

"What happened to you?" demanded a nearby voice.

He wasn't alone. Good or bad? Most likely good, since he remembered he was tied and blindfolded when he was shoved down the rabbit hole, and now he wasn't. Perhaps he ought to thank them, and he would when he found a way to speak.

A hand braced the floor as he sluggishly rose, his other arm remained fastened to his ribcage.

A dark, steady gaze centered on him from across the room.

He paused half-way up and discovered his voice

although it hurt like hell to speak. "What the fuck?"

"Nice to see you, too."

"How did you…?"

"Long story." Darla slumped against a far wall. Her legs were crisscrossed. She circled a curl around her finger. "FYI. Our current situation sucks."

"Yeah." Eric glanced at his former girlfriend. "And it's getting suckier by the minute."

Chapter 6

Darla raised to her tippy toes, grasping the sill's edge, and peered past a tiny porthole. The speedboat scattered a dull beam across the deep, providing a speck of light. Water spewed below, splashing the pane with a liquid sheen, obstructing her view further.

She turned within to inspect indoors, searching to locate a possible escape. The cabin was slightly deeper than most. She judged the hatch above to be about six feet. However, the width appeared standard and amplified the tight quarters. Someone went to the trouble and gutted the room, but even then, space was limited.

A long sigh seeped from her lips as she palmed the cool glass. Except for the trapdoor overhead and this miniature window, she didn't see any additional exoduses.

"We need to find something heavy to smash this."

"Sure we do." Eric sat on the brig's far side. He'd scarcely mumbled a word since he awakened. Arms crossed, face defiant, his quiet, but surly attitude projected the depiction of disgruntled. "And then what?"

Amazed he responded, she ignored his dourness. "We break out."

He scanned the bare cuddy. "And go where?"

She examined the span of murkiness outside. "Not

sure."

"You're not sure because our options are nil."

"We can swim."

He stretched his neck as if to peek past the aperture, although it was too high for him to view outside. "I'm speculating we're nowhere near land. Breakers are rough. Sky's gloomy. Can't tell if it's day or night. Plus, I'm not in the best shape. We might or might not live by hanging out with Gargantuan upstairs, but I have serious doubts we'll get to Tluq Cay if we jump into the water. We'll either drown or sharks will devour us. Neither's appealing." He leaned into the bulkhead. "Which puts us in deep shit."

Darla transferred off her perch and lowered to the floor. She struggled to not let his brusque demeanor bug her. They were not on great terms, heck, they weren't on terms, but at the moment, they shared a number of dire situations, this being the worst. She couldn't let his curtness diminish her efforts to find a way out.

Eric wrestled to sit higher. "You never explained how you got caught."

"Yes, I did. A giant man captured me while I was on the beach. End of story."

He eyed her skeptically. "One sentence is never your story's end. Hell, your beginnings are at least two chapters long and crammed full of details. Giganta abducting you oughta be at least three hundred pages."

She preferred not to continue this chat. In spite of their present condition, she was still mad at him and clearly he remained angry with her. Her explanation wouldn't succeed in satisfying him and most likely expand their fight.

"Isn't Giganta female?"

"Semantics. Tell me what happened."

Darla held in a huff, resigned that she would have to offer him a fragment of what occurred earlier. "Everything went down quick. I walked along the shoreline, and a super tall person apprehended me. I fought, but he was stronger and faster." She grinned. "I did manage to get in a couple of good kicks..." her smile faltered, "and I may've ticked him off. He threatened to suspend me from the mast by my ankles if I didn't behave."

Eric chuckled as if he got a visual and relished in it.

A shoulder raised. "That's all."

His doubting features mirrored his disbelief. "Let me make sure I got this. You went for a hike on the beach by yourself, *late at night,* attending to your business when Godzilla, who I'm sure is male, catches you and carries you here."

"Sums it up."

"No, it's vague. You're avoiding details and keeping something from me."

"Glad we're on the same page." She tugged at a curl. "Do you suppose this group of pirates will demand ransom for us, too?"

"I don't think this guy's a pirate."

"Why not?

"Something is off. The pirates who have Blaine never called last night."

Alarm shot through Darla. "I wonder why?"

"Yep. That was on my mind, too. Until Godzilla showed up.

"So, how does he fit in?"

"Dunno. But he came to my room specifically for

me. I don't believe you're a part of the equation." The blue in his eyes intensified. "Fess, Darla. How'd you wind up on this piece of ship?"

"Cute pun."

"No deviations."

"You won't give me a pass, will you?" His glare pierced into her. "Fine. I followed you. Happy?"

"You followed me? From where?"

Added discomfort riddled her. She so didn't want to reveal any more. "Your bungalow," she murmured uneasily.

"My bungalow? You saw that ogre manhandle me and did nothing?" Eric exploded. "Fuck, he marched me five kilometers until we reached the pier. Why didn't you go for help?"

"I called the police, or I tried to call them. Cell service is awful. Zero signal. It was four in the morning. No one was around. I went to plan B, and I followed you."

"Which helped, how?"

"I brought my Sig Sauer and had it aimed. I wanted to wing him and give you a chance to get away." Her head shook. "But he moved too fast, even carrying you. Darkness was a major factor, too. I couldn't shoot and risk clipping you. So, I tailed you, hoping he'd possibly lead me to his hideout. Then I could alert authorities. Except he brought you to a boat. I was scared he would sail off before cops arrived. My final gamble was to sneak on and somehow save you." Her chin dropped. "My plan didn't work."

"Where'd he catch you?"

"On the dock." She paused. "Funny. He knew me. Knew my name."

"Strange. Was he the only person on deck?"

"I didn't notice anyone else."

"Hmm, swore he had a helper." He hesitated. "Still no bars on your phone?"

She shrugged. "He took it. And my gun. My favorite."

Eric acted sympathetic—briefly. Then his expression altered to confusion. "It was late. How come you were on the beach and near my bungalow?"

Darla gulped. New questions she'd rather not answer. She braved a glimpse his way. He wouldn't let this pass, either.

"I was kinda watching your hut."

"Interesting. Kinda. Why?"

"In case you needed me?"

"Really? Did you believe me too unqualified to carry a briefcase? I mean, I had to hike a whole kilometer."

"The briefcase was loaded with cash. Tluq Cay hasn't proved to be the safest place, and you were scheduled to meet pirates. Blaine's kidnappers who are also known to kill their victims."

"I brought my pistol, too."

"I assumed. Where is it?"

"I dropped it when big, mean, and nasty attacked me."

"See? My having your back isn't a bad thing."

"It wouldn't have been if he hadn't grabbed you."

"Semantics," she cracked.

Eric shifted, releasing a groan. Her brows dipped as she conducted a long-distance inspection. A bruise darkened his left cheek. His movements indicated more severe injuries beneath his clothes.

"Your turn to tell me how you got hurt. Did you lose a fight?"

"Lose? Never made it into the fucking ring. Asshole sucker-punched me and kicked my butt b'fore I had a chance to react." His hand touched his ribcage. "He cracked my ribs. I'm unsure what else is fractured. Probably my entire body."

More upsurges of alarm engulfed Darla. "I can check your ribs."

"Why? They're broke. Nothing you can do'll unbreak 'em."

"You may have other injuries. You're not moving well."

"No shit." He glanced at the hatch above. "I didn't use a ladder to get down here, either. Bastard tossed me through the hatch after he beat the hell out of me."

"No wonder you're a mess."

"You think?"

"Can you run if we find a way to escape?"

"Doubtful."

"Great. I'm not certain I can carry you."

He crossed his ankles and propped his legs on a built-in storage bin. "Didn't I say we're in deep shit?"

"You're not thinking positive."

His face squelched. "I am too. I'm positive this isn't gonna end well."

"That's not the right attitude. He may not be a pirate, but he could be associated with them. He might take us to where they're located. We could find Blaine. Then the three of us can figure a way out. Strength in numbers, right? Blaine's smaller than you, but together we can help you."

"Seriously, I hurt so bad, I feel faint wiggling my

pinky toe. If Blaine buddied up to someone like our guy, his condition is probably comparable to mine. Or worse. Another problem, we lost our firearms." He paused. "Deep shit, remember?"

"Regardless, if an opening presents itself, we'll have to roll with it."

"Cause we've done a great job of rolling so far."

She rose, turned to the window, and touched the glass. "I wish we could crack this. I'd rather take on waves and sharks"—she glanced toward the ceiling— "as opposed to him."

"Forget it. I'm too big to crawl through that little hole. I'd get stuck. Plus, just breathing kills me. If worming through that hole doesn't do me in, then attempting to swim would."

She sat, casting a glance in his direction. He sounded friendlier, but his features remained rigid and irritated.

"I know it hurts, but you should move to work the soreness out of your muscles. And proactivity beats sitting around."

"Then be proactive." He tilted his head farther back as his lids gradually drooped until they shut. "All this rockin's putting me to sleep."

"Fine. Sleep. Better than you nixing all my suggestions."

"One suggestion. And it can kill us in seven different ways. None of which thrill me."

"Better than opting to play the wait and see game and discover what other surprises your new bestie has for us, later."

"We're lost. Surrounded by a sea of turquoise, ambushed by the fucking hulk. Choices are limited.

Can't be too many surprises left."

She tugged her legs to her chest and draped her arms across her knees. "We could figure out a way to surprise him."

"We could, but I got nothing." Eric reshuffled as he tried to find a comfortable spot. "Happy brainstorming, luv."

Darla opened her mouth to retort, but her vocal cords briefly froze. "You called me luv."

"Habit."

"Habit," she repeated dully.

"What do you want, Darla?" His eyes opened and stared her down as he worked to realign himself. "Until we exit this floating bucket, I gotta act civil. M' energy's drained so I could slip into the past, but don't envision any subliminal signs, if I do."

"No worries. I don't expect anything subliminal or otherwise coming from you. I won't make the mistake, again."

"What mistake?"

"Never mind."

No point in letting the exchange continue. Their environment was already hostile, and their mutual animosity closed in on boiling. An extra battle would escalate their antagonism, which they didn't need. They had to unite to stay alive.

"Whoa." Eric cautiously straightened. "You can't just announce something like that and leave it. Explain."

A lock of hair twisted tight, restricting the circulation in her finger. She blew out a puff of air, disregarding her resolution the previous moment, prepared to weather another tempered firestorm.

"I expected you to understand."

"What? You breaking up with me? Nope. My brain's still boggled. I've yet to understand why you walked."

"You let *me* leave."

"I did not. You left because you didn't get your way. You tried to back me into a corner when I wasn't ready. When I told you how I felt, you threw a tantrum, and took off b'fore we finished our discussion." He relaxed against the wall. "Shitty move, by the way."

"What else was left to say? You'd given me your final answer."

"I don't know...you could've considered my views? Oh no. You said we're done and slammed the door. You blindsided me. I never imagined us apart. I loved you." His lips flattened as his eyes narrowed a fraction. "I thought you loved me, too."

"You know I..." she choked.

"Do I? We're in love, but let's split anyway? What the fuck is that?"

"You'd know if you listened."

"I heard. Every word. You're not happy with our living arrangements. If you and I lived together, we'd see each other more often, and we should consider takin' the next step in our relationship. I didn't miss one word."

She digested this. Between the shouting, he did pay attention. Obviously, he still didn't agree.

"If our living situation was problematic," he aimed a finger at her, "then you share equal responsibility. You should've told me sooner. Instead you let it build up and chose to drop a bomb when you decided to hold the, *where are we going* talk without alerting me what I was in for."

"I never implied I was innocent, but you're correct. I procrastinated on the subject too long. Except when I did come to you, I didn't come at you and attack. You're the one who detonated and blew up. Not part of the deal, either."

"But I didn't dismiss you."

"Nor did you attempt to compromise."

"Whatever. You did what you had to. Message received."

"You heard what you wanted to hear. I suggested we reassess. Put *us* in perspective and determine how to find a happy medium."

Blue eyes snapped toward her. "We had to do it separately? Huh. I'm calling foul. I say you were looking to find a way to leave."

"I was not." Darla uncurled and stood. "I was trying to find a way to wake you up."

"I wasn't aware I was asleep."

"Don't be an ass."

"I don't know what else to be. You love me, yet you dumped me because I'm not to the point where I'm ready to become permanent roommates."

"Why is living with me such a terrible idea?"

"It isn't a terrible idea. I adored every moment you and I spent together."

"But you'd rather not share your house with me? We spent nearly every night together when you were home. I presumed you liked having me around." Her voice trembled. "Evidently, I was wrong."

"No, you're not."

Silence crowded the cabin's insides. Forceful waves pulverized the outer hull as their power strengthened. An approaching storm flitted inside Darla's mind, but she was too distracted to ponder the prospect further.

"Darla, we became a couple super-fast."

"I said something similar when we got together. I believe I even suggested we slow down."

"You did, and you were dead-on. My fault. Because of my excitement of falling in love, I convinced you to hurry. Can't fix it, but I learned, and I didn't want to rush. We *both* had to be willing to make a change. And you don't automatically leave someone you love because they're not where you are."

"How long was I supposed to wait for what I wanted?"

"Until the time is right for both of us."

"I tried that before. It didn't work."

Eric's features softened. "Morgan."

"I waited four years, and what'd I get? Burned. I refuse to repeat my past."

"No worries. Wilmington's prepared to un-burn you whenever you say the word."

Darla elevated her chin to accept his challenge. "Seriously, you're going there? I'm not the one who picked up a pair of bimbos on a plane ride and brought them to my best friend's wedding. Morgan and I *do* have a history."

"And history's ready to repeat itself." His face reddened. "As far as my lady friends? I'm single. I'm allowed."

"What you're allowed is constantly splashed across the internet." She painted the room with her emotions and should bite her tongue, but she couldn't stop herself. "Or rag mags in checkout stands. Everywhere."

"Can't help photographers snap my pictures and post 'em."

"Sure you can. Stay home. You claimed you loved me so much and are devastated because we broke up. Show me and what we had some respect before you go boasting about your latest conquests."

He realigned his position and stared at her. At first, she feared he'd tell her to keep out of his business or go to hell, but he didn't.

Instead, he slackened into the wall. "You're right. I'm sorry."

She went speechless.

"Doesn't matter what we do at this point. The bottom line is you didn't confide in me on something that really mattered to you until you were ready to burst." His manner calmed. "Or make the reason clear as to why you felt the need to move forward at this particular time. So, I didn't get a chance to tell you."

"Tell me what?"

"I may not've been ready to move to where you were in that moment, but I wasn't going anywhere. I was working toward it, because I wanted forever with you."

Their gazes locked. Darla's mind froze. The air thickened as the diminutive cabin shrank. For a second, a familiar glint brightened in his eyes. The sexy tease he used to taunt her, right before he kissed her. His look ignited a deep-seated hunger inside her.

"I wanted forever with you, too," she softly confessed. "I guess I was ahead of you."

He broke their visual link. "I guess." His inflection reverted back to its harshness, demolishing their tender moment. "You shouldn't have waited until this problem consumed you. It made you impulsive and dump me in an all-out brawl."

"Terminating our relationship wasn't predetermined. It happened in the heat of the moment."

"Really? I think it was stashed somewhere in the back of your mind."

"It was not."

"Okay, how about this? You just accused me of disrespecting you and what we had. You did too. You didn't believe in me or us."

"Not true."

"Is true." He shook his head as if to search for the right words. "Didn't you know? I would've moved every mountain on earth to make you happy. Done anything to please you. Died to make your life perfect so you'd know how much I loved you. And you wouldn't share your fears with me. You never trusted me, did you?"

Her heart practically stopped. She trusted Eric Boyd with her life.

She opened her mouth to protest, but he held up a forefinger to stop her. "We're not moving," he whispered.

Darla listened. Engines had shut down. "Did we dock? Maybe he's left the boat."

"The guy nabs us, berthed, and leaves us on our own?" His brows furrowed. "Don't think so."

Darla hated to put their conversation on hold. Although no resolution had been reached, they'd communicated, and gotten things out into the open. Regrettably, staying alive was more important.

She twisted toward the window and surveyed the water. They sat dormant, drifting amid high breakers. "I don't see any land on this side. I assume we anchored, or we've stalled."

"Dunno. I'm not keen on this sitting duck situation. I don't hear any noises upstairs." He stood and swayed, then moved toward a wall ladder. His actions were jerky, like he'd doubled in age. He stopped and looked up at the sealed exit.

Darla joined him. "Can you tell if he left the hatch unlocked? I never considered checking, figuring he bolted us in."

Eric stepped around her and cautiously hoisted a foot to the bottom rung. "One way to find out."

"You can't just climb up and open the door. Big and creepy navigated us to this spot. He's bound to be aboard."

Eric ignored her and mounted the ladder, climbing at a cautious pace. Easing the flap ajar, he scrambled up further and poked his head into the openness.

He retreated two bars lower. "Nothing."

"You're sure?"

"I s'pose he could hide and maybe set a trap for us, but why? He already has us." He returned to the top. Gingerly, he hoisted to the surface on deck and then peeked back through the opening. "You coming?"

She snagged a rung and boosted a leg. "On my way."

Due to moistness caused by humidity and the rocking, her short scale was treacherous. She stumbled several times before her upper body jutted outdoors. Blowing breezes felt wonderful. Strong winds caressed her face, lifted her hair, and awarded her with fresh air. Much improved circumstances compared to the staleness below.

A huge gust raged across the sea. A mass of water slammed into the vessel. Surfs tossed their boat as if it were a bathtub toy. Darla's foot slipped off the ladder. Releasing a soft scream, she caught the hatch's edge and grasped the border tight. Both legs dangled in the air. She prayed another surge wouldn't smash her to the underbelly as she fought to find a rung.

Warm fingers clasped around her wrists.

"Easy," Eric mumbled.

She let go of the side and clutched onto his forearms. Gently, he pulled her up. Standing her on her feet, he let his palms skim across her bare arms.

His inadvertent caress liquefied her interiors.

He eased back, but his hands remained on her shoulders. She raised her eyes and stared at him. Gales whipped his lengthy locks off his forehead as hard raindrops soaked him. His gaze skated across her. A sprinkle of chills coated her skin.

A fiery glow covered her cheeks, aware where this moment could take them. She missed him, missed his touch. Darla fought to curb her spiraling emotions.

Every morsel of willpower strained against her desires, but it kept her from throwing herself into his arms. She severed eye contact and whirled away to stifle her passion that was slowly stealing control.

Eric's palms slapped his sides. He cursed under his breath and stomped to the cruiser's port side.

Shaken, Darla strolled to the helm. She devoted a full minute to reroute her concentration and focus on the cockpit.

"Where the hell did he go?" Darla flinched. Eric had moved beside her. He studied a dark cloud bank on the verge of rupturing. "Not a lot of places to just hop off."

"Water's squally," she observed, forcing her voice to sound normal. "This cruiser is older and not been tended to properly. He shouldn't have piloted out this far. He could've fallen overboard."

Eric's hands gingerly went to his hips as he watched the spray shoot from underneath the boat. "We can only hope." He squinted and leaned forward. "Is that a ship or...?"

Darla searched the bobbing swells until spotting a small dot bounced amid spurts of water. "Did he swap boats?"

"He left a second anchored in the center of fricken' nowhere, unmanned? Not even logical."

They continued to watch the vessel until the blotch vanished into a hazy shield of fog.

Darla glanced across the deck. "Well, he's somewhere and it's not here."

"So you're saying a guy kidnaps us, brings us out in the middle of nowhere, switches boats, and takes off without us. And leaves us transportation?"

"Maybe his aim was to scare us."

"Well done."

"And he has a partner who met him out here."

"Makes more sense." Eric's lips stretched into a flat line.

"What's wrong? Or more wrong?"

"Blaine's ransom. I wonder if he stole it when he kidnapped me."

"Where did you stash the money?"

"On the floor. By my bed."

She held in an inappropriate giggle. "Next to your handgun?"

He shot her an aggravated look. "You didn't notice the suitcase when you came onboard, did you?"

"No, but he covered my eyes, which now seems odd."

"Like any of this's normal."

She lowered into the captain's chair. "I say we accept his generous gift and start back to the island."

"Won't hear me argue." He glanced over the side. "Those waves are high. Will you have problems maneuvering them?"

"No." She inspected the switch board. "Because we're not going anywhere."

Eric appeared confused.

"The key. This old boat requires a key to start." Darla seized a strand of hair and twirled the curl around her finger. "And it looks like he took it."

Chapter 7

Brutal gusts swept across the water, creating massive whitecaps and propelling the crests into the port side. Eric maneuvered forward toward the bow, holding on to whatever protruded to maintain balance and prevent him from toppling into the cycloning brine beneath.

He shivered as he progressed. Temperatures dived and transformed humid airstreams into a cool draught. Add dousing surfs and rain, chills were inevitable.

Eric attained his mark, the starboard bow. Exhausted, he sank into a drenched seat and examined the gloomy skies. Loitering dark clouds had begun to reel toward them. Ribbons of light zigzagged downward as sequences of muted growls announced their impending visit.

"We're screwed."

"What's wrong?" Darla came up behind him. She had disappeared into the cabin below and emerged topside without him noticing.

Eric carefully twisted so not to tweak his ribs. "Besides the obvious, why would you s'pose something's wrong?"

She strolled to him and stopped close by. Too close. Wafts of her familiar scent intermixed within the strong breeze. He rejected the idea of even a slight peek her way, but her intoxicating aroma was a forlorn reminder of what he lost and what he yearned to find again.

"Word choices. You're sounding pessimistic."

He circled away, unable to curb cerebral rewinds. He was mega-pissed at himself for letting his guard down earlier. He'd fought to not ponder over their previous conversation below deck, where he overshared his feelings, and laid them at her feet.

Now, he sought to resurrect his protective barrier and keep his distance.

"Restrain your negativity. We have to be optimistic if we intend to find a solution to our problem."

"You can't assume I'm pessimistic because of my tones or expressions."

Another grumble erupted. She glimpsed at the incoming weather, then back to him. Her brows climbed up her forehead.

"You're way off. My attitude isn't negative. I'm confident. Confident the typhoon approaching will convert us into fish food."

"That's not a typhoon. I've experienced plenty of adverse conditions while sailing. It won't be pleasant, but we can survive."

"You're tellin' me we're safe?"

"Not even. We're stranded. Surges are high, and lightning's everywhere." She evaluated the ominous bank churning straight at them. "No, we aren't safe."

As if to reinforce her prophecy, squalls began to shriek. Rogue breakers arched and collided, pitching the boat carelessly into the air. Eric grasped the gangway to prevent from hurling overboard.

Darla tumbled backwards. She lengthened her arms to catch a floor cleat and held on before plunging farther. Strong gales diminished and shifted its fierce sprays into merely rough. Within a flash, they resettled among the sharp rollers.

He forced a smile. "Point made. But still not cool." A hand raked through his hair, squeezing additional droplets from his follicles. "You okay?"

Saturated, Darla scrambled to her knees, before she stood. Eric squished the urge to help her. Not that he could do much, given his condition, but he certainly wanted to.

"No. I'm soaked." She stomped her feet, splattering drops around her. "We need life jackets. I rummaged in those cabinets downstairs but couldn't find any." She strayed to the stowage bin. A loud squeak echoed as she boosted the lid. She romped inside. "Great. Three are here, and we only need two."

Extracting the vests, she tossed one to Eric and slid the other across her torso. He snared the preserver with one hand, and though the task was difficult, he managed to wrangle into the armholes and fastened the front.

A soft rumble in the opposed direction diverted his attention. A subsequent set of thunder clouds had formed. The original bank was created in the southern region, while this new set was building on the western side. Eric judged their ship's coordinates the potential meeting site as the two monsters were preparing to convene.

"Another storm's brewing."

"Wonderful. Just what we need." Darla wandered to the cockpit and squatted to inspect numerous cubbies situated within the helm's central section. "We have to find cover, but I'm not sure where."

A second blotch amid the rolling waters netted Eric's interest. Eyes narrowed, he concentrated on the murky patch jutting beyond the aquatic sphere. This time, a genuine smile curved across his lips. "Would land work?"

She shot him a doubtful glance.

"Land." He gestured at the portion of earth swelling beneath the sea. "An island. Dunno, could be a part of the Turquoise Archipelago."

Darla raised to stand. She squinted at the mass. "I doubt if the Turquoise Archipelago's chain reaches this far. If I remember correctly, they're all populated, and designed to attract tourism. This one seems secluded, although we're still too far away to say for certain."

"Whatever. Dry ground's more secure. If we can guide this tub to the island, sans a working engine."

"Unfortunately," she fell to her knees, reviving her hunt, "it isn't so simple."

"What's simple about steering a boat, minus a motor?"

"Nothing. But even if the mechanics did work, we're still at risk. High drafts will change directions several times during downpours. We could end up adrift, which is the least of our worries."

"You're saying it makes no difference if we can move or not?"

"I'm saying to keep a watch on our bearings."

"Can't do that if we leave our bearings up to Mother Nature."

"We're not leaving anything to anyone. We're taking control." Darla rose, her face beaming as she displayed a screwdriver. "Ever hotwire an engine?"

"You're joking, right?"

"Nope." She knelt by the switch. "I can teach you, if you don't know how."

He left his bench, ambled closer, and slanted toward her. "Wish I was surprised you know how to do this, but I'm not. How'd you come by this talent?"

She loosened the tiny rivets skirting the control panel to expose various reedy wires. "Let's just say, I didn't always date upstanding types."

"Yeah, TMI. Let's not go there."

Piercing booms bounded overhead. Eric peered upward. The thunderstorms loomed low, swirling practically on top of them. Flickers bounced off one vapor to the other, stalked by more threatening growls.

"You might wanna hurry. Storm number one's ready to invade."

"Almost there. I just have to tap these wires to the starter." She linked the connections, goading the motor to whine.

Flashes popped, followed by a chain of explosions. Sheets of rain began to flow, pounding, and stinging their skin.

"Eric," Darla yelled between crashes and flares. "It's dangerous out here. Go below."

"What about you?"

"I'll be okay. I have to steer us away from this mess."

His arms folded as he reversed and sat in his perch.

"Eric." She seemed exasperated, but chose not to waste time arguing, which he counted on. Grabbing the wheel, she rotated. "Fine. If you're thrown overboard or struck by lightning—"

"Yeah, yeah, warned." Eric twisted half-around and paused. His jaw fell. "Holy shit, Darla, starboard side."

She turned and gasped.

A wall of water towered above them. The enormous upsurge held, then swooped under them, lifting their boat and angling it sideways. The brine fizzed and churned. Spurts kicked up and lashed as the vessel creaked and buckled.

Eric attached to the side's trim. His legs bicycled to stay aboard. Darla flew across the base. She snatched the tip of a coiled rope. The tie unwound as she was flung toward the violent spins below.

Helpless, Eric clutched the manrope tight. He couldn't allow her to submerge and be sucked into the revolving depths. Releasing his hold, he flattened, lying on his stomach and belly-skated toward the gunnel. Heavy spurts concealed his vision, and his cracked ribs throbbed like hell, but he kept pushing.

The swell released, levelling the craft. Eric crawled to his feet and sloshed to the last place he saw Darla. Whirling tides swayed the liner. Explosive blasts ricocheted throughout the atmosphere. Enormous raindrops battered his chest, driving him backward, but the rain didn't deter him. He fought until he grasped the vessel's flank.

He found Darla. She'd been slung overboard. Violent green water surrounded her. Clinging to a line, she skimmed amid the deep's spinning summit.

"Hold on." He tugged at the lead. Furious swells towed the bind in the opposite direction, tightening around the underside, and refused to yield. Eric wrestled, but relented after a brief tussle. Raging seas wouldn't wait. A sturdier apparatus was required. He scanned the craft's interior.

Oars were secured to the aluminum border. Effortlessly, he untied the sweeps, rushed to Darla, and extended the paddle to her.

"Grab on."

Another monstrous roar detonated. The vessel lurched again, sending Eric airborne. Gravity overruled his flight attempt and smashed him into the freeboard. Without hesitation, he ignored his aches, hopped up, and raced to Darla.

But she was no longer suspended. She wasn't anywhere. This latest eruption triggered currents to spool. Solid flows had captured and dragged the line underneath the hull.

Tamping down his panic, he snagged the dangling cable and leaped in. Fluxes raced, ramming him into the craft's larboard. Struggling, he swiped a hand underwater, inching lower, and repeating the process as he went.

He found nothing, and dread clutched his heart. He descended sixty meters when he grazed something odd. Skin.

Combatting the elements, he dove past the surface, and swam the course where he estimated she drifted. Luck finally went his way. It took a meagre instant to locate her. As he suspected, Darla had been pulled underneath and knocked unconscious. The lanyard, along with the tide's pull had pinned her against the exterior.

Explained why her life-preserver hadn't performed its function. He jerked the cord and found it to have plenty slack, rendering the fix uncomplicated. No longer confined, he enclosed an arm around her middle, and drew her to him. Although his palm burned after gripping the thick twine, he maintained the attachment, lunging to the top with Darla in tow.

Hoisting her past the edge, he gently eased her to the boat's floor, then scaled inside. He placed her on her back and positioned two fingers on her inner wrists. A healthy pulse thumped.

He shook her. "Darla? Darla."

Her eyelids lifted. She sprang upright and coughed. Water gushed and spewed from her apertures amid hacks. Her head dropped between her legs to spit out the leftover sea. Laying back, she breathed heavily.

"Are you all right?"

Soggy curls laced across her face. "I'm great," she choked.

"You don't look so great."

She heaved another hoarse hack. "Thanks."

Eric carefully removed his shirt, folded the wet material the best he could, and tucked it under her head. "Why'd you let go of the rope?"

"I didn't. Those huge waves yanked it out of my hands." A forearm brushed across her mouth to wipe away access water. "I'm glad you found me."

He clutched his ribcage and settled next to her.

"You're in pain," she observed.

"Been an intense hour."

"Seriously. Did you do more damage?"

"Dunno. I'm still breathing. After what we just went through, I'm happy with that."

"Um, I appreciate you saving me."

He grinned. "I do owe you."

"You do." She raised and stretched, combing her fingers through her hair. She removed her life-vest, gripped the hem of her t-shirt, and twisted. Liquid flowed from the material. "We're even, now."

Eric tried to avert his eyes, so he wouldn't stare. The perilous moments evaporated as his mind emptied. The shirt she wore was his, one she usually slept in. The wetness caused the thin cloth to become transparent. It clung to her curves, revealing the outline of her pert nipples.

He forced his eyes away. The air may be cool, but blood roasted his veins, inciting a searing hunger. Memories of her skin beneath his fingertips wavered inside his thoughts. Eric held onto his impulses. He couldn't go there. The discussion concerning their relationship seemed eons ago, only in reality, an hour had scarcely passed. Because of their circumstances, his anger had dwindled. Instincts told him Darla's did too, but they'd solved little, nor was he certain they would agree to a mutual resolution.

He reverted to her. Unusually quiet, he feared she may suffer unforeseen issues after her prolonged dip. She didn't. Instead, she sat cross legged, allowing her hair to dry in the sweeping gales as inclement conditions dissipated.

Eyes shut, chin tilted, a tiny smile touched her lips. An uncomplicated enjoyment for her, and a stimulating one for him as his libido spurred into overdrive. Her head tipped to the side.

Alarm transported him back to reality. "You're bleeding."

She regarded him, surprised. Crimson streaks trickled across her cheek.

"You must've hit your head."

"I don't remember." Fingertips traced her temple. She studied the scarlet liquid and frowned. "Is it serious?"

Eric inhaled, laden with apprehension and spiraling emotions. Unsure he could be near her and not try something stupid, he resisted attending to her basic, but immediate necessities.

"You're not dizzy?"

"No, but I am nervous. Head injuries require monitoring. I want to know what this is."

Enduring a mixture of reluctance and eagerness, he rose to his knees and tilted slightly to detangle her locks.

Gentle fingers pressed against his chest. "Um, can you put on your shirt?"

His mouth curved upward as he grabbed the t-shirt by the sleeve and tentatively tugged the wet fabric over his head. Then he edged closer to examine the wound. "Does it hurt?"

"It's starting to throb." Her voice sounded stronger, though he detected a slight shiver.

Working through her tresses, his fingertips became warmer each spot he touched. It didn't take long for him to find the glob of plasma congealed near her hairline. "I can't tell much. Blood's clotted, and it's hiding the gash. I gotta clean it' b'fore I can tell anything."

"A rag is stuffed in one of the nooks by the wheel."

"Not sanitary. You can't afford an infection."

"Rinse it first."

"Your gash has affected your thinking. The ocean isn't sterile either."

"Benefits of ocean water have been touted to ward off infections for centuries."

"You spent ten minutes in the sea. You ought to be

halfway healed."

"So more should completely restore me."

"Your call." Eric gradually heightened to stand. He lumbered to the cubbies.

"Third cube to the left, I think."

As usual, she was correct. He quickly inspected the material. Not clean, but not filthy. He cautiously leaned over the boat's frame, dipping the scrap of fabric into the water until it was doused.

He crouched near her and dabbed. She hissed at his initial stroke. A warm palm grabbed his and squeezed.

"Hurting worse than before?"

"A little." Her voice cracked. Flush crept up her face as she broke their connection.

"Still not sure this is the best idea. I always heard leave wounds alone if they're clotted."

"True, but if the wound is slashed to where I require stitches, then I want to know."

"What's the point? It's not like we can call 911, and they'll arrive in thirty minutes or less to sew you up."

"You're confusing emergency services with pizza? Medical assistance is free if they aren't here in a half an hour?"

"You think they'd bring food, too?" A stern guise flickered his way. "Lightening the moment, luv."

Her head bowed as a smile inched across her lips. Eric gave himself a mental kick for his nickname slip. "I'll try to keep m' touch gentle and to your satisfaction."

She snapped a glare his way, then once more lowered her head, and grinned.

Eric also smiled as he cautiously blotted away the

gunk, exposing the laceration to investigate the scrape before forming his diagnosis. "It's not bad. I doubt it'd take one stitch." Lowering next to her, he bathed the washcloth in a leftover stream to drain. "The side of y're face is worse."

A palm stroked her cheek. "What's the matter with my face?"

His knuckles nudged her hand. "Move." He cupped her chin to level her head. "You gotta bunch of squiggly red lines runnin' down." He chuckled. "You're full of errors."

"I've made a few."

"Not as many as me."

Tenderly, he daubed the stains, hovering and leaning into her as he worked. Her fresh breath feathered and caressed his skin. Insides of his mouth moistened as cravings to taste her sweet lips mounted.

Her eyes lifted to unite their gazes. Dark pupils dilated as if she sensed his desires. They knew each other too well, and he knew her hunger matched his.

Could he? Or better question, should he?

Forgiveness was automatic when it came to Darla Hennessy. But would they reunite? As much as he wished they would, he'd have to say no. She didn't believe in him, and her lack of trust didn't just disturb him, it sliced his heart in two.

Despite the love they shared, an absence of trust would end them. Except the knowledge didn't block his growing appetite to physically have her. If he didn't shut off his longings, he would lose control and give in.

"Done." He abruptly withdrew and stretched to stand, discarding the bloody rag, careful not to look directly at her. "Feeling well enough to begin my hotwire education?"

"Oh, sure."

She gradually rose. He paced behind her to the bridge and waited several feet away. He should give himself a break. He did the right thing.

She crouched by the open board to work, presenting him a full view of her sweet, tight ass. He spun away. Sometimes the right thing sucked.

The engine revved and died. She made a second effort and received identical results. She gaped at the regulator, bewildered. "I wonder why it won't turn over."

"Dunno." Eric relocated to the cockpit and thumped the plastic seal covering a petrol gage. "Gage's sitting on E. No fuel, maybe?"

"Oh, don't tell me." She checked the meter. "Betcha that's our problem. We're out of gas."

"Ideas?"

Darla scanned the surrounding aqua deep. "Swim?"

"Oh, hell no."

"The trip isn't too far. Five miles, tops."

"Five miles? Are you nuts? We're both drained. I have fractured ribs, and your head is seeping blood. Don't you have a headache?"

"Yes, and a swim will be tough, but we'll wear our life vests. We can stop and tread if we need to rest."

"Not safely. The waves aren't calm, and the ocean's got its own version of Sea World, starring creatures I'd rather forgo meeting face to face."

"Do you have a better plan?" She toddled across the deck to retrieve her vest. "What are our alternatives? Stay and hope what? We'll drift inland? I can already tell you we're floating farther out. You suppose a ship will sail by and rescue us? I haven't spotted so much as a rubber raft, have you? Or what if that ogre reappears, realizes we're not dead, and finishes us off." She stuck an arm through her life jacket armhole. "Better odds are on Shamu."

Thoughts of spending more time in the unstable depths, especially with his ribcage on fire didn't appeal. Plus, her head had begun to show a huge knot. But even so, Darla was right. Their picks were limited. They would certainly die if they remained onboard. The only other option was a swim.

He staggered to the edge and pondered over the breakers. While the concept didn't get any better, the waves did appear more frolicsome as opposed to menacing.

"Contemplating or measuring?" Darla appeared by his side. "Here." She passed him a pair of worn sneakers.

"What are these, and where'd you find them?"

"They're sneakers, and I found them in the cabin."

"And you're giving me someone else's smelly, used shoes because...?"

"Because the land may be rocky or a jungle. Or the island may be the home of slimy, toe eating reptiles, and you're barefoot. Wear them for protection."

His nose wrinkled, but he accepted the sneakers, silently not agreeing with her logic.

"Quit acting so disgusted and put them on. They'll wash in the ocean."

Stepping down, he slipped a foot into the shoe, holding back his grimace, and laced it tight, doing the same with the other.

He climbed upon the brink, emptied his mind, and

vaulted into the green-blue waters. Rigid, liquid skulked over him like a thawing iceberg slithering deeper into the whirling depths.

Darla jumped in behind him.

They sustained slow and easy strokes to conserve strength. Neither wasted their momentum on conversation. Concentration centered on treading the blustery breakers, resisting aggressive tides, and maintaining their endurance.

No curious or famished marine life interrupted their swim. Storms drove most fish and company to the bottom. They did have to dodge a smack of jellyfish and masses of seaweed. More than once, Eric wished friendly dolphins would materialize and provide them a ride, but they'd gone into hiding, too.

Eric's mind became as waterlogged as the rest of him. He couldn't estimate the number of hours they swam. They approached the isle as the sun descended, dipping behind the horizon. Exhausted, they crawled onto a sandy beach. Eric elevated high enough to unfasten and take off his life jacket before he collapsed.

Darla whipped off the vest and tossed it aside. "I wish we had a flashlight to investigate and see if this island's inhabited."

Eric stretched his tired, throbbing body. He didn't move. Couldn't move. His throat was dry, and his nostrils burned. The night currents whispered across his wet skin, provoking a rush of prickly needles to stipple his body. Cooler air didn't bother him, he was too tired to care.

"What you're suggesting involves moving. I don't have another step in me."

"We're camping here? On the beach? I'm cold."

She chafed her arms to reiterate. "Can't we find a better place, one that shields us from the wind?"

"You're welcome to seek five-star lodgings. Me? I'll sleep wherever. As long as it's not in water." His lids drooped as the fire in his lungs cooled. "Not water. I never want to swim again."

Darla rustled next to him, but his strength was too zapped. Eric didn't waste the energy to speculate the cause of her restlessness as his world faded further into nothingness.

"Eric? Eric?" Someone shook him.

"Sleeping," he mumbled.

"Eric. Come on. We're in trouble."

"Listen to your lady. Git your arse up."

His eyelids fluttered. The voice sounded familiar, but the person who spoke was a stranger. Bit by bit, he awakened. An image developed, at first blurred, and then a form fully emerged.

"Shit." Eric sprang to sit, promptly wide awake.

A group of scary-looking men had hemmed them in. Some had flashlights and others didn't. They all had weapons. Trained on him.

The massive guy who beat him senseless, kidnapped him, and left him on a useless barge in a turbulent storm arched over him wearing an expression of malice. His gun was targeted at Eric's forehead.

"Not sure how ya' escaped." The firearm inched closer to his brow. "But we gotta rectify the situation."

"Darla?"

"I'm here. So is island hospitality, if you haven't noticed. They've come to welcome us."

He scanned the men until he found her. Two men restrained her off to the far side. One held her arms behind, and the other aimed a pistol at her temple.

"Thanks, guys." Eric eyeballed the chunk of steel leveled in the middle of his brow. "Your kindness is givin' me the warm and fuzzys."

"You ain't felt nothin' yet." The big guy laughed. "But you will. And don't count on it bein' warm or fuzzy."

Chapter 8

The bandit jabbed Eric's ribcage with his machine gun muzzle. "On your feet, mate."

Darla winced, experiencing Eric's agony. Worried he would counteract the rib poke and suffer a volatile outcome, she leaned forward to catch his eye.

Eric slightly nodded. Clasping his middle, he balanced a knee to the ground, and slowly pushed to stand. Once on his feet, the giant prodded him again, urging him to join the ring of men.

Two men hemmed him in on either side. Each carried an automatic assault rifle aiming the barrels at his temples. Holsters were attached to their waists, containing handguns.

Darla's mouth watered, spying her weapon of choice. If she could snatch a pistol—logics derailed her. Her and one revolver against approximately forty equipped men and duel rifles targeted at Eric's head? Conditions weren't favorable to win against these guys.

The group disbanded and hiked into the darkness. Chatter amongst the quiet crew emerged. Most spoke French, a language Darla understood well, but she only caught a word or two as they progressed, since their backs faced her.

The huge man strolled straight toward her. "C'mon, Lady." The firearm aimed at her side fell away. He snatched her forearm and spun her the other way as he passed. "Let's you and me have some fun."

"Awe, Auster." Her guard smirked. "Don't enjoy her too much, or you'll piss the captain off."

"Ain't worried 'bout no captain."

Darla withdrew her arm and treaded backwards. Surprisingly, Auster didn't attempt to restrain her. She considered running. Her gaze swiped the landscape.

Surrounding shadows afforded numerous underground options, but to elude this goon would be a near impossible challenge. Incorporate her exhaustion and headache, she doubted she would advance far.

Auster surveyed her and smiled.

Darla back stepped again, wider, this time. Straight-faced, he induced bone chilling danger, but his grin heightened his sinister appearance.

"You mean to fight me?" His fists clenched. "Won't win, ya know. Just come with me. Promise you'll appreciate me if you keep your mind open."

A glance across her shoulder revealed the band of men were gone. With Eric. Fate may well decide their survival on this quest.

"Follow me, girlie."

Once again, Auster didn't try to physically restrain her. Without checking to confirm if she was behind him, he sauntered across the beach in the opposite direction from his cronies.

Confused, she stayed put.

He paused and turned back. "Lass, you ain't gonna escape pretendin' to be a statue. Now c'mon."

She shook her head to reassure she heard him correctly. "Escape?"

"S' what I said."

"You're letting me go?"

"Part of the deal, Lady." Then he mumbled, "'bout got m' ass reamed for leavin' ya on da boat."

Darla frowned. She summoned her courage and deliberately marched to where he stood, but safely halted out of his reach.

"What's the deal?"

"None your business. Just, I ain't s'pose to kill ya. To be sure no one else does, you need to do as I say."

"Is this release happening before or after your *fun* with me?"

"Now listen." A large hand waved at the shoreline. Moonbeams gleamed across the sandy beach and offered a semi-clear view. "Go that way till ya come to a fork. It's some ways, so don't panic if ya don't sees it in awhiles. Take the right side, leadin' to the jungle. Carry on into the woods. Mind yourself. Unfriendly residents sleep in them bushes." He chuckled. "Might extend a meet and greet if you're too loud. Stay on the trail to the isle's other side. You'll see a big cabin and a pier. Jet skis are parked on da bank. Wait till dawn when the crew's sleep'n, before you start any engines. Head north, and ya 'll get back to your fancy resort."

She tried to determine if he was joking or if this was an attempt to ambush her, yet he still didn't make an effort to apprehend her. Maybe he really was truthful and turning her loose?

This whole night puzzled her.

"Ya better get movin' before they"—he gestured at the area his buddies recently vacated—"come huntin' for ya."

"What will you say when you return? They'll wonder what you did to me, won't they?"

"Might." He spat a wad of dark matter between his

gigantic boots and stared out toward the sea. "If they ask, I'll tell 'em I had my way with ya, and I kilt ya, cuz ya tussled with me." He chortled again. "They'll believe me."

Darla snatched a curl and twisted. She ought to express sincere gratitude to her guardian angel and bolt. Even if his so-called pact with whoever instructed him not to murder her, he didn't offer any assurance he wouldn't hurt her, or renege on his agreement if he deemed it necessary.

Except, she had another reason for not taking off. "And Eric? Are you releasing him, too?"

"Nope." Auster's jovial demeanor altered into severe. "Gonna put a bullet in him as soon as y' go. You better scram before dat happens. Hate for ya to witness a violent act toward your man."

"What did Eric do?"

"He's gettin' what's comin' to him, s'all I'm sayin'. Now, you're askin' too many questions, same as ya did when I caught ye before. Gettin' on my nerves." He gestured toward the water. "Now go, before I change me mind."

Darla ultimately conceded, determining she wouldn't obtain the answers she sought. She scurried along the shores, not wasting time to check if anyone tailed her.

Newly formed clouds blanketed the moon and obscured her passage. She regarded the murkiness as double sided, beneficial and a hindrance. No one could spot her without a lot of effort, yet her view was obstructed. Following her instincts, she sped across the surf, scampering around a long, sharp bend.

Her momentum dipped halfway. Yesterday and

today were exhausting. Her head pounded, sleep had been sporadic, and she hadn't eaten since…she couldn't remember her last meal.

She operated on pure adrenaline and longed to stop for a rest.

Except her intuition screamed. Evil lurked near. Or maybe her imagination overreacted. Trusting her instincts, she summoned her reserve energies and pressed on.

Her run persisted, straightforward along the banks until a fork in the road materialized. She stopped for a moment where the road pronged and studied the two paths stretched before her. One hooked to the right, while the second paralleled the seashore. She didn't hesitate and rounded the curve farthest from the water. Shapes of a tower mass loomed in the distance. She studied the contour and deduced this was the rainforest Auster directed her to enter.

Reservations mounted as she approached.

Normally, she investigated places she vacationed prior to her arrival. She preferred to review and avoid any adversities. Eric called her an adventure buzz-kill, in which she countered preparation created satisfying trips. She gazed at the community of trees swaying wildly in the breeze. He couldn't accuse her of spoiling the venture now. No doubt, she was not prepared.

Darla braked and skimmed the forest outskirts, hoping to detect an alternate route inside, but her efforts were useless. If one existed, she lacked the knowledge and sight to locate it.

Every nerve ending kinked as she searched to find a tiny clearing that looked secure to enter. Setting foot in any jungle was a risk. Setting foot in an unknown wilderness at night deprived of supplies or protection was foolish.

Similar to these past few hours, her choices were zero. She shoved a cascade of shrubberies aside and trudged into blackness. Brush crackled nearby, indicating she'd disturbed a dweller's outing.

She stopped and remained motionless until her eyesight adjusted. This forest visit was her first. Air was steamy and dense. Darla sniffed as her eyes watered. Aromas of over-fresh, damp earth, cypress, and the exotic flowers smell was strong, and extra potent.

Winds whistled within the heavy, twisted growth. Branches clicked overhead, rustling the thatches of leaves hanging heavy on the trees. Normal sounds transformed into eerie and strange.

An array of scenarios flitted through her mind as she began to move. Ignoring the creepiness, she made plans to locate the jet skis, find and save Eric, because leaving him wasn't an option.

She also had to consider Blaine. She and Eric temporarily overlooked their original goal after the storm struck. If this landmass was also pirate infested, they might've stashed Blaine in the vicinity. Hopefully, she could perform a double rescue and end this nightmare.

She trekked across a crude course. Dense undergrowth and coiled vegetation congested every passage. A canopy of blackened green veiled the night sky. Slivers of moonbeams peeked past thick foliage, casting spectral vapors, and presented a supernatural glow.

Leaves crunched as branches groaned and scraped.

Occasional squawks and peculiar hoots didn't ease her anxieties. Darla loved outdoors. She grew up on the Texas coast, but she wouldn't pass as a woodsy girl. Fears of a bad guy reunion were surpassed by encounters with non-humans who called the forest home.

Wandering into exceedingly high thickets, her pathway diminished into nothing. She hesitated to study her predicament. Walls of prickly hedges fenced her inside. Fists planted on her hips, she swung toward the access. Brush swayed in the breeze and concealed her entry.

Now what?

Kneeling, she patted the terrain, praying she didn't smack something slithery. Her taps uncovered a bulky stick.

She nodded and bounced the hefty limb in her palm. "This'll work."

Wielding the branch, she battled to divide the spiky shrubs, and creeping past, short of scratching off too much skin.

Her mission proved difficult. The constant swinging motion triggered a piercing pain in her arms, while the endless bending burned her back.

Humidity coated the air. Sweat drenched her clothes, her hair stuck to her head, capping her curls as perspiration trickled down the side of her face, blending with blood from her reopened gash.

Finally, she did enough damage to sidle through.

Frustration surged as she stood on the other side and faced yet another obstacle. A patch of overcrowded trees grew behind the brushes. The grove was heavily branched. Tree limbs interlocked and swept the turf.

"I'm too drained to do any more."

A reluctant grumble seeped, while she separated the tiers, and wormed inside. Headway was slower than a snail's race. Snaking vines tangled and clutched her ankles as she fought miles of overlapping foliage.

She shoved until she created a sizeable clearing. This side appeared obstruction free. Relieved, she took a giant step forward and put a foot down.

The earth gave way beneath her. Plunging into murkiness, she descended rapidly, smacking against a hard surface, and crumpled. Lying on her back, her legs ended up propped against a clay wall above her head. Itchy grasses, chunks of rocks, and dirt clods followed and pelted her body.

She swiped the debris away. "So not my day." Struggling, she sat with her knees pressed into her chest as she squeezed into the diminutive space. "And definitely not five-star lodgings."

Darla peered upward. A precise rectangle was cut above. Undoubtedly a hunter's animal trap, or just another island welcome feature for unsuspecting tourists.

Next on her list. Find a way out of this mess. She gaged the climb around eight feet. Only she required something to help her scale the sides. Another sprinkle of dirt sailed downward and peppered her face. She brushed away the soil, spurting dust off her tongue. A sudden quiver tickled her stomach. Hair on the back of her neck rose.

Grappling to stand, she froze to listen. A noise, resembling a *human* hiked around the hole's outer edges. Darla was no longer alone.

"Hello," she whispered.

No answer. Scuff-like footsteps continued to thud.

"Hey." She raised her voice. "I'm stuck and could use a little help."

Pops and crunches resonated overhead. A silhouette stood above the gap. Darla backed into the wall, unsure whether to further reveal her presents.

"Hello?"

"Can you help me?" Darla yelled.

The dark profile dropped to examine the cavity's interiors. "Darla?"

She stretched, straining to see. "Eric?"

"What're you doin' down there?"

"Sunbathing, what do you think?"

He laughed quietly and stood.

"Seriously? Get me out of here."

"Hang on. I gotta find something to use as leverage."

"Hang on," she muttered, leaning on the wall, then shouted, "Like where would I go?"

Grating clunks and bangs mingled amid groans vibrated. Eric's shadow reappeared. He hauled a long cylindrical object across the pit's brim.

"I'll lower this to you." He huffed, struggling to inhale. "Grab on after I drop it, then give me a shout when you've latched on, and I can pull you up."

"What is that?"

"Dead tree trunk." He straddled the log, leaned forward to retain control. Gradually, he slid the shaft to her. "Once I've lifted you, put your feet on the side of the wall, and take small steps. That'll help get you up."

She grasped the end to embrace tightly. "I've got it."

The log slowly elevated her off the floor. She did

as Eric directed, positioning the soles of her sneakers onto the side and took tiny steps while he inched her higher.

Maneuvering in such an odd stance was difficult and became close to impossible as she ascended toward the top. Loose bark grated against her exposed skin, and the tree's rotted smell made her queasy.

He raised her crest high and held it steady. She stretched to clutch the edge. Her hold slipped. Nails penetrated the soft wood, retaining her grip. She grappled to find the rim.

Eric freed the timber and grabbed her wrists. "I got you. Let go."

Darla relaxed her grasp. Eric swung a leg across the trunk, allowing it to fall into the hollow, while simultaneously yanking her upward.

Once her feet were planted, he released her. She collapsed to her knees and crawled safely away from the abyss. Dusting debris off her clothes, she finger combed the fragments of rubbish out of her curls, then she sank and lay in a mound of dry leaves. Eric crept to her and flopped down beside her. His shoulder overlapped hers. Whether the merging was conscious or inadvertent didn't matter, neither moved.

His warm contact awakened Darla's exhausted body. Her shirt was dampened with sweat and helped resist the urge to snuggle against him. She lay still, barely breathing so not to breach their link.

A deep sigh discharged from his side. She peeked to check on him. His eyes were shut, and his chest moved up and down in even strokes.

He'd fallen asleep.

Disappointed, Darla eased onto her temporary bed

and nestled closer. Stealing a memory, she sniffed, inhaling his musky scent, invoking a soft hum to rattle in her throat.

"How'd you get away?"

She jerked. "You're not asleep."

"Too tired, if that makes sense." He paused. "And I'm eager to hear how you ducked big, mean, and ugly."

"Um, Auster told me to leave."

"Auster?" He raised his head. "Who the hell's Auster?"

"Big dude who messed you up."

"You're on a first name basis, now? When did you become besties with him?"

"There wasn't a formal introduction. I overheard a guard call him by his name."

"Wait a minute." Eric stopped as if her words had just reached his brain. "He let you walk away?"

"He also told me where I can steal a jet ski. And he provided directions to our resort."

"His playmates were ready to use me as target practice, and the fucker was givin' you goodbye gifts?" He relaxed back into the leaves. "What's up with that?"

"Apparently, I'm not a part of the plan, whatever that is."

"Interesting. I think I said something similar a while ago. Am I a part of the plan?"

"If the plan is to eliminate you forever, then yes, you are."

"Nice. Did he mention why?"

"He said you would get what's coming to you. I don't understand. He didn't mention a ransom. He seems to just want to kill you, so I don't get his vendetta. Are your past actions more dishonorable than you've admitted to?"

He croaked a weak chuckle. Darla propped on an elbow and tapered her eyes.

"I bet you have secrets, too," Eric defended.

"I never saw a reason to bury my past."

"Hmmm. Don't agree. You never revealed Wilmington's still in love with you."

"Because he isn't."

"Yeah, he is. Why do you think he attacked me?"

"He didn't. You challenged him. Which is curious. What made you do that?"

"His nose is in my business, and it doesn't concern him."

"Wrong. He paid Blaine's ransom."

"I'm not having this conversation. You know where I stand."

Darla lay down, fuming and disappointed. She hoped he'd get past his animosity, considering their perilous circumstances, but he seemed set on preserving a portion of his anger.

She braved a glimpse his way. A dim moonlight reflected his tenacious frown. Arms were folded across his chest. His annoyance made her realize their semi-truce was only temporary. Once life went back to normal, their hostile ex status would resume in full force.

His tone softened. "How's your cut?"

He rose to bend over her as soon as the question popped out of his mouth. He swept wayward strands away from her forehead.

Nimble fingers traced across her wound with extreme gentleness. "You've bled a little." A quiver shimmied through her. "It's re-clotted. As long as you don't keep hitting it, you should be okay."

She swallowed to moisten her arid mouth. "I'll do my best."

He lay back, emanating another lengthy moan.

"Your ribs? They're bothering you."

"Broken ones are."

"I would offer to help, but you'd say no."

"You'd be right. Nothing you can do for 'em." A hand glided across his torso as if to sooth the soreness. "Doc confirmed that when I broke a couple a long time ago."

"A long time ago?"

"Impulse's first gigs weren't booked in the most respectable clubs. We played in lots of seedy bars and backstreet rooms. Blowups occurred just because some drunk bloke didn't like another's stripe on his shirt. I usually tried to lay low, but I ended up drawn into a few brawls. Broken ribs, smashed nose, and one concussion."

"You've never told me this."

"In the past. I didn't see a reason."

"Glad I taught you to shoot. You suck at fist fighting."

"I fight just fine. My opponents wouldn't've won any beauty contests after a round or two with me. 'Cept a shithead who gave me the concussion. Asshole got me on a sucker move and blindsided me, using a chair. Knocked me out cold."

"Speaking of knocking out. Did you cold cock your bodyguards, or did they give you a free escape pass, too?"

He laughed, then groaned. "Hardly."

"I sense a story."

"Nope." His shoulder closest to her raised as if to imply he successfully fled men yielding weapons with means to kill him, daily. "The herd had gotten ahead of us. My buddys' friendship was shaky, and they bickered most of the time. One had to go into the bushes. They kept fightin' while he did his business. The other guy shoulda watched me but he didn't. He was too involved tryin' to win his fight. I saw a chance, snuck into the forest, and slipped away b'fore they realized what happened."

"Did they come after you?"

"I assume. They can't return to their mates if I'm gone. It's their asses if they do."

"Which means, they'll stay on your tail until they catch you."

"I guess they will. A good reason for us to get out of here. I suggest we rest an hour, stick to Auster's idea, and leave this miserable piece of rock. I'm not comfortable returning to our hotel, but it's a hell of a lot better than this place."

"Did you forget Blaine? I think this island is a pirate hideout, too. Isn't it possible he's stowed here?"

"Why would you believe pirates are on this island?"

"Gut feeling. Regardless, we should scout the area and see if Blaine's here. His safety should be our priority."

Eric was silent. "It is. Just wish we had a place to start."

"We can backtrack to the shore and follow the trail from the beach."

"Backtrack. We're in a jungle. Don't see a way to

retrace our steps."

"Why not?"

"What have we found, so far?"

"You found me."

"Deep in a hole." He rose again and slanted over her, close enough to bump noses. A curve formed across his lips as a playful twinkle entered his eyes. "Pure chance, luv."

Their gazes locked. Eric's spirited gleam transformed into dangerous. Darla identified the expression and knew what was on his mind. Her body trembled, her desires screamed, shouting for her to seize the moment. But his unwillingness to compromise still stung. Until he developed flexibility regarding her emotional requirements, she couldn't adapt to satisfy his physical ones.

Even if it killed her.

He lowered to get closer to her. "Some fortunes are better than others." His voice dropped to a sexy, Scottish rasp. "This one might be the best coincidence I've ever run into."

"Count me as thrilled over your good luck." She pressed a palm into his chest and gently urged him back into his spot. "We should rest. Then we'll search for Blaine before we leave."

Chapter 9

"Seriously, you're not starved?"

"A little." Seriously, Eric wished Darla would find another topic. Her constant hunger jabber reminded him of his hollow stomach, and how delicious a plate of linguine and salmon would taste about now.

He stifled a yawn.

Sleep almost sounded better than food. His catnap had worn off ages ago. His ribcage warbled in pain. Plus lying on the ground for the short rest they did get hadn't done his broken body any favors.

"I'm thirsty too," Darla rattled on. "A huge bottle of water sounds sooo good. Oh, and a soft pretzel with tons of mustard. I'd give away my granite collection if a convenience store would appear around the next corner."

"Don't place bets on that happening. Only place you'll find anything to munch is on the ground. If you're okay nibbling on bugs."

"They're starting to look tasty."

"There's plenty of 'em, every shape and size." He chuckled. "They're organic, too, so they'll be crunchy when you bite into them."

They approached a rare range, vacant of undergrowth. Two sufficient trees shaded the lot.

Darla fluttered her fingers. "Break?"

After trudging hours amongst the jungle's entrails,

dodging thorny bushes, and ducking low hung branches, a break sounded good.

Eric tripped over a half-covered pointy rock, nearly splattering into a huge entwined root, but caught himself in the nick of time. "I think we have to."

He lowered to sit underneath the closest tree, tilted against the trunk, and shut his tired eyes. But sleep didn't come. His brain refused to relax.

They had to regroup. Or just make a solid plan. This constant drifting wasn't working. They required an extended timeout as in a good night's sleep, and food.

If they didn't tend to their basic needs, the conclusion of this trip wouldn't end with a cheerful finale.

"We need to find those jet skis, and head back to the resort."

Darla had reclined against the other trunk. An arm covered her eyes. She straightened as the arm collapsed into her lap. "And forget Blaine?"

"Blaine isn't on this shitty rock. We've trekked across it dozens of times and have yet to encounter another human."

"We haven't even cleared half."

"Well, it feels like dozens. Still, we should go back to Tluq Cay."

"Again, Blaine?"

"We'll get 'im, but we're nearly asleep on our feet, and our energy's zapped because we're hungry. Neither of us can run or fight, and I expect we'll need to do both in a rescue attempt."

A full minute of silence passed.

"You win." She lay back again. "We can go back. I am exhausted. And if you haven't noticed, starved."

"You mentioned it once or twice." He paused. "We can also bring my Glock, if I still have it. One's better than none."

"Auster took my favorite gun. I brought four. I'm well-armed."

Eric stared, but held back his response.

"I can't guarantee I have enough oomph to budge from this spot, but a shower and a soft bed does sound heavenly. After I order room service. I want an extra-large pepperoni, mushroom, pizza with extra cheese."

"Pizza. Official grub of the over process, anti-nutrient gods and the creator of heartburn."

"Totally worth it."

"If you say so. You can spend an evening eating a bottle of antacids for dessert."

"You're confusing me with you. Unlike yours, my digestive track is perfect."

Eric disagreed, but he was too exhausted to argue.

"We also need to check in with Stephanie. I'm worried about her."

"Me too. And the ransom's bugging me. I can't rest until I know the kidnappers are paid. Hopefully, the satchel's still in my room."

"I'm at a loss what we'll do if Auster stole it. Blaine's already in a jam. If we don't have funds to pay…" She swallowed. "I'd rather not consider the outcome."

"Me either. Plus, I'd hate to be indebted to Wilmington for cash we didn't use."

"He'll work out a reasonable repayment plan if the money is missing."

"I'm sure."

Darla ignored his smartass remark. "I'm more

concerned about Stephanie's emotional state. She's probably going crazy since we've vanished. I hope Finn's supporting her."

"He's not."

She shot him a frustrated look. "I get you and Finn aren't best friends, but he's not a total ass. Unless Tequila Sunset, booze, and cheap women take precedence over Blaine's kidnapping. Seriously, he wouldn't desert Steph at a time like this." Darla paused. "Would he?"

"Finn caught a flight home."

"What? When?"

"Same night we made our acquaintances with Auster."

"Why did he leave?"

"This island gives him freaky vibes." She didn't reply. "Finn carries a lot of guilt since his brother and Drake were murdered."

"Why? He didn't cause their deaths."

"Regardless, he was the target, so he holds himself responsible."

"I'm still not understanding why he left."

"Blaine's kidnapping scared him. He spouted a bunch of senseless shit. Even hinted he should replace Blaine in the band if the unthinkable happened."

Darla looked outraged. "I can't believe the thought entered his mind, much less him voicing it."

"I told you, he's bonkers. Anyway, since he was so upset, I suggested he go home. He jumped at the chance." Eric stopped. "A little too quick, if y' ask me."

"Poor Finn."

Darla straightened her backbone and hugged her knees to her chest. She observed the sky as the sun beamed upon the towers of foliage. A wispy breeze lifted her tangled curls off her shoulders. Long waves flowed and caressed her back.

The vision of her messy and pretty roused a familiar ache Eric wished would go away. But no matter how hard he tried, he couldn't squelch the powerful emotions she invoked.

It wasn't difficult to figure out why.

Rockers were known for dating super-models and high-profile actresses. When Eric fell in love with Darla, not a single rock and roll compadre questioned his reason for choosing her over one of the glamor girls from his past. They identified with her realness. Her inner beauty outshined the numerous fabricated females who traveled within their circles. She was one of a kind, and she was the one for him. She stirred him in a way no other did or ever could.

He glanced her way. She lounged on her elbows, extended her legs, and displayed her lovely calves.

A fiery tingle roused in the bottom of his abdomen and shifted downward. He fought to maintain restraint, but his self-discipline disintegrated as old memories rolled in like high tide. She might have pushed him away last night, but he felt her resistance waning.

A forefinger snapped to her lips as she shot a meaningful look his way.

"Wh—?"

She silenced him. "Listen," she whispered.

Eric sat still. The adjoining woods swished. The wind picked up and carried the echo of voices. The words were indistinguishable, but someone was near.

"Shut up, ya' idiot. Ya givin' him fair warnin' you're on his tail."

Darla met Eric's gaze and mouthed, "Auster."

Auster brought a partner, and they were searching. For him.

Hiding seemed the logical way to go. Their current spot was on a small hill in an open range, and in plain sight. Auster's height gave him a double advantage and improved his chances of noticing them if they didn't quickly take cover.

Darla must have drawn the same conclusion. She rose and motioned for him to follow. With difficulty, Eric inched off the ground until he stood. They crouched, staying low, and scuttled in silence toward a brush-filled embankment. They dipped behind the brushwood the exact instant Auster appeared, marching uphill.

The giant man paused near the location where Eric sat seconds prior. He squatted to inspect the topsoil.

Eric seized in air as his heartbeat vibrated in his chest. Instincts told him this man was an excellent tracker. He feared dirt hadn't sufficiently withered, and his footprints were etched into the earth's floor.

The hunter stood and wandered to the tree Darla had just vacated. A boot scrubbed across the soil as he tipped his head back and sniffed the humid air.

"Not here," he yelled to his anonymous associate. He inspected the terrain once more, then gradually paced backward until he vanished into the woods.

They stayed put. "Close call." Darla finally edged from the shrubberies and stood. "We ought to follow him. He might lead us to Blaine."

"He wants to kill me. He might do that, too." Eric didn't stand but stretched his neck to see over the thickets. "Wonder if he and his colleague are tag teamin'. If that's their game, one will hang back and wait until we show ourselves."

"I doubt it. I'm standing in the open. They can't miss me." Darla's concern had been drawn farther away. "Eric?" She aimed an index finger past a thick of trees. "Lights."

"What?"

"I see lights across the field."

He scrambled to his feet and peered above the treetops. A radiance glimmered miles away, bright enough to reflect in the sunlight.

"Wanna wager Auster's heading that way."

"I'd lose. Are you sure you'd rather not follow him? He may lead us to where the jet skis are parked." She rose to her tippy toes. "I can't tell if the light's near water."

He walked to her and offered a hand. "Let's go find out."

She flattened to the soles of her feet and accepted his outstretched palm. "I so hope this place has a Starbucks. A chai tea would really hit the spot."

"Maybe you'll get lucky. You can usually find one on every corner."

They strolled toward the low glow. Their strides held an added bounce, embracing hope their dire circumstances would conclude soon. But their speed slowed as their journey dragged. The village, camp, or whatever was set farther away than they anticipated.

Coarse terrain amplified their travel difficulties. Flatter regions contained severe ridges and uneven planes. Fatigue and their nutrient-lacked physical conditions added further danger to the perilous journey. Steps became cautious. An inadvertent slip could result in an acute sprain or broken bone.

Eric checked on Darla after a hairy maneuver past a wide crevice. "You all right?"

"I am, and I'm just being careful. I tumbled into a hole once already, I'd sooner forgo a repeat."

"You quit talking 'bout eating. I'm starting to worry."

"Daydreaming isn't working for me anymore. I've been speculating how clods of dirt might taste."

"Grimy and lumpy, I suspect."

"Kinda like the oatmeal you make at breakfast."

"Bet you'd devour a bowl if I heated a pot now."

"It'd be a tossup between it and the dirt." Darla slowed to a halt.

Eric stopped behind her. "What's wrong?"

"Watch the brush farther up. It's swaying kind of odd."

Eric shifted and studied the vegetation's movement. His height advantage gave him a clearer view. A sudden chill washed over him.

"You're looking at a person. Someone's hiking ahead of us and movin' the weeds. Auster's possibly our leader."

She narrowed her eyes, straining against the setting sun. "It's hard to tell. Should we hide? If we can see him, then he can see us, right?"

"Yeah, and he's got an invisible friend. They could be lurking around, and we'd never know." Eric sank to sit at the edge of a gap. Pain shot through him. He tilted toward the side to alleviate the ache, placing a palm on the ground to balance. "Let's wait and allow whoever to get farther ahead."

Darla sat by him, dangling her legs over the ledge.

"You're still in a lot of pain, aren't you?"

"Scares me how well you know me, luv."

"Scares me too, sometimes." She cut a look in his direction. "Question. Are we mad at each other?"

"Technically."

"I can deal with technically as long as we're friends."

"Us friends?" He chuckled. "I could never see us as friends. Too much history. Then there's the other thing."

"Other thing?"

"I shouldn't have to spell it out, Darla. Sex. I don't care how mad we are at each other, it wouldn't stop me from wanting you, physically."

"You mean you still want to…?"

"Can't help what's on my mind." He hesitated. "Or should I apologize for my thoughts?"

"You just said you can't control your thinking."

Eric released an awkward laugh. "I can't control anything when I'm around you." Darla's face reddened, although she didn't react.

He'd said too much. He needed a quick diversion to get out of the deep hole he'd dug himself into.

An odd smoothness slid across his perched hand. Eric turned to shake off what he believed was a weed brushing his fingers. He paused. His body flexed as he swallowed what surely would've been a girly scream.

"How long should we wait before we start again?"

"Now's a perfect time," he hissed through clenched teeth. "Get up slow and easy."

Darla reeled her legs in and turned on her butt. She froze. "Eric?"

"Yep, and it's a big fucker, too."

"Actually, it's a snake. Slithering across your hand." She slanted and studied the skating reptile. "I don't believe this one's poisonous, but don't make any abrupt moves, just in case."

"Thanks, luv. Your advice is golden."

Their slinky guest continued to glide across the top of Eric's fingers and flowed downhill into the crevice next to them. Finally, it vanished into the hollow. A mutual gasp discharged once the snake disappeared. Placing his rib pain on the backburner, Eric crab crawled backward, desperate to distance himself from the snake's address.

Darla smiled and stood. "How exciting."

"Because we haven't 'ad enough excitement so far." He inched to his feet and dusted his sweatpants. A shudder zipped across his spine. "A snake crawling between m' fingers isn't exciting. It's more like a mess in your pants and haul ass kind of situation." He dangled an arm to the side and flung his hand back and forth. "I can still feel the slimy bastard."

"Reptiles aren't slimy." Darla peered into the cavity where the snake had disappeared. "I'm curious as to what kind it is."

"Excuse me if I don't wait around while you find out. I'd rather face Auster and his buddy." He paced the length of the hole, struggling to not break into a run. "I'm declaring our rest stop over."

She followed him, but a bit slower. "You know, my eighty-year-old granny comes across snakes all the time when she's working in her garden. She just chops their heads off and goes on. Do you need her to teach you how to deal with them?"

"Glad your humor's intact, luv."

Darkness arrived rapidly, void of the usual sunset fanfare other isles underwent. The faraway glow flickered vivid in the fading sunlight. Obscurity grew around them and provided a straight shot to their destination.

"What if Blaine's held in this compound?"

Eric kept his focus on the brilliance ahead. "We stick with our original plan, after you get your Starbucks. Steal a jet ski and head to Tluq Cay. Refuel, rest, load our guns and come back."

"We can't just leave him. What if we return to the resort, gorge ourselves, catch up on our sleep, and he's executed while we're away? Stephanie wouldn't ever forgive us. Heck, we wouldn't forgive us."

"Why do you ask my opinion if you intend to disagree?"

"I figured you would agree. I never imagined you'd bail on Blaine."

"I'm not recommending we bail, but we need support." Eric halted. "We're not in a position to pull off a rescue, especially by chargin' in spontaneously. We'll be shot the second we bust through the door."

"Just you." Darla maneuvered around him. "I'm not a part of the equation, remember?"

"They can kidnap and torture you until you wished you were dead."

"Pleasant image, thank you."

He resumed walking. His tone changed to thoughtful. "I hope this route actually leads to somewhere, and the light isn't a memorial to a three antlered antelope."

The pair advanced the final link and quickly arrived. Subtle beams glistened within a grove of greenery. They squatted behind brush and peeked above the bushes.

Primitive huts were built close and squeezed in tight rows. The primeval shelters were constructed of logs, loose pebbles, and mud. Roofs consisted of branches and jagged strips of bark. Pillared torches glimmered and encircled the village to serve as protection.

"Sorry, luv. No chai tea."

"Bummer, right?" She scanned the compound. "What should we do?"

"Dunno."

"The sheds appear deserted."

"'Cept who lit the torches?"

"Good question. Let's check out this place. We want to make sure Blaine isn't stashed around here."

"Remember, we can't count on finding Blaine in one piece. We might have to carry him. Are you ready to haul him across the territory we just crossed?"

"Why don't you want to save Blaine? He's your best friend."

"He is. But we'll probably have to risk our lives to save him. I'm too tired to go against his kidnappers."

She glared.

"If Blaine's here, we'll rescue him." Eric drew a long breath. "Somehow."

"I don't believe he's here."

"Then why argue?"

"So we're ready."

"I'm as ready as ever. For goin' on hardly any sleep, no food, and cracked ribs."

"We hiked all this way, let's explore." Darla rose and walked toward the village. She tossed her hair over her shoulder and glanced back. "Are you coming?"

Hesitant, Eric followed her into the soundless, well-lit village. "Place is creepy, luv. Looks haunted."

"Stay alert. You never know what's hiding inside waiting to pounce." Muted flames exhibited a teasing sparkle in her dark irises. "Seriously. Ditch the blood and gore horror movies and find another hobby while traveling on the tour bus."

He lingered in the middle of a dusty pathway, while Darla explored the lean-tos with animated curiosity.

"Stone cookware," she squealed. "I've only seen these in books and museums. This is so cool."

His desire didn't expand to bouncing in and out of ancient lodgings, but he had to admit, he found observing Darla springing from one hut to another, entertaining.

Engrossed in her antics, he sidestepped to stay near her. He stood outside the final hut while she explored. A sharpness pricked his neck.

He flinched and slapped at the sting. "Damn bugs." He grazed the bite with his fingers. Warm stickiness saturated the tips.

A chill rippled across his spine. Slowly, he rotated.

A spear was trained directly at his forehead. An angry man stood at the other end.

Eric gaged their newest situation. "Um, luv? We've got a problem."

A group of native men appeared from the darkness and joined their friend. Gathering in a tight cluster, they crept toward him, with spears targeted straight at him.

"Luv. I think I know who lives in these huts."

She emerged from a cabin. "Did you say

something?"

"I've met the neighbors." He stared at the spike pointed at his nose bearing a dot of crimson. "And they're not friendly."

Chapter 10

"Oh my." Darla paused to review the scene, wishing she'd been discreet when exiting the hut. A group of primitive, young men cornered Eric. Each possessed a spear, and they aimed their weapons straight at him.

Poised to run, she assumed a segment would break away and come after her. Hopefully the diversion would provide Eric an escape option. Surprisingly, not one person budged. Or bothered a glance her way.

Odd. And perhaps a positive, which is something they could use for a change. If they continued to ignore her, and she found a way to relieve Eric, they could resume their jet ski search, return to their island, and regroup. Void of an inkling on how she would pull off a rescue, she paced with ease to the site where the group restrained him.

"Careful, luv," Eric cautioned in a quiet voice as she approached. "Those javelins deliver a mean stick."

She gestured at the tiny stream of blood trickling on his neck. "You discovered this through experience, I see."

"Nothing like learning firsthand."

"I'll take your word for it." Curious, she strolled the ensemble's outer perimeter. "They don't seem to notice me. Do they speak or understand English?"

"Dunno. Spike's done all the talking so far."

She did a quick inspection as she walked. Skin tones were deep brown, but Darla couldn't distinguish if the shade was natural or due to time spent in the sunshine. Dark eyed, their scarcely past adolescent faces remained void of facial scrub. Their hair color was blacker than coal, worn long, and tied loose at their necks.

Their clothing consisted of pants made of dense pelt, sewn with thick thread. Chest and feet were bare. Weapons were also handmade. They used long tapered hardwood as handles, and the shafts were constructed of flint or jasper.

No one stirred or made eye contact as she progressed. "Their culture must deem females as insignificant."

"Hmmm. Not too smart."

"I won't disagree, but it isn't uncommon among primal civilizations."

"You gonna prove 'em wrong and spring me? We can stick with our run like hell plan."

"Because it's worked well, so far."

"Hearts are still pumpin', luv." A dart inched closer to Eric's nose. "For the moment, anyway. We better find an exit soon. I'm gettin' they expect me to hang around until this game is over."

"You may not fare well."

"My thinking, too."

"Let's see if I can help you." She ducked amongst his captors and entered the sphere. Dodging the pointed barbs, she edged ahead of Eric, shoving the most threatening spear outside of pointing range.

"Tread lightly," Eric whispered. "Don't provoke 'em."

"I won't. I plan to be friendly and approachable. If we're lucky, they'll get we're not the enemy, and let us go." She plastered on a bright smile, raised her hand, and waved vigorously. "Hello," she shouted.

Their frozen stances shifted. Expressions of confusion replaced intimidating glares.

She patted her chest. "I'm Darla." She motioned at Eric. "Eric."

"Your plan is to mime?"

"Of course not. Mimes don't speak. My gestures are extending friendship."

"You might want to extend a little clearer. Don't think they're gettin' it."

"Just smile and be pleasant." She mimicked clasping a glass and then pretended to gulp. "We would like a drink of water." Another frantic wave followed. "And we'll go."

A moment creeped by. Collective features transformed back to ominous, and postures resumed their strike-mode stance.

A spear swung toward Darla and targeted the center of her neck. She gasped and swiftly crisscrossed her hands in front of her throat.

"Charades aren't working, luv." Eric paused. "You might've misjudged their opinion of females too. They don't seem to care which of us they kill first."

"Great time to find out I'm wrong."

Spears advanced toward them seemingly in slow motion. She and Eric exchanged a glance and took a giant backstep. They were being maneuvered near a crude, but solid structure.

"They're boxing us in. We have to do something quick." Darla scouted the outer territory. "I say we find an opening and haul ass."

"Agreed. There's small gaps on the left and right sides. You head one way, and I'll go the other. We might get lucky enough to throw 'em off."

They continued to close in, the points of the spears centimeters from their necks. "Count of three?" She didn't wait for him to reply. "One, two, thr—"

A screech erupted amid the darkness. A sequence of indistinctive sounds trailed. The youngsters froze. Their aggressive façades converted into tense or fearful.

Darla frowned at a confused Eric. "Wonder what that was?"

"Not sure, but I'm grateful. And a little disturbed."

Loud clacks drew their attention back to the crowd. Their foes tossed their lances onto the ground, into a pile. No longer armed, they retreated, leaving Darla and Eric unguarded.

"Should we leave?"

"That was our original plan." Eric used his collar to wipe off the oozing blood. "I say we stick to it."

Darla rotated toward the blackness and took one step. "Eric?"

He looked past her. Horror crept across his face. "What is that?"

She squinted. "No clue."

An entity materialized amid a cloud of murky vapors. It lingered too far away to distinguish, but the spectral figure seemed to float toward the torch-lit compound, emitting cries and shrieks as it loomed.

Darla tossed Eric a glimpse. "Suggestions?"

"Mind's gone completely blank."

"How about we run now?"

"Oh, hell yeah."

Neither made the effort to bolt. Both were too mesmerized by the approaching shape.

The presumed ghost closed in. Glowing, beady eyes emerged out of the darkness, morphing into a petite, older woman. Stout breezes billowed her black, flowy gown, giving off the impression she glided on air.

"You lost your pointy hat," Eric muttered.

"Don't offend."

"Cm' on. You can't tell me she didn't fly straight in from Oz."

The frightening newcomer surged across the complex's borders and slowed to a halt next to Darla and Eric. She cut a watchful gaze at them. Dull, gray hair pulled into a stern bun accentuated her hawkish features and enhanced her witchy appearance.

She looped around Darla letting loose a loud cackle. Darla's frame stiffened. She paused near Darla's backside. A light touch brushed against her hips.

Darla's head snapped to look at Eric. "What is she doing?"

He angled back. A corner of his mouth lifted. "I think she's measuring your butt."

"What? Why?"

He chuckled. "She's appraising your assets?"

"Not funny."

She shifted to Eric and orbited around him.

Darla giggled. "Your turn."

She faced him head on, bent down, and eyed his lower frontal region.

He backed away. "Whoa, this is not okay."

"Right? How does it feel to have *your* endowments

evaluated?"

The woman straightened and flashed a jagged smile. A wrinkled hand slipped inside her robe's ballooned sleeve.

She removed a long, sheathed knife.

"Holy shit." Eric overlapped his hands to protect his privates.

"It's getting more amusing by the second, huh?"

He backstepped several more paces. "Nothing's amusing 'bout slicing off my manhood."

The witch's grin broadened. She tilted her head back and chirped a succession of chants.

Strong arms encircled Darla's torso. She struggled to disengage. She glance behind. Two men held her. She opened her mouth to call Eric, but he couldn't help her.

He was in the same predicament.

Both were forced to face the witchy lady. One man held Darla steady. The other stretched out her left arm. Eric's position was identical. The men balled their hands into a fist, protracting their thumbs.

Scary lady nodded and smiled. She slipped the dagger from its case, then quickly hurled it into the air. Steel glimmered in the firelight as it swiveled, handle over blade. The woman caught the handle in mid-air. She wheeled the blade overhead, then brought the cutting edge downward, smoothly slicing the razor sharp lip across their skin.

Both winced, but Darla didn't have the courage to cry out.

Their bloody digits were fused together, held for seconds then they were released. Swabbing the knife's rim, the woman shrieked again. She re-sheathed the dagger, bowed to Darla and Eric. She turned and ambled into the darkness.

Darla examined her cut. "What just happened?"

"Dunno. She made us blood related?"

"Weird, considering our past relationship."

"We can talk to a shrink later." He checked out the group of men, who remained in their tight circle. "We don't seem to have any opposition. I suggest we scram."

A thunderous noise shattered the quiet. Bushes and shrubs around them shook and shimmied.

Eric gaped at the ruckus. "Now what?"

People surfaced from everywhere. Men, women, young and not so young, an entire community appeared from nowhere. The youngsters who held them disassembled and intermixed with their latest guests.

"You had to ask," Darla groaned.

Four men and four women raced to them. Two ladies entwined their arms with Darla's. The third stood ahead of her and the fourth, behind. Males surrounded Eric in a matching pattern. They urged them forward.

Darla and Eric exchanged worried glances. Darla feared they had no choice but to comply. They were walked toward the inner-village. Once they attained the town's midpoint, they split. Darla was led one way, and Eric went in the opposite direction.

"Eric," Darla pleaded over her shoulder.

He fought to wrangle free, but the cluster of men detained him. Within seconds, he was out of viewing range.

Darla's panic soared. None of her companions, noticed. Chattering cheerfully in their native language, they steered her in an unknown direction.

They bypassed the row of huts she explored when she and Eric arrived. She was guided to the last shanty, where they stopped.

The women motioned for her to go inside. Darla refused, shaking her head, hoping the meaning was universal. The beckoning suddenly ceased. They gathered to confer, leaving her alone. She gaged her escape route, but by their tones, they seemed to relent, so she didn't feel the need to run. She could just walk away.

Or so she imagined.

She spun to leave. Quickly, they divided into pairs. Two on each side of her. The front duo snatched her arms and tugged. Darla planted her feet, burying her heels into the dirt.

The other second pair picked up her legs.

They carried her inside. She wriggled to get free, but she was no match against four women. They released her in the middle of the room.

Darla sat on a dirt floor, panting. She scanned the space. An abundance of manmade candles refreshed the drabness. The fragrance was pleasant, too.

In the central section of otherwise stark quarters, sat a wooden bathtub, filled to the brim.

She jumped to her feet, squealing at the sight. Her palm patted her upper chest. "For me?"

Grins, nods, and gestures at the tub was their response. She didn't require a second invitation. She grabbed her shirt hem, then abruptly stopped. Although not particularly modest, she preferred to bathe solo.

She smiled and motioned toward the exit. "Um, I'd rather do this alone."

Her request was ignored. Still chatting, they

surrounded and undressed her as she protested. Once stripped, they helped her into the warm water. She sank blissfully into the tub with a satisfied hum and relaxed to enjoy the soak.

A slight tinge of guilt tweaked, because she wasn't more worried about Eric. She hoped he was having the same experience.

The women gave her a while to relax, then returned to her. Although she found them bathing her and washing her hair awkward, the feeling of clean was refreshing. She smiled and gratefully accepted a soft pelt to dry once they were finished.

She glimpsed toward a corner. Her soiled shorts and t-shirt lay in a heap. A sense of dread swept over her. She hated the idea of putting on her sullied clothes.

A different woman slipped past the doorway. She carried a white dress, which was parallel to what the tribe compound women wore.

The cluster congregated and slipped the garment over Darla's head. Off the shoulder, simple and elegant, it fit perfectly. Swirling, she grasped the ankle length skirt and held out the sides.

"Lovely." She beamed at her hosts, who seemed pleased by her admiration. One produced a fearsome shaped comb and fluffed her drying curls, then positioned a ring of white flowers on top of her head.

She was steered out of the lean-to and back outdoors. A considerable blaze ignited the night sky as drums pounded in the distance.

Darla sniffed the air. Warm winds transported a divine scent in their direction. She emitted a famished hum. Food. She couldn't identify the sort, but her hollow stomach growled. Foregoing deliberations, she allowed the ladies to escort her toward the bonfire.

Drumbeats grew louder as they entered the carnival like atmosphere. A choir sang in their native language, while young men danced to the rhythm, circling the inferno, twirling fire-lit lances. Other performances also took place throughout the festivities.

Her new friends showed her to a square of material spread across the ground and indicated for her to sit. She nodded and thanked them before they vanished into the crowd.

"You look enchanting, luv."

Darla whirled around. Eric appeared from the roving partiers.

His lips curved into a roguish grin. "You really clean up nice."

She smiled and rushed to meet him. "I was about to go search for you. Did you—" She stopped and gasped. Her hand covered her mouth.

Eric's wardrobe duplicated the native males, meaning his chest remained bare. Though he'd been shirtless earlier, she was too out of it to notice much. Black and purple bruises covered a huge range of his upper torso.

Instinctively, Darla extended an arm. Her fingertips traced the discoloration. "This is bad."

He flinched and pulled away. "Looks worse than it feels."

Darla dropped her hand. "If you say so."

An awkwardness fell between them. Her gaze drifted to his arm. His favorite tattoo artist had scripted her name, *Darla* onto his bicep. He also inked a Wiccan symbol below to disguise the scar created by a bullet.

The combination was invented to signify their

unbreakable bond. Rumors circulated he removed the artwork after they split. A wisp of joy trickled within her, happy to discover the reports were false.

Her eyes moved farther down. A huge grin spread across her face. "Those are, um, really tight pants."

He performed an unusual shift as if the movement might loosen the constricting fabric. "Not a one size fits all, for sure."

"Those look like they came from the kids section." She aimed a finger at his crotch, unable to hide her amusement. "Where's your…?"

His mouth flattened. "No room in front. I had to tuck it underneath."

She laughed. "You look like a Ken doll."

"Funny, luv." He gave in and smiled. "Very funny."

A cluster of locals intervened and indicated for them to sit. Darla sank onto the tarp, bowing her head so Eric didn't see her laugh as his extra snug pants hindered his ability to easily stoop. He almost had to perform a backbend to reach the ground.

"I think they're serving us dinner," she observed.

"Hopefully, they're not serving *us* as dinner."

"They wouldn't." Her eyes widened. "Would they?"

He rubbed the day-old stubble dotted across his chin. "Might be the reason they insisted we clean up."

Adolescents brought them wooden plates piled with food. The cuisine was unrecognizable but oozed an appetizing aroma. Neither cared what they ate. Both were so starved, they dived in.

The entertainment continued while they dined. Once they completed the feast, the same youngsters collected empty dishes, performance props, and gathered remnants scattered on the grounds.

"Wonder what's next."

"I'm imagining sleep." Darla stifled a yawn. "Clean and a full stomach. This is the best I've felt in a long time. The only thing missing is a decent night's rest."

"Sleep sounds great." Eric glanced and pointed. "But I don't think it's gonna happen."

The party goers had formed a sphere and walled them inside. Faces didn't appear enraged. In fact, they maintained their festive expressions. Various members motioned at them to stand. Something momentous was about to occur, and they were the lead characters in the event.

Darla gradually rose. "What's happening?"

"Dunno. But my happy feeling is fading fast."

Two girls, in their mid-teens approached. They gestured, urging them to bend. Darla and Eric exchanged a glance.

Eric searched over the girls' heads. "Wicked witch didn't bring her trick sword to finish us off, did she?"

"I don't think so, why?"

"We're bein' told to bow. Did you see that blade? It could decapitate us in one swipe."

"This experience is weird, but we seemed to have developed a friendly relationship. I don't believe they'll kill us." Darla nudged him. "Now bend."

Both lowered their torsos. The girls carried identical beaded necklaces and placed them around Darla and Eric's neck.

A heavy silence fell as the teens backed away. A long moment passed. Drums began to softly beat. A feeble, elderly man emerged from the rear. He hobbled keeping in rhythm with the drum's thump. His dress was similar to the tribal males, except the man's exposed skin was painted, and he wore an elaborate beaded, flowery headdress.

Eric opened his mouth, but Darla nudged him, and shook her head. Whatever this was, the ritual was a somber occasion, and they should be respectful. He could save his smartass comments until later.

It took minutes before the little man reached the front. Once he made it, he took his place in front of Darla and Eric.

Another male appeared and stood off to the side. He handed the leader a fire lit pole. The elderly leader balanced the burning stick horizontally on flattened palms. Huge flames smoldered at both ends.

"This is a ceremony," Darla whispered. "Perhaps they're welcoming us to their tribe family."

"Or he's blessing next week's groceries."

"Will you stop?"

The chief raised the staff into the air. He tilted his head back, closed his eyes, and softly began to sing. Wielding the blazing stick, his song became louder. Drums pounded every time he elevated the pole. The audience clapped, keeping in time with the beat.

The procedure carried on until the melody faded to a low hum. The man extinguished the fire. He tapped Eric's shoulder, then Darla's. He bowed and retreated into the mass of people.

A man and woman appeared, clutching the ends of a vine. The vine's edges were entwined around Darla and Eric's wrists. Once bonded, their arms were thrusted high in the air for everyone to see.

Drums thunderously banged, while cheers exploded. The couple led them amid the spectators, who patted their shoulders in the same spot as the tribal leader.

Once everyone touched them, they were ushered away, back into the compound. In silence, the duo guided them to a semi-hidden refuge, built similar as the bathing shanties, except this hut was positioned farther off the grid.

The man tugged back a drape guarding the entrance and showed them inside.

Eric glanced at Darla. "Hope they're just here to tuck us in."

The pair placed a palm on their shoulders, then disappeared.

A lit candle radiated a muted glow on a table made of branches. A man-made bed was placed in the center.

Eric snapped the vine. "I'm too worn-out for this much strange, especially in one day."

Darla walked to the table to inspect an odd figurine next to the candle.

Eric eyed the bed. "Do we share? Or am I expected to be the gentlemen and take the floor?"

"That ceremony was to bless a union."

"Okay. Bed or floor?"

She held up the statue so he could get a better look. "This is a unity statuette. Many tribes believe these figures create an eternal bond between a husband and wife."

"Interesting. Bed or floor?"

"Witchy slashed our thumbs and combined our blood. The bath, wardrobe change, feast, and entertainment were preludes to a rite." She fingered the necklace draped around her neck. "These are comparable to wedding rings. The old guy's rants translate as a purpose of intent or a crude marriage vow, and the intertwined vine links us together for an eternity." She elevated her wrist, displaying the torn vine. "Eric."

"Yeah, luv?"

"They married us."

"It's settled, then." He tumbled onto the mattress. "We share the bed."

Chapter 11

"You comin' to bed?" Eric drew a thin blanket to his waist. Since they didn't have pillows, he'd stuffed both hands underneath his head as a substitute. "I'm ready to get some real sleep." He stretched excessively then added a loud yawn. "I'm beyond beat."

Darla stared at the shirtless, mouth-watering man, lying in flutters of candlelight. "Seriously, is sharing a bed a good idea?"

"We've laid on the ground next to each other. Why's the bed any different?"

Nothing made a difference. Except it'd been ninety plus days since they were intimate, and the longer they were together, the more she craved to recapture the magic they once created. Could she lay next to him with her desires swelling, and retain her sense of logic? Or would her body betray her?

"So what's the verdict?"

His invitation was irresistible. It also signified she should refuse. Skip this impromptu slumber party and forgo another possible heartbreak. Yet, despite her internal chaos, she was exhausted, and comfort beckoned.

Leaving her—where?

Placing her cerebral debate on hold, she surrendered to her tiredness and strolled to the bed's edge. She lingered by the side until Eric scooted to the left. Scrambling under a soft pelt blanket, she sank into squishiness.

Eric propped onto an elbow, pursed his lips and blew at the lone candle. Darkness cast a soothing shadow about the room. He settled back into the mattress. "So we tied the knot, huh?"

"I'm ninety-nine percent sure the ceremony was a wedding." She paused a moment. "Our wedding."

"Strange, don't you think? First, those kids acted like they're gonna skewer us, then the evil witch shows up."

"Perhaps the boys were supposed to hold us for the woman?"

"Do you get why she fucked up our thumbs?"

"Engagement ritual, maybe?"

He lay still in the darkness. "This is too weird. They had clean clothes ready, a feast prepared, and the ceremony was arranged."

"Like they expected us, yeah, I noticed that too. I wish I had an explanation."

A tiny shift came from his side. "Glad it wasn't real."

"Me too. It didn't come close to my dream wedding."

"Huh?"

Darla tensed. Strong winds whistled through cracks slit within the walls magnifying the razor-sharp silence that spiked between them.

"What's your dream wedding like?"

Just what she needed. A loaded question. One she preferred not to answer. Except, this was her fault. She'd opened her big mouth.

"I prefer something traditional."

"I already got that, and it doesn't answer my question." He hesitated. "You're dodging me."

"No, I'm not."

"Darla, I know you. If you imagined your wedding, then you've planned it. Location, colors, every particular is in place."

Her heart battered. Couldn't she just pretend she fell asleep? "What do you want me to say."

"The truth. You imagined us getting married when we dated." A pause ensued. "I thought about it, too."

Warmed tingles shimmied inside as her excitement soared. "You did?"

His announcement truly stunned her. She assumed marriage was an experience he'd rather avoid. Neither had brought up the subject while they were together. Her reasoning was she thought he would tell her marriage wasn't for him.

She had tried to convince herself she was okay with them as more than companions, minus legitimacies, but the idea never quite jelled.

Now, her imagination surged. Her once futile wedding plans came to life. Then she halted and backtracked. She was getting carried away. He referred to the past, not the present, where their relationship was muddled and untidy.

"Actually, I did more than think about it. I looked at rings."

Darla's delight heightened again. "You did?"

"Yeah. I also wrote a few possible songs we might use for a ceremony."

"Eric, I had no clue. Sooo romantic."

"Hell, I even contacted Barry to draft a sample prenup."

Darla's pretend preparations suddenly hit a brick wall. She popped up. "I'm super drained, and I think I hallucinated. What did you just say?"

"I checked out rings, composed some music, and spoke to Barry about drawing up a prenup."

"A proposal from you comes with a contract? This is a first."

"We never discussed getting married. If we had, my attorney would insist both of us signing a legal contract to protect our assets."

"Your lawyer is my half-brother."

"And an excellent legal advisor. He wouldn't allow me to enter any type of partnership without protection. I pay him well to ensure my finances stay reasonably healthy. I didn't watch my money b'fore, and a crook swiped every penny from under my nose. I won't let that happen again."

"Of course not. What's more significant than your ripening portfolio?" She flopped back, landing in crackling softness. "You accused me of not trusting you. You apparently don't trust me, either."

"Darla." A heavy sigh resonated amid obscurity. "Is there a point?"

She jerked to sit up again. Pulling her knees to her chest, she rotated on her butt, faced him, and pushed her feet into his hip. "Here's the point." She gave him a solid shove. "Get out."

"Careful. My ribs are cracked, remember?"

"I'm not touching your ribs. Although that can change if you don't move." She rammed him again. "You've been warned. Your fault if I hurt you. Leave or suffer. Choose."

"And I'm supposed to sleep, where?"

"Outside. On the floor. I could care less."

"You're being irrational."

"So? Technically today is my wedding day. *My* day. I'm the bride, so I get what I want, and I want you to vacate this bed. Put that in your damn prenup."

Using every muscle, she delivered a final heave.

"Shit." His foot thumped the ground. The makeshift mattress lightened. "All right, all right, I'm gone."

Arms tightened around her middle, she flung backward. She couldn't believe him. A vision of his proposal formed in her mind. Eric on one knee presenting a sparkling diamond, marred by the addition of a pen and legal document.

"I love this whole marriage perception as a business concept. So dreamy."

"Not so much business, but practical. You'd be smart to insist on an agreement when the time comes."

"I don't have a need. My resources don't compare to yours. I earn enough to pay the bills and a little extra, but I don't have a lot set aside or own much of value. Why would I worry since my bank account isn't equal to yours?"

"I don't mean to sound harsh, but how's that my fault?"

"It isn't. You can afford to purchase whatever you want within reason."

Her eyes adjusted to the darkness. A dim light flickered in the small window. The torches' glow outlining Eric's form standing by the bedside.

"Why are you so pissed? Most women would be thrilled if their future mate wants to guard their financial interests and give them a good life."

"Unless a split happens. Then the wife is screwed."

"Everyone should protect themselves so that doesn't occur."

"Right." She huffed. "After all the crap we've endured, why would you even imagine I would accept a penny of yours if we divorced?"

"I don't. You're taking this as personal. This isn't about you."

"Of course, it's about me, and yes, I am taking this personal. You're prepared for us not to last, and you're afraid I'll legitimately find a way to steal your money."

"We didn't last."

She ignored the sting of his comment and spouted, "And you kept your precious cash."

"Sorry, luv."

"That's all I get? Sorry, luv?"

No response. Instantly, she wished the topic had died minutes ago. He was right. They were no longer a couple. How did a lighthearted chat drift into such murky territory and conclude into a dispute?

Because he mentioned the stupid prenuptial agreement, that's how.

"I understand you're mad. But I don't believe it has anything to do with a non-existent paper. You're still upset I wouldn't let you move in with me."

Darla squashed farther into the mattress as her annoyance expanded. She hadn't thought of that, but now that he brought the subject up, she couldn't fathom a reason for him to not want to share a home with her. It's not as if she'd already scheduled movers. He could've considered the idea for at least a minute.

"Darla? Are you asleep?"

"I'm awake."

"I wanted to explain something to you on the night we broke up. Only you said we were done and stormed out b'fore I had a chance." He stopped to inhale. "I'm gonna tell you now. Maybe you'll appreciate my reason for not asking you to live with me." A second hesitation succeeded. "I don't want to just cohabitate. I preferred we marry before we moved in together. My thoughts weren't organized, and my priorities weren't aligned, but I was one hundred percent sure I'd ask you to be my wife someday. Old fashioned, but I wanted to do right by you."

Speechless, Darla lay motionless, unsure how to respond. She replayed their horrible squabble in her mind many times, and she always changed the outcome to positive, but this unexpected confession floored her. "I didn't know."

"You never wanted to hear me. Just so you understand. You nearly killed me when you left."

"I'm sorry." Darla paused to digest his confession. It pained her that she hurt him so deeply, but something else bothered her, too. His current antics didn't quite gel with his admission. He may've been devastated but didn't hang around the house eating gallons of ice cream like she did. "On the upside, you bounced back nicely."

"What do you mean?"

"The tons of photos of you and numerous women."

"My way of dealing."

"Seriously?"

"How am I supposed to act, Darla? Show the world how your walking away destroyed me? Shout to let everyone know my self-esteem, self-worth is laying shriveled in a gutter. Nope, I'm not tellin' the fucking universe how dead I am inside, or I don't know if I'll ever feel alive again." His footsteps pounded the dirt floor as he paced. "The media stories are a load of crap. I posed for pictures with other women, but I went home alone. For the last three months, I've slept by myself."

"You're saying…?"

"In plain words, I haven't had sex with anyone since you. If you need additional details, I'll give you more. I haven't kissed, touched, or even held hands with anybody else."

"What about your dates who accompanied you to Blaine and Steph's wedding. You three appeared extremely cozy."

A mischievous chuckle emitted from the darkness. "You saw us, eh?"

Darla gasped at his implication. "Jerk."

"I have my moments." He walked back to the bed. "Since you know my reality, can we let my fake social activities drop? I'm tired of quarreling about it."

"Subject's closed if you give me a break from seeing you with other women in the media." She snuggled into the mattress. "Realize you got off easy. If you proposed, and suggested I sign a prenup? Let's just say the pictures of you with women on your arm argument wouldn't compete."

"I got that, luv."

"Good." She waited. "You can come back—"

"Shit." Eric vaulted off the floor, then came down hard. His silhouette twirled around the room his arms flailed. He roared again, springing over the bed, and landed on top of her.

Darla lay motionless, trying to catch her breath. Eric's breathing was labored, also.

Unsure what had just occurred, she flattened her hands against his chest. "What is this? A new move? FYI, it's not working."

He raised with a groan. "Something crawled across my foot. Twice. I had a snake flashback. I freaked a little."

"A little? You pirouetted, did a high dive, and used me as your landing pad as your finale."

"Okay, I overreacted."

"You think?"

He wrapped an arm around his middle and clutched, clearly struggling in the shadows. "I'm movin'."

A hazy beam haloed his face, displaying his agony. Guilt stalked her. Perhaps she shouldn't have been so adamant he leave the bed. Her forced supplemented activities may've aggravated his injuries. Her palms remained pressed into the warmth of his chest. A hand slid to his ribcage. He hissed at her touch.

"Hurt?"

"You're a first-rate detective, luv."

"I could stabilize your ribs. I just need to find some material to wrap around and hold them in place. You might still have pain, but not as much."

"You could also puncture my lungs if you accidently move a bone the wrong way."

"Whatever. I won't help you. You can pierce your lungs yourself performing your next high dive act."

Without thinking, her fingers instinctively raked through the fine hairs speckled across his pecks. Memories of when her world reveled in the freedom to caress him whenever desire struck her. Her fingertips continued to trail over his skin, tracing across a broad shoulder, until she brushed the silky locks coiled behind his neck.

"Darla?"

His voice snapped her back to reality. She untangled her fingers and withdrew her hand.

"You stopped." Torch lights flickered across his face. The corners of his eyes crinkled as his lips curved upward. "Too bad."

His naughty grin widened. He manipulated the lower half of his body to sync with hers. His growing firmness was positioned into the heated junction between her thighs.

She inhaled a shaky breath as her heart assaulted her ribcage. Swept away in upsurges of emotion, she had instigated this situation, and allowed the circumstances to escalate. Her behavior would cost her bigtime if she didn't stop this.

Easing in, he smoothed the curls away from her face.

She gently shoved him back. "I can't."

"What?"

"I lost control. As I always do whenever I'm near you."

"Gotcha." He eased off, moaning softly as he relocated.

"You do?"

"Not really. I've yet to comprehend much since the day you left me."

She didn't know how to respond, or how to contain this newly unleashed remorse since she was to blame for their split. Her only argument? When she broached the subject, he exploded right away. No discussions. It escalated into a full-blown fight. She still didn't get his reaction.

Finally prepared to ask him about his vocally fierce retort that night, she turned, but found him snoring softly, leaving the air unsettled between them.

Without recourse, she relaxed and dozed too, but rest was sporadic. Her subconscious needled her and demanded she awaken.

Her eyes cracked.

The climate comfortable room was stifling. Her body soaked in sweat. She punted the cover off her legs. A loud crash came from somewhere. She flinched and popped up to listen. Scents of smoldering wood fused amid a blistering breeze. Debris swirled. The air had converted into a thick mass. Something was on fire. And not too far away. Flames weren't obvious, but the churning fragments were actually smoke produced by the blaze.

Tamping down her panic, she shook Eric. "Eric. We have to leave." He didn't budge. "Eric? Wake up."

"S' hot in here," he mumbled, rolling onto his back.

"Something's caught on fire, and it's close."

"No shit?"

"Yes. Let's get out of here."

He spun off the bed and toppled to the floor. "Comin'."

"Are you okay?"

"Yeah."

"Are you crawling out?"

"S'pose to, right?"

Her lungs began to burn. She followed Eric's lead, and dived to the ground. A hand protected her mouth as she performed a one-handed scuttle. Thankfully, her instincts helped her find the exit.

Once outdoors, she leaped to her feet, and sprinted. After she was sure she was far enough away, she tumbled into a mound of weeds. Climbing to her feet, she checked the compound. Their shanty was enflamed. A torch had tipped and fallen onto the edge of the roof, catching it on fire. Combustions blackened the thatched cover. Embers shot upward as sparks lit up the night sky.

She circled to Eric. "That was close, wasn't it?" She scanned the area. "Eric?" Chills pricked across her neck. Dread froze her insides. Had Eric not followed her? "Eric?" she shouted, hoping he fell on the run. "Eric, where are you?"

She looked at the crumbling shack. Every safety rule forgotten, she retraced her steps to the incinerator-consumed shelter, hoping she'd find him along the way. Except she didn't.

She advanced toward the burning hut.

The doorframe was enflamed, blocking the entrance. She tried to battle her way inside by other means, but the searing firestorm drove her backward. Interior walls had collapsed, but she still couldn't penetrate the inferno.

Darla refused to surrender. She sank into the dirt and crept toward the baking building. Sweat intermixed with soot and ash trickled across her skin.

She ignored the burn and stretched over the threshold, carefully inching inside. Hot soil sizzled beneath and scorched her palms. Smoke saturated the air, pilfering every bead of oxygen.

But she didn't care. She had to save Eric.

"No ya don't." An arm snaked around her midriff

and lifted her off the ground.

"Let me go." Her fists hurled and legs swung. "I have to save Eric."

"Stop fightin'. Ya ain't goin' nowhere." Auster returned her to her feet. He snatched both her wrists and crushed them in a gigantic hand. "He's dead. I made sure this time."

"You're lying." She jerked her wrists. She had to break away before it was too late.

He tightened his grip and yanked her to him. "Now listen. Ya gotta get back to where ya belong, like I told ya ta do the other day."

"Not without Eric." She twisted her arms to wrangle free, but still wasn't successful. His hold remained firm.

"He's dead."

Darla abandoned her struggle as his words sank in. Eric was gone. Her chest constricted as her heart was primed to explode.

"Fine." She swallowed a scream. She couldn't allow her emotions to dictate her. Not yet. She had to know why. "You won, Auster."

"Ain't notting 'bout winnin', girlie. Just gettin' me job done."

He let go of her and stepped in front of her. He nudged her to walk as he passed by. She followed as he led her away from the grisly scene.

"Where are we going?

"Like I said. To y'r fancy resort."

"What's to stop me from running away?"

"You'll stay wit' me," he warned in a voice that would cut through an iceberg. "I might can't hurt ya, but ya got friends. They're not protected." He forged ahead until he came to a wall of brush. He divided the cascade of leaves, holding them aside. "Understand, do ya?"

She marched to the foliage tunnel, pausing at the entrance to glance at the burning hut. Her attention returned to Auster. "Eric? Are you sure?"

"No help for him. Nothing be left 'cept charred bones."

She stumbled but caught herself before she fell. Taking a deep breath, she fought to hold onto her control. She must have answers before she broke. "You shoved the torch into our hut and set it on fire."

"Didn't move itself."

"Your goal was to murder us."

"Just da man. If ya hadn't got out, I'd saved ya."

"You have rules forbidding you from kidnapping and murdering women?"

He laughed. "Naw. We take anybody. Kill 'em, too, if da price is right. Males, females, kids, too."

Unable to process, she mentally bypassed his admission. "Why didn't you just kidnap him and ask for a ransom like the pirates did for Blaine?"

"Not the plan. Ransom ain't the only way to get paid."

"What are you saying?"

"Ain't sayin' notting. Job's done, notting left to talk 'bout."

Darla struggled to restrain the explosion building within her. She sought to pound her fists into this man's chest and shatter his heart into thousands of pieces, just like he did hers.

"Ya shouldn't be too sad, lass. Eric Boyd just achieved every rock star's dreams. He's joined the greatest band in heaven, and he'll be a legend on earth. Don't get better than that in his world."

Chapter 12

Auster maneuvered his jet ski next to a dock adjacent to Tluq Cay Island. Darla swung a leg across the Sea Doo's extended seat to dismount. She stood zombie-like on faded, wooden planks. Exhaustion and disbelief seized her will. So much, she couldn't muster a morsel of terror or disgust at the man who stole Eric's life.

An engine rumble startled her, rousing her from her private darkness.

Auster relaxed on his watercraft. The massive predator displayed an ominous grin, "Too bad 'bout your loss, Missy, but don't worry. You'll survive without 'em."

He saluted and pointed his craft toward the west. Moments later, he and his jet ski vanished. Not that his exit mattered. He eliminated the most significant person in her world, and the process was irreversible.

Darla stayed at her location, not shifting an inch. Outwardly, she felt powerless, but inside, her emotions were agitated like the churning sea below. Was Auster right? Would she survive? Could she psychologically endure a life minus Eric? She didn't need to ponder. The answer was a distinct no.

They had separated but talks during their mutual turmoil began to heal a lot of wounds. The idea of Eric alive and thriving gave her hope there was a possibility they'd reunite and achieve a greater level of happiness through their love.

Now hope was gone, and Eric was dead.

She would never experience a connection so powerful and intense with another human again. Leftover pieces of her disintegrated soul might regather enough to progress forward and exist, but she wouldn't allow love to seep into the crevasses of her broken heart. Those stakes were too high, and her losses cut too deep.

She fingered the native necklace secured around her neck. Grief flared and overpowered her. Salty wetness saturated her cheeks. At first, her sobs were soft and noiseless. As her anguish soared, her mild weeps evolved into wails that echoed across the bay.

Indifferent to nearby islanders, agony flooded her. Her cries extracted and freed her sorrow. Losing a loved one was hell. Eric's demise left her with a multitude of impossible reservations, and the cruelness of how he departed added an extra layer of regret.

Clutching her stomach, she heaved and folded in two, her lungs demanding air, seeking relief. Unable to stand any longer, she lowered to her butt and dangled her legs above the wharf's edge. Cool waves licked the soles of her bare feet. Gradually, her emotional meltdown faded, leaving her feeling shattered.

Her mind drifted as hours elapsed. Consciousness only fully reverted when she gazed up into the night sky. Tonight, no iridescent moon or twinkly stars appeared. A dark veil covered the sky as the universe mourned with her.

She ought to head to the resort, check in with Stephanie, and explain her disappearance, but Darla didn't want to abandon this spot. Here, she felt bonded to Eric. If she budged, she feared their link would break, and she would lose him forever.

Her theory was irrational, she got that, but it took a while until her brain convinced her heart. Finally, she reluctantly scrambled to her feet and walked to her bungalow.

****

The next day, Darla sluggishly emerged from her bathroom after a long, hot shower. She draped a towel around her wet tresses, and clad herself in a thick robe, cinching the belt tight around her waist. Pausing at a set of French doors, she examined the mid-morning skies. The weather outdoors looked on the verge of storming, matching her gloomy disposition.

Uninterested in the overcast view, she stepped away from the glass, confused what to do next. Possibly go back to bed? She found Stephanie last evening. The friends talked, cried, caught up, and consoled each other the rest of the night.

Once she left Steph and was alone in her bedroom, sleep evaded her. Yet, excluding her stress of dealing with Eric's death, she was beat. She headed to her room with the anticipation of catching a few winks.

A loud click resonated throughout the room. She stopped short. Hair prickled on the back of her neck. She whirled to face the doorway and glanced at a clock. Too early for housekeeping to arrive. The knob twisted slow and deliberate.

Auster?

Backstepping to the desk, she slid a hand into her waiting travel bag where she stored her concealed handguns. She withdrew a loaded Glock.

Pistol aimed, a thumb dragged the striker backward. The door opened quickly, smacking an inner wall. Darla froze, poised to shoot. Stephanie backed inside, wheeling a cart.

Darla relaxed, rapidly stuffing the gun back into the bag.

A foot shoved the door, slamming it shut. Stephanie turned to her and waved a hand above the trolley. "I brought sustenance."

"I'm not hungry, Steph."

"Fantastic, because I didn't bring food." She held a crystal pitcher loaded with an iced, orangey liquid face high. "This is much more satisfying."

Darla's nose wrinkled. "I'm not thirsty, either. I especially don't want juice. That's juice, right?"

Stephanie poured the drink into one of two tall glasses. "Yes, but this isn't ordinary juice." She smiled, and tipped the decanter, dispensing the concoction into the second tumbler. "This is mind numbing, help you survive, I don't give a shit about anything, juice."

She held a glass out to Darla. She gingerly accepted.

Steph sipped at her beverage. "Scrumptious." Her tongue swept across her lips. "Great for deadening pain."

Darla's expression paralleled her doubts. "What is this amazing cure?"

"A fuzzy navel. Ever tried one?"

Darla shook her head and timidly tasted the alcoholic mixture. "Gees, Steph. How much booze did you add? Schnapps, right?"

"Peach flavored. And the amount of booze? I can only warn you. Drink with caution." Stephanie snatched the carafe off the handcart. "Let's drink our attitude infusions on the patio." She didn't wait until Darla replied, but led the way past the twin doors, and onto a tiny terrace overlooking the ocean.

The pair perched on a settee. Neither spoke, which was fine. Darla had described the previous forty-eight hours last night to the police and Stephanie. She preferred not to speak of yesterday's horrors ever again. They sat in a compatible silence, watching the sky clear as newly formed, puffy, white clouds drifted.

"Have you heard from the authorities?"

Darla removed her towel to allow the warm winds to dry her damp curls. "I did a while ago. Their response was as we expected. They can't do much. Eric's murder site isn't in their jurisdiction.

"The magistrate stated he would try to send an investigator to the island to do an unofficial analysis, although he's hesitant to risk his men's lives, since the area is considered dangerous." She huffed to show her aggravation. "They're appeasing me. They don't intend to explore any further."

Stephanie snorted. "Local cops are worthless. They've yet to lift a pinky or offer any help to rescue Blaine."

"Unfortunately, those in charge are clueless as to where they're holding Blaine. However, we are sure Eric's dead, and who lit the fire that killed him. I expect an investigation and Auster arrested. I also would like Eric's remains flown home, so he can be given an appropriate burial." Her eyes watered as she swallowed back a bucket of tears that threatened. "I'm not asking too much, am I?"

"No. You're not. The man who killed Eric deserves

to spend the rest of his life in jail, and Eric's family will want his body transported to Scotland. They need to say their final goodbyes."

"You'd think Eric's fame would light a fire under these guys." Her voice cracked. "Apparently not."

"Speaking of his family, did you notify his mom and dad, yet?"

"No. I'll have to soon. I'm worried they will learn about his death due to some rogue reporter grasping to get his fifteen minutes and broadcast the news before I get a chance to tell them."

"How come you haven't phoned them?"

"I'm too scared to make the call."

"So get that."

They settled into an uneasy quietness. Sunshine broke through the clouds and shined bright, but the cooler breeze kept the air comfortable.

The day equaled perfection, but the surrounding serenity didn't compose either woman. Both stared blankly at the gorgeous waters, resting unobtrusively, lost in reflections of endless what ifs.

"Darla?"

She and Stephanie snapped around to determine the identity of their approaching guest. Morgan surfaced out of the blaring sunlight and entered the undersized gateway.

He rushed to Darla and knelt by her side. "You disappeared two days ago. I've been worried. Are you okay?"

She inhaled and nodded. "I'm fine."

"You don't look fine." He backed to sit on a low rise table positioned close by and rested his elbows onto his knees. Tilting nearer, he examined her features.

"You're not fine, at all. Can you tell me what happened while you were gone?"

She glanced at Stephanie. Her friend gave an encouraging nod.

"I'll try."

Her voice trembled as she gave him the basic facts, choosing to omit personal details. Those were her business.

Morgan sat back once she ended her story and eyed her suspiciously. "Are you sure Eric died in the fire?"

"What kind of question is that?"

Morgan might've despised Eric, and feasibly invented a non-existent competition between them, which was forgivable, but this was way over the line.

"Of course, he died in the fire. *I* tried to save him." She gulped. "I couldn't."

"You didn't find his body, did you?"

"I was clear on what happened. Auster made me leave. I didn't get the chance to stay and search. What are you getting at?"

Stephanie glowered at Morgan. "Why are you grilling her so hard? You do get she's gone through a horrible experience. The love of her life has died."

"I do understand."

"Ease up, then."

"The ransom money's disappeared." Morgan interlocked his fingers, his knuckles whitened. "Police and I have corresponded since I informed them I funded Blaine's potential escape."

Unease filled Darla's chest. With her surplus of agitation, she'd forgotten about the briefcase full of cash, nor had Stephanie provided updates concerning the ransom.

She rotated toward her friend. "I'm so sorry. I didn't ask if the kidnappers were paid."

Sympathy spread across Stephanie's face. "No need to apologize. Your soulmate was just murdered, and you're in shock. You would've remembered once the craziness died down."

Darla's stomach tumbled. "The money wasn't delivered, then."

Stephanie's expression saddened as her head shook.

"Auster kept the cash."

Morgan's throat cleared. "That's one concept the law enforcement's contemplating."

"They have others?"

"They lean toward the idea Eric stole it and disappeared."

"They suspect what?" Darla inhaled deep, attempting to control her rising temper. "Why would they think that? They never mentioned their suspicions when I spoke to them concerning Eric's death."

"They probably felt you're too emotional."

"Auster took the money."

"Police have their doubts." Morgan paused. "If a Les Brigand were to discover Auster stole their ransom money, then his life would come to an abrupt, ugly ending. People like Auster respect pirate boundaries. Someone on the outside stole it."

"Eric was murdered, and Auster took the money." Darla caught a curl and wrapped it around her finger. "Seriously, where do they think Eric and the ransom disappeared to?"

Morgan lifted the dark lensed Ray Ban's concealing his eyes and positioned them on top of his head. "I just talked to the police. They believe he planned to take it all along."

"How did they come up with that theory? I mean, really? They think he would let Blaine die?" Her head shook violently. "He'd never do such an awful thing to anyone, especially his best friend."

"You're sure? Steph said the band hasn't toured much this year and profits were down. His finances might've suffered enough for him to do the unthinkable."

"Eric's careful with his money, plus I was with him through the entire ordeal. He didn't have the briefcase."

"There's more." He hesitated. "They kinda suspect you're in on it, too."

She straightened as her anger soared. "I'd never betray a friend."

"I explained that, Darla."

Stephanie leaned across the cushion and patted her hand.

"I did my best to convince them you wouldn't steal from anyone. I think I did a pretty good job." Morgan's look became more foreboding. "But they aren't sure Eric isn't guilty."

"He wouldn't. I found him tied and beaten. I freed him. His ribs were broken. He could barely move. We were trapped on a boat in the middle of the sea during a storm, then on an island. I can attest he didn't have access to a dime. I can assure you, he died in that fire."

"You also assumed he followed you out of the burning hut," Morgan pointed out. "You can't be certain he didn't bolt in a different direction."

"Auster told me more than once he was supposed to kill Eric. He claimed he succeeded before he brought me back to Tluq Cay. It sounds like a paid job. How can you explain that?"

"Think, Darla." He stretched across the short space, took her hands in his, and gazed into her eyes. "Eric could've paid this…Auster to do his dirty work."

"Paid him with the funds set aside for Blaine's release?" She jerked her hands away. "Wouldn't it be considered cheating the pirates if he helped Eric?"

Morgan reset his shades. "I can't explain their rules, Dar. I'm telling you what the police believe."

"Well, they're wrong. And you are, too. You barely know Eric. He wouldn't do this."

"You're right, I don't know Eric. Maybe you don't either."

She whipped around and glared at her best friend. "Tell him, Steph. We both *know* Eric well."

"I agree with Darla, but I've already explained, Morgan, and the police, too. Eric is one of the most authentic people I've ever met. He's straightforward and brutally honest. He wouldn't take anything that doesn't belong to him."

Morgan rose and repositioned his sunglasses. "Maybe. For your sake I'll speak to them again, and possibly get them to look in another direction."

Darla slightly relaxed. "Thank you, Morgan. Your word carries a lot of weight here." She turned to Stephanie. "Are the pirates corresponding with anyone now that Eric is…gone?"

Stephanie shoved away a lock of hair hanging in her eyes. "Blaine's dad returned, and he has Eric's phone. They've communicated. The pirates aren't happy about the missing money. They're threatening to kill Blaine if they're not paid. We're going mad trying to figure out what to do."

"Oh, Steph. Why didn't you tell me?"

Her tears welled. "I didn't want to burden you. You're still dealing with Eric's murder, and your ordeal. The kidnappers have ordered us to pay three times the original amount. If we don't, Blaine's dead."

"Did they at least extend the time?"

"One more day."

Darla gasped. "Have you had luck securing more funds?"

"We've gathered a small sum, but no, we're nowhere close. And the clock's ticking."

Morgan's fingers brushed Darla's exposed knee peeking from underneath her bathrobe. "I'm on my way to work. We're preparing a big fireworks display tomorrow night."

"Here? On Tluq Cay?"

"Summer Solstice celebration." He sauntered toward the gate, then stopped, and lingered as if he preferred not to go. Darla's fists coiled, digging her nails into her palms.

Shades hid his eyes, but it was obvious he had something else to say. She wasn't ready to have the conversation she feared was on the brink of happening.

"I realize you've suffered a huge setback, and now's not the best time, but why don't we try to get together tomorrow before the show? I'd like to get some concrete information about Eric to take to authorities. We can have that drink we discussed the other day while we talk."

She debated whether meeting him was appropriate. She wasn't in a social mood, but he spent a lot of time on these islands, and he was in good with the authorities."

"One drink and a short conversation is all I'm up for."

"Then that's what it'll be. How about we meet on the resort's deck before dusk?"

"I'll see you tomorrow evening."

Stephanie swirled the liquid in her beaker, clinking the ice cubes against the glass as Morgan strolled away. "Seriously? A date with Morgan?" Her frown deepened. "So soon?"

"Not a date. If he plans to talk to the police about reversing their opinion about Eric, and arrest Auster, then I'll force myself to sit with him for an hour."

"Whatever you say."

"Don't judge me. I want Eric's name cleared."

"I'm sorry. It's all so emotional." Stephanie paused. "Try to talk him into forgiving our loan while you're at it. We can't raise the total sum demanded and repay him, too."

"I will. He may have some ideas where we can find the extra cash."

"What's your next move?"

"Make sure Eric's reputation remains clean and see that Blaine's released." Darla sighed. "After that, there's nothing to do but head home, deal with my misery, and somehow go on with my life."

They exchanged a grim look.

"Such a pragmatic ending, isn't it?"

"This is no pleasure trip, for sure. Sad. It should have been wonderful." Darla squinted against the brightened sun. "I do want to do one last thing before I leave."

"What's that?"

Darla drained her glass and set it aside. "Give Eric a proper send-off."

"Once his death is confirmed, his parents will arrange a service and we can attend." Stephanie drank the rest of her spiked concoction, then reached for the pitcher to refill her and Darla's flutes. She sank back into the cushions. "Thousands of memorials and tributes will be arranged around the world when the word leaks."

Darla touched the beads she silently vowed to never remove. "I mean a private ceremony." She searched the sky as if to find some sense of the last twenty-four hours. "With just Eric and me. I prefer to say my goodbyes without an audience."

"How perfect. A perfect way to show how much you loved him. I suppose you could hold a ritual on this stretch of beach. It's private."

"Nope. I plan to go to the last place I saw him and have it there."

"Darla, no. You can't. Not by yourself. The island's dangerous, and probably a pirate haunt according to police. Auster hangs out there, too, and he could come after you. He released you once, but he may not feel as inclined a second time."

"We only ran into natives. Auster was there to track Eric and kill him."

"What about the welcoming committee who met you when you arrived on the island?"

"They were part of Auster's gang. I can avoid them. They don't scare me."

"They should. They definitely scare me."

Darla gazed at her friend. "I have to find what's left of Eric and take him home. I can't be afraid."

"Forgive me, but I'm selfish right now. I can't stand to lose anyone else. If anything happens to you, my closest group of friends will diminish to one. Finn."

"Not a great example of a friend. I'm so mad he took off and left you by yourself. He should've bucked up and stayed. Seriously, how's that friendship?"

Stephanie appeared confused. "This nightmare must have affected you more than your realize. What are you talking about?"

"Finn left the island to go home."

Stephanie's scowl deepened as she shook her head.

"Eric told me he grabbed a flight the night Auster abducted us." Her eyebrows drew together. "He didn't?"

"No, Finn's still here. Camped in his cabin, ordering room service, and charging crap out the wazoo."

"Seriously?"

"Yeah. He's extremely busy, so he orders everything in."

"Busy doing what?"

"I can't say. He's been very secretive."

"Strange. Say what you want about Finn O'Conner, but his life has always been an open book. He usually tells you stuff you'd rather not know."

"True, but his recent behavior's been super-secret and super weird." She and Darla swapped glances. "Weirder than usual."

"Eric did say Finn mentioned replacing Blaine as Spiraling UP's base player if Blaine doesn't return. He thought that was way off base. Even for Finn."

"He hinted the same last night when we were at dinner with Blaine's dad." Stephanie's shoulders squared. "I threw a loaded breadbasket at him. It made me sorry I made him leave his room and join us. Which reminds me, when I went by his bungalow, I saw a ton of boxes inside."

"What kind of boxes?"

"Medium size boxes. Wrapped in brown paper. They almost filled the main room. I asked him what they were, but he wouldn't tell me."

"This is so peculiar." Darla finished off her drink. "Finn's always strapped for cash, yet he's ordering stuff?"

"Blaine's ransom money was in his bungalow. And that was the last place it was seen."

"Interesting theory." Darla stood and smoothed her palms across her terry cloth robe. "It's time to have a long, heart to heart with Mr. Finn O'Conner."

Stephanie placed her glass onto the table. "I agree."

After Darla dressed, the two women sprinted across the hotel grounds, straight to Finn's cottage. They stood on the small porch, and both pounded on the door. No one answered. They knocked again, getting the same results.

"He's probably asleep." Stephanie placed her ear to the door. "It's quiet inside."

Darla exited the doorway and hurried to the window. Curtains were drawn, but there was enough of a crack to see in. She peered through the split. Stephanie was right. Boxes were everywhere. A laptop sat on the coffee table. It was opened, the screen facing the window. Photographs of Blaine were plastered on an unfamiliar website.

"This doesn't look so innocent," she mumbled under her breath.

"No, it doesn't." Stephanie had moved behind her. "He's up to something, and whatever it is he's up to, it involves Blaine."

Chapter 13

Darla maintained a solid grip on the rented jet ski as she cruised within a swell of breakers at a gradual pace. Winds had gained momentum. Fierce breezes jerked and jolted her, making her excursion rougher than she anticipated.

She steered due east. Auster had journeyed west on her return, so she assumed this way was correct. But she may be wrong. Thus far, her hour-long expedition produced nothing but the barren sea. Darla tried to recall the timeline and distance when coming back to Tluq Cay, but deep shock caused her memory to go blank. She barely recalled a second after she left Eric.

A bubble of misgivings grew as she zoomed upon vast openness. What if she couldn't find the island and never found Eric's remains? No, she wouldn't consider failure. The isle was near, she just had to determine where.

Another ten minutes passed without success. A sigh escaped. Time to call it a day. She'd try again tomorrow. Possibly study maps and pinpoint her quadrants first. She circled around.

A tiny image captured her attention in mid-loop. She released the throttle until she slowed to a halt. Legs extended, she remained straddled and stood, squinting against a mass of blaring sunrays.

Her heartbeat quickened. A miniature shadow

peeked beyond the horizon surrounded by a ring of turquoise. Land, and perhaps her destination. Mentally, she calculated the amount of distance between the realm and her, gaging the span.

Piece of cake.

She lowered to her seat, gunned the engine, and cut crossways amid the sea's jarring surges. She passed a huge rock formation. She remembered seeing this before. She was on the right track. The murky shape transformed into a lush landmass as she closed in.

Skillfully, she reduced speed, guiding her watercraft forward. She accelerated seconds ahead of touching the coastal threshold and beached the jet bike with ease. Motor off, she removed her life vest, hooked an armhole through a handlebar, and dismounted, ensuring her key's coiled band stayed attached to her wrist. Snatching a backpack loaded with supplies, she trudged across a hill of moist sand.

Pausing at a drier site, she dug into her pack's side pocket, grabbed her spare sneakers, and tossed them to the ground. Once her shoes were secured and tied, she was set to hike the treacherous range. She headed toward a dense tree grove. Shrieks soared behind her.

Darla's heart leaped. She spun to the noise, unzipping her backpack, ready to draw her weapon. Her terror instantly shrunk, and a slight panic took its place.

Stephanie barreled recklessly across the ocean's plane aboard a Sea Doo.

"Help, Darla," she screeched. "I can't stop."

Darla dropped her belongings, sprinted to the shoreline, and waved her hands above her head. "Turn, Steph. Bring it around this way."

Stephanie yanked the handlebars left and punched

the engine. The unstable craft rocketed, zigzagging out of control. It bounced onto the shore producing a loud smack. The nose pointed straight at Darla.

Darla didn't wait and see if Stephanie would veer the other way. She dove onto the shore and rolled away, moments before Stephanie skimmed the watercraft upon the silt.

The jet ski skidded diagonally, spouting a wet powdery muck over the banks. "How do I turn this thing off?"

She smashed into Darla's parked ski. An explosive bang shook the immediate atmosphere. The impact brought the commotion to an instant standstill.

Stephanie jerked forward. She summersaulted headfirst over the water bike's apex, landing on the ground, ending with a decisive thump.

Darla sprang to her feet, breaking into a run. She slithered to a halt next to Stephanie. "Are you all right?"

Stephanie lay flat, struggling to regain her breath. Gradually, she raised to sit, brushing at clumps of mud clinging to her. "I believe so."

Darla flicked a look toward the ensnared jet skis. "That was—an interesting dismount."

Stephanie stood with more dignity than Darla deemed possible. "Where are the brakes? I couldn't turn the damn thing off."

"That jet ski's an older model. Manufacturers didn't install brakes until a few years ago."

"Then how do you stop?" Wiping her palms, she slapped them against her thighs, splattering heavy droplets of mud. "A person could get killed riding one of those things."

"You decrease your speed and use the beach as a way of bringing it to a halt." Darla gestured at their entangled vehicles. "Works much better than crashing and tumbling off headfirst."

Stephanie grumbled, unfastened her lifejacket, and slammed the vest to the ground. "Excuse me. I'm not like you. I didn't grow up driving androids before I could walk. I was raised in Montana."

"I get that, Steph." Darla wrestled to reel in her flippantness. "And I'm sorry for joking, but you frightened me. I'm just relieved you're okay. You could've snapped a bone. Didn't anyone coach you on how to operate a jet ski before you attempted a long distance voyage?"

"Not exactly."

Darla's brows lowered.

"You were almost out of sight. I didn't know which way you were heading. I had to leave, or I'd lose you. I mean, the guy at the rental shop asked if I needed lessons, but I told him no, I could drive a jet ski." She glanced at Darla sheepishly. "He probably guessed I lied once he saw me sputter around the harbor."

Darla sauntered to the dented Seadoos hoping for only cosmetic damages. She easily separated the two machines to assess the losses. Each powered up without a problem. The charter company insisted renters purchase insurance for added costs, so they should be fine.

"The exteriors were already scratched, and there's a couple of new dings, but that's it." She detached the keys from the ignition and pitched them to Stephanie. "Keep those with you." Her face clouded. "Why'd you follow me?"

"A better question is, why did you come here? We agreed to deep six this weird island adventure because of the danger." Stephanie's eyes flickered a hint of irritation. "Or did you forget?"

"That was your agreement. Not mine."

"Yes, I got that, which is why I came after you. You need backup in case trouble arrives."

"I appreciate your concern, but I can take care of myself. Natives are harmless, plus I'm prepared if bad guys hassle me."

"The natives aren't dangerous? You mentioned some hairy instances when you first met. Auster and his friends also made an appearance." Stephanie ambled to the lapping water and squatted. Splashing her exposed skin, she rinsed away the excess grime, then shook her hands dry. She rose and returned to Darla. "But I guess since we're already here, we ought to explore, locate Eric's remains, and make arrangements to transport him home."

"We? I wanted to do this alone, Steph."

"Nope." Arms clamped across her chest. "I survived the waterpark ride from hell chasing you. I'll tail you every inch of this island if I have to, but you're not doing this by yourself."

Darla regarded Stephanie's sparkled, thick-soled flip-flops and freshly pedicured toes with a touch of inner humor. Her friend might hail from Montana, a state known for wildlife, mountains, headwaters, and real-life cowboys, but her every cell was girly girl.

She didn't do rugged, remote, or uncivilized. The fact she agreed to Blaine's request and hold her wedding outdoors surprised Darla. Even so, she doubted Stephanie would tolerate their upcoming precarious trek devoid of difficulties.

"That's not a great idea," Darla cautioned. "The wind's blowing the sea pretty hard. The water's choppy. You should head to Tluq Cay now. I'm right behind you as soon as I'm done."

"I'm not leaving unless you are. Besides, if Eric was hounded and murdered nearby, then conceivably the pirates are holding Blaine here, too."

"We haven't seen pirates, Steph."

"The police told me they won't go to this set of islands. The area isn't just inhabited by people like Auster, but all underworld types. As in pirates."

"Interesting."

"Isn't it? Tourist and locals are warned to stay away." Hands on her hips, she scanned the area. "Yet, here we are."

"So you're considering...what? They're holding Blaine here?"

"I'm not sure what I think. I intend to investigate, though.

Stephanie strolled to the edge of the jungle and waited. Darla expelled an exasperated breath. She swiped her backpack off the ground, walked to her friend, and assumed the lead once they penetrated the interiors of the forest.

"Do you remember the way?"

"Not really." Darla scanned the heavily wooded region. "But I estimate we're close to an hour and a half away. Keep your eyes open and stay alert."

As if to reiterate her caution, a series of screeches echoed above them, trailed by multiple fluttering flaps.

"And just to prove your point, we get to experience a reenactment of the opening of a horror movie."

"Wait until after dark."

"Don't even." Stephanie studied the surroundings.

"So this trail isn't familiar?"

"Other than brambles and a ton of water? Nope. We moved after dark or hid under a canopy of trees when we were here before. It felt like night the entire time. I'm almost positive this way will get us there. Every path seems to lead into the same direction."

They continued their expedition in silence. Darla's mind drifted. She fantasized she found Eric, only he hadn't died. He was alive and well.

A gush of wind rustled and howled among the treetops. Needles puckered over the base of her neck, shadowed by a peculiar sensation.

Eric was waiting for her.

A spark of optimism ignited. Perhaps he somehow survived the inferno. There was a slight possibility. She had been dragged away, and without confirming he'd died. She only had Auster's word, which meant what?

Nothing.

Her heart sang.

Yesterday's conversation with Morgan suddenly highlighted her memory. If he had lived, it may substantiate Morgan and the local police's suspicions. An investigation would occur. Inconvenient at best, because she knew Eric well. He never faked anything, nor would he steal cash slated to rescue his closest friend. His innocence would prevail.

"I wonder…" She spoke aloud, but didn't finish, unwilling to expose her outrageous idea. The likelihood was too farfetched, and Stephanie wouldn't hesitate to call her on it. Even if Steph was right, Darla preferred not to listen to harsh reality.

"What do you wonder, Dar?"

"Nothing. I'm thinking out loud."

"Can we rest a while?" She didn't wait until Darla replied, but crashed onto a mound of earth set in an exposed section of the forest. Kicking the once shimmery flip flops aside, Stephanie crossed one leg over the other and inspected a blister developing on her big toe.

Darla assessed their whereabouts, seeking signs they traveled on an accurate course. "We've made good time. I'm guesstimating, but I'm thinking we have about forty-five minutes to go."

Stephanie slackened against a tree trunk. "We should be back to the resort by nightfall, then?"

"That's the plan."

"We need to find Finn."

"Definitely. Hope he's there, this time."

Darla unzipped her pack, extracted two water bottles, and handed one to Stephanie. They revisited Finn's bungalow three times yesterday, and once again this morning without seeing or speaking to him. Neither she nor Stephanie could verify if he was inside and ignored them or if he left the cottage. They peeked through the window on each trip, hoping to catch him. But luck dodged them and apparently so did Finn.

Darla settled next to the foot of a scaling cliff and uncapped her water.

"This place is pretty, but it kinda gives me the creeps," Stephanie observed. "Like something sinister is lingering under our noses."

"Auster murdered Eric a few miles away. This island is filled with evil."

"Eric's death is incredibly painful, and not

knowing if Blaine is dead or alive is driving me nuts. None of this makes sense. Take your and Eric's primal ceremony. What was that about?"

"I'm not sure what you're asking."

"The impromptu wedding. Extremely bizarre. Doesn't it strike you as strange a feast and ceremony was arranged prior to your arrival? They even had clothes prepared for you to change in to."

"Honestly, so much has taken place, I haven't given it too much thought. Eric and I discussed it later, and we agreed the night was strange."

"Almost as if they knew you were coming."

"I believe Auster orchestrated the whole thing. He was hired to murder Eric. Creating a celebration so Eric would relax and lowering his defenses would've given him an opportunity to ambush and kill him."

"Rather elaborate, don't you think?"

"He hadn't been successful up until that point. Auster waited until after Eric was fed well and exhausted, consequently, when he least suspected it."

"Which should tell you, those native people you insist are so kind are in cahoots with Auster, and they helped him execute the love of your life."

"I suppose."

"Any clues why Auster wanted to kill Eric?"

Darla snatched a curl to twist around her index finger. "He just said Eric was getting what was coming to him."

"How come you didn't mention any of this to Morgan?"

"Although he says he wants to help, I sense he doubts Eric's innocence. He agrees with the local cops."

"Are you setting him straight on your date?"

"Not a date, and no, I'm not getting into Eric when we meet later, other than to answer Morgan's questions. I might have misread Morgan's intentions in the beginning, but I'm starting to suspect the same as you. He's aiming for us to get back together."

Stephanie awarded her a sly look. "Hmmm. Didn't I tell you?"

"You did. I'll make sure he understands we're totally over. Even with Eric gone, we won't reunite as a couple."

****

"Aren't you afraid to go in?" Stephanie probed as they approached the edge of the shambled village.

"Yes." Darla's voice quivered as they traipsed inside the compound. "But I can't let fear get to me."

"You're sure if these people show up, they won't harm us?"

"They're different. They threatened us at first but turned accommodating the rest of our visit. But no, I'm not sure of anything."

An eerie, dark silence hovered around them.

"Lots of shacks, but they're intact. None are burned." Stephanie's head tipped to study one of the small huts. "Where did the fire happen?"

"This way."

Darla led her behind the rows, to the reclusive area where the hut once sat. The space was cleared. Searing fragments should rise and linger over a destroyed home. But remnants of the rectangular shelter were gone. No traces of smoldering ash or residue. And no indication Eric was ever here.

"I don't understand." Darla gazed at the bare plot

of dirt. "This is the exact spot, I'm sure of it."

Stephanie motioned to a sequence of lines etched in the sand. "Everything's been raked."

Darla stared at the elongated strips imprinted in the soil. "He's gone," she whispered. "Eric's gone."

Stephanie placed a hand on her shoulder. "I hate to sound cold, but it's only a body, Dar. Nothing but a vessel we utilize while we're here on earth. Eric no longer needs his vessel. His spirit is what matters…" She choked on her words. "I'm sorry. Would you like some time alone?"

"I don't know. I'm on mental overload. I can't concentrate."

Stephanie patted her. "I'll give you a few minutes to sort through your feelings."

Darla scraped a foot on top of the fresh earth and sank to the ground. Due to the smothering chaos surrounding them, she hadn't truly begun to grieve. Burying Eric would put a finality to his life and give her freedom to mourn.

Except, she didn't have anything to bury.

She sat still as her emotions reeled. Raw pain ruptured, on the verge of an overflow. She gaped at a span of vacant terrain.

Tears filled her eyes. "I don't want to tell you good-bye. It's too hard to let you go. If I knew you'd leave me forever, we wouldn't…I wouldn't have fought with you. I'm sorry we argued, and I so regret we broke up." She sniffed. "You may've never known this, but you're my world, and that'll never change."

"Dar?"

Swallowing her frustration, she twisted to Stephanie, who emerged out of a cluster of bushes.

"I hate to interrupt your private moment, but I found something you'll want to see." She advanced, extending her cupped hands.

Darla stared at the object lying in her friend's palms.

"A necklace, like yours, but this one's larger, and sized to fit a man." She lifted it by the tip. "Eric's?"

"Yes." She accepted the necklace and clasped it to her chest. "Where did you get this?"

Stephanie nodded at a patch of undergrowth. "Past the thicket. It's in good shape for toasting in a blaze."

Darla tied the strand around her neck as she rose to her feet.

"Perhaps you can bury it? Symbolic to laying his body to rest?"

"Or maybe it's a sign, telling me not to hold a memorial, just yet."

Stephanie's eyes narrowed. "You don't expect to find Eric alive, do you? I get you want to alter his outcome, but you can't allow yourself to fantasize impossibilities. You're set to suffer a major fail, if you do."

"My head's aware, but my heart won't let go of the possibility." She flashed a sad smile. "Don't worry. I understand the difference between fantasy and reality."

"You normally do, but this is Eric. Has his death truly sunk in? I'm traumatized that he's gone. Your head must be spinning."

"It is." Darla preferred not to discuss Eric anymore, fearing she may suffer an emotional breakdown if the conversation continued. "I want to examine the native colony closer during daylight hours." Her head tilted upward. "The sun is still high. We have plenty of time.

Do you want to look for Blaine?"

"Wouldn't you prefer me to stay and help you, and we search for Blaine after."

"I'm afraid we'll lose the light. I would rather not tackle the ocean after dark." She turned an unsettling gaze upon her friend. "Plus, there's Finn. I expect we'll get more out of him than we'll find here."

Stephanie nodded. "I won't go far."

Darla paced down the colony's rugged path centered between the lines of shanties. Odd. The space remained deserted. Where were all the people? And why did this commune have the distinct ghost town aura.

She wandered to the festival grounds. Again, the space resembled a neglected stretch of territory. She walked the perimeters, trying to unearth a single item to show a party occurred two days ago, but she found nothing.

She rambled toward the bath house and peered inside. The tub remained. Darla sighed, relieved something stayed the same. Hiking farther in, she gave the room a quick onceover. Half burned candles were scattered about, but her dirty clothes and everything else had vanished.

She stepped outdoors. A wind gust sent a cluster of dried leaves skittering over the dusty trail. She shivered. Chilly air, laden with dread coated her skin. Reaching behind, she unfastened her backpack, and dipped a hand into the opening to retrieve her 9mm.

"Ya' just couldn't obey, couldja?"

Darla dropped her bag to the ground. She slowly rotated toward Auster's voice, raising her weapon as she turned. She halted, aiming her gun at his forehead.

"Darla don't," Stephanie shrieked.

Auster wore a formable smile. An arm was hooked around Stephanie, gripping her hands in one of his. A machine gun-pistol was pointed at the back of her skull.

"Now ya gone and done it, missy. Told ya to leave here or your friends would end up dead."

Darla winced. A gun directed at her friend rattled her, but she couldn't let Auster see her weakness. Showing vulnerability would give him added power. His gun outpowered hers times ten. She must stay in control. She would have to outsmart and outshoot him to save Stephanie.

"Ya better put that toy of yours away. Ya know your little pea shooter don't got a chance against my cannon."

He could provoke all he wanted. She wouldn't fall for his head games. Darla grasped her weapon steady, her concentration focused on his trigger finger. Adrenaline rushed through her veins.

"Guess ya gonna watch me kill her." He smirked then chuckled "Ya gonna go home a sad lady, losin' all your friends."

Patiently, she delayed movement, waiting until he presented her with an opportunity. His finger twitched. Darla restrained a breath as her heart bounced erratically. She slid the striker backwards, priming it to discharge.

A muffled thud boomed.

Auster's frame straightened. His face became distorted, then stunned. A blotch of red formed on the side of his head. Blood oozed down a whitened cheek.

He released Stephanie.

His large body folded and crumbled to the ground.

Darla's eyes widened, keeping her firearm trained forward. A chunk of iron pipe waved over an unconscious Auster.

"What do you think, luv." A half-grin spread across Eric's lips. "Did I hit him hard enough to call us even?"

Chapter 14

"Are you okay, Dar…Steph?"

Eric divided a bewildered look between Darla and Stephanie. Both appeared shocked, and he didn't understand why. He assumed Darla stumbled upon the jet skis, stole one, and hauled ass. Now, she returned to take him back to Tluq Cay with Stephanie in tow.

Except they acted stunned, like they didn't expect to see him. Or maybe Auster's threatening Stephanie threw them into a panic, and they hadn't recuperated.

He refocused on Darla. She'd yet to budge. Auster lay unconscious in front of him, meaning her 9mm was aimed straight at his heart. Not a comfortable situation if she were frightened out of her trance and reacted aggressively.

"Darla." His speech elevated. "Everything's fine. Lower your gun." She flinched but continued to stand in hold position. "Put your weapon down. *Now.*"

She blinked. Although her poised-to-shoot posture relaxed, she kept the revolver level, still eyeing him like he was a ghost from her past. "You're dead," she whispered.

"Dead?" He wiggled the hand clasping an iron pipe. "Pretty sure I'm not."

A squeak emitted from his other side. He twisted toward Stephanie. Another gurgle discharged, then her eyeballs rolled, and retreated into her head. She folded at the waist and collapsed.

Darla took a step, but Eric was nearer and reached her first. Kneeling, he dropped his rod and positioned two fingers on the side of her neck. Her heartrate had slowed; however, her breathing seemed regular.

He shot Darla a glance. "She fainted, but she's fine. Give her a moment, and she'll wake up."

Darla continued to study him, still seemingly unsure if he was real or a walking corpse. "How did you escape the fire?"

"Dunno." Eric brushed his hands and rose to his feet. "I remember you waking me and telling me we had to leave." He shrugged. "The rest is a blank. I think I passed out. I came to later inside a commune."

She released her firearm and gestured at the rows of empty huts. "Where? I came back that night and again today. It's deserted."

"No one lives here. Not sure why. The village where I stayed is next to a range of mountains, and residents live there. I ran into everyone we met the other night, except for Witchy and Preacher Man."

"Weird." She walked to her backpack and swept it off the sand, tucking her weapon into a side pocket. "Did you attempt to find a way back to Tluq Cay?"

"First, I searched, trying to find you. A woman at the compound understood what I was doin' and explained through motions you'd left."

An abrupt fear materialized. What if his information was incorrect or he misunderstood and something else happened? Maybe that's why Darla behaved so strange, like her believing he was dead.

Darla relieved his worries and nodded. "Was she able to describe how I exited?"

"If she did, I didn't get what she meant." He paused. "You didn't find the jet skis?"

She shook her head.

Eric's eyebrows lugged together. "How didya' get to the resort?"

"I'll give you details after you finish what went down during your stay."

"Not much left to tell. I kept exploring the island, hoping to uncover the jet skis and steal one, but I didn't have any luck. I was never too worried 'bout finding a way back. I figured you'd come and rescue me." Eric aimed a broad grin her way. "Was I right or what?"

Angry crimson spread across her cheeks. She abandoned her bag, took three long strides, and pounced. Hands balled into fists, she hammered them into his chest.

Eric's arms crisscrossed, covering his torso. He tried to reverse the other way, but she matched his movements, her fists reeling as he attempted to disengage.

"Hey, what's with the hostility?"

"I thought your sorry ass was dead." She pummeled at his forearms. "Do you know how awful these last two days were? I came here to collect your ashes, so I could send you home to your family for a proper burial."

"Darla." One-handedly, he seized her flailing limbs. She gritted her teeth and jerked, but he firmed his grip. "Darla."

She stopped fighting him and simply glared.

Tugging her close, he gazed into her eyes. "I never intended to upset you. I couldn't have known what you thought. I'm not so cruel I'd let you think I died. Not on purpose."

"What else would I believe?"

"Same as me. We split due to the chaos, and we'd find each other later."

"You were trapped inside a burning hut." Tears shimmered in her dark eyes. "I tried to get back inside, to rescue you, but he stopped me. Auster. He told me he'd killed you. I didn't think I'd ever see you again."

Releasing her wrists, he slid his hands to her waist, and drew her into a protected embrace. While he bore no fault, guilt coiled around and wrenched his gut.

"I'm sorry, luv. I had no idea." He swiped a kiss across her brow. "Dry your tears. I'm right here, and I'm not going anywhere." Her arms circled his neck and rested against his shoulder. "I hate that I made you sad," he murmured, stroking her hair.

"Sorry, I punched you."

He chuckled. "Multiple times."

She unburied her face and eyed him, alarmed. "Did I make your injuries worse?"

"I hurt all over." A corner of his mouth lifted. "I need medical assistance immediately."

She edged backward to inspect his mending bruises. "Can I help?"

"Hmmm." His chin raised, pretending to contemplate. "If I remember right, your lips have an amazing healing power. They can bring life back into a dying man."

Suspicion spread across her face. "And if I kiss your boo boo's, they'll get well?"

Eric's head bobbed as his smile widened.

She gave a profound sigh and stooped to align with one of the larger discolorations. Tilting forward, she positioned her mouth over the bruise. Feathery strokes traced across his upper body.

His palms slid to her shoulders and squeezed. His eyelids closed as he expelled a satisfied moan.

"I'm glad you're not dead," she breathed against his skin.

"I'm thrilled about that, too, luv," he murmured.

A rage of suppressed hunger ignited, searing his blood and sent it tearing through his veins.

Her tongue skimmed his nipple. A sharp breath escaped. His spine stiffened, tightening his grip around her shoulders.

She pulled away. "Did I hurt you?"

Eric's lids opened and peered at her concerned face. "No, why?"

"You tensed. I thought I pressed too hard."

"No, luv. Your press is perfect."

Hovering above her, he gazed into her pleading eyes. Her face lifted higher, offering an invitation to taste the sweetness of her lips. Their three-month disagreement completely faded as their mutual desires skyrocketed. He bent toward her, ready to devour her.

Whimpers arose toward the rear. Alarmed, Darla spun around and mouthed, "Stephanie."

A reluctant Eric freed her the exact moment she untangled herself from his hold. She flashed him a quick smile, and he repaid her with a warm grin of his own.

Darla hurried and knelt by Stephanie, placing a hand on her upper arm to help her sit. "Are you all right? You blacked out."

"I did?" Stephanie sat. She shoved away strands of hair covering her face. She looked at Eric. Her jaw plunged. "Eric? You didn't die?" She frowned at Darla. "Eric's alive or did I inhale some hallucinogenic seaweed when I fainted?"

"You're not hallucinating. Eric's here, in the flesh, and yes, he's breathing."

Stephanie rotated to him and beamed. "I'm so happy you're here.

"Believe me, I'm glad too, Steph."

"What happened to you? Where were you?"

"We'll explain on our way back to the jet skis," Darla put her hand underneath Stephanie's arm to help her up. "We probably need to leave before Auster awakens."

"Can we do a quick search for Blaine?" Stephanie motioned to Darla she wasn't ready to stand. Her gaze focused on Eric. "Finding you is a positive sign. I predict we'll track him down soon and end this nightmare."

"I hope you're right." Eric strolled to the women, attempting to keep his movements vertical. A problematic feat as the result of an inferno still burned between his legs. He wobbled as he awkwardly lowered to kneel by the women. "I scouted the area during my stay. I might have found where they're keeping Blaine." He waved a hand. "I thought we'd been over this island, but there's a whole section that we haven't explored. I've spotted a lot of unsavory looking characters making frequent trips that way."

"Why are we waiting? Let's find out." Stephanie leaped to her feet and then swayed to one side, off balance.

Darla swiftly sprang up and caught her. "You're talking about an extensive hike. Are you sure you can make it? You just came to, after fainting."

"I'll walk a thousand miles in a coma if it leads to Blaine."

Once sure Steph stood steady, Darla went to snatch her gear. "If you're certain you can walk, then we better get started." She squinted at a sprawled Auster, sleeping off his inflicted stupor, then looked at Eric. "You may want to go back, now. He's going to come after you when he wakes up"

"I'm not leaving you." Eric retrieved his rod off a leaf pile and strolled toward the jungle. "But you're right. He's gonna be nail spittin' mad after he recovers from his headache."

"And he'll want payback."

"Thanks for the reminder, luv."

Traipsing across a littered track, the trio plodded farther into the forest with little conversation. Damp patches of moss and numerous fallen branches were in the middle of the trail, hindering their trip.

Stout airstreams whistled inside the dense vegetation, while insects and amphibians entertained with their preferred species' melodies. Streaks of sunlight beamed past tiny cavities and jutted through the foliage canopy, creating specks of light, and dotted the landscape in shadowy outlines.

Stephanie suddenly released a high-pitched giggle. "What's up with those pants?"

"Um, this is my wedding suit." A twisted root protruded in the center of the trail. He swerved to miss it. "Did Darla tell you we got married?"

"Yes, she did, but she failed to mention you were married in a pair of snuggies."

He chuckled. "I'm in good with the locals. Want

me to ask 'em to make Blaine a pair?"

"Thanks, but I'll pass."

"Speaking of our ceremony," Darla stated. "Stephanie agrees with us. The ritual was prearranged prior to our arrival. I haven't told you what occurred after you and I became separated, but it coincides with that belief." Without encouragement, she proceeded to recall the incident the night of the fire and afterwards.

He considered her theory after she finished. "Your concept has a slight problem. If you're right about the wedding being a set up, then the natives are tied with Auster and his secret partner. I don't believe they're involved. They saved us, then saved me again during the fire. Doesn't add up."

"They also held us at spear point when we first met to keep us here for the ceremony. Auster or someone he's connected to may have control over these people. They're spiritual and easily swayed by outside influences. Their behavior tends to make me think they believe in magic and spirits. They might believe he's a god or spirit and threaten to curse them unless they do as they're told."

"But why go to all the effort to set up such an elaborate ceremony?"

"To catch you off guard." She sighed. "Someone is determined to end your life and will go to any length to succeed."

"That's becoming disturbingly clear." Eric jammed his fingertips in his hair and combed through the thick layers. "I'd like to know who's behind this shit."

"Me too, but the puzzle isn't piecing together."

"Nothin' but a puddle of mud, and I'm not feeling reassured."

Darla glanced at Stephanie. "What about Finn?"

Eric scowled. "What about him?"

"He never left the Turquoise Archipelago, and he's acting stranger than usual."

"How?"

"He's put together some secret operation, and he is managing it out of your bungalow," Stephanie revealed. "I've asked him what he's doing repeatedly, but he won't say."

"You two are saying Finn is behind all of this?"

"You never got along, and you said he was still upset about his brother and Drake's death. Maybe he snapped," Darla suggested.

Eric paused. Had Finn hooked up with Auster and been behind these attempts on his life? The idea seemed farfetched. Finn was a peace-loving soul, who would never consider hurting another human being.

"Finn and I aren't best friends, but I can't wrap my brain around him hiring someone to come after me."

Darla stared him down. "Then who wants you dead?"

"No fuckin' clue." Eric stomped through the brush. Some psycho meant to kill him, and he didn't know how to stop it. Confirming his fears didn't help his frayed nerves. He was tired of shit going every way but right. "We'd better hurry if we hope to get to the other side of the island and back."

Eric slid to a halt. "Where did Finn find cash to finance a project? He's broker than broke. Other than royalties and oldie shows, he doesn't have money comin' in."

"A pot of gold?" Darla twisted a curl around her forefinger. "Or maybe Blaine's ransom? That's missing, by the way."

"Fuck. I knew it."

"Finn had access to it. All he needed to do was to get you out of the way."

Aiming his pipe at a rotted tree trunk, Eric swung it hard. Decomposed roots lifted from the ground, tilting the trunk sideways. The ladies watched, but neither spoke, giving him the time he needed to absorb the information in his own way. It didn't take long, because nothing added up.

Once he calmed, they resumed their hike, trudging across the dusty trail. Eric worked to process their mounting problems. The girls tailed him but seemed to forget their issues and chattered about a big to-do the resort was hosting later tonight. Their talks continued until they approached the trickiest section of the journey.

There Eric slowed and signaled to the women. "I've tried to get around this way twice, and both times I saw some mean looking dudes lurking near the bog. We gotta stay quiet."

The ladies' chatter silenced, and the trio treaded toward a swirl of choking mist with caution. A repulsive odor that didn't belong in this world reeked where the road narrowed. Most of the path ebbed into a reedy marsh. Carefully, they maneuvered the thin course, their senses on edge, and primed to retreat if necessary.

A gentle shatter of twigs broke the silence. The three froze. Maybe an animal prowled amid the blackened shadows. Chills pricked across the back of Eric's neck.

Maybe not.

The brush rustled louder. A conversation in rapid French rattled inside the hedges. Darla inched her backpack off her shoulders and removed the pistol. Eric tightened his grip on the pipe and signaled for the women to flee.

Before they managed a step backwards, four men emerged from the bushes. They were spotted right away.

"They see us," Eric roared. "Go."

They scattered, instantly in a footrace. While not the best fitting footwear, he managed to salvage his borrowed sneakers at the natives' camp. Darla also donned running shoes. They stayed far enough ahead, but Stephanie flapped in flip flops, and lagged way behind. If their circumstances didn't change quickly, she wouldn't out distance their pursuers.

Darla also recognized the problem. She slowed and grabbed Stephanie's arm and tugged her around a corner. "Separate and hide."

Eric snatched a low tree limb, hoisted up, and scaled high enough to blend in with the thick vegetation. Stephanie ducked behind a hollowed tree trunk and climbed inside. Darla dived into a dry culvert, quickly and quietly covering herself with withered leaves.

Though well hidden, they were all easy prey if spotted. Eric inhaled, waiting, hoping their hunters wouldn't notice them as they rushed by.

He gazed downward. Ominous shadows appeared past the bend. Soundlessly, they performed a speedy scour and moved on.

The three waited nearly ten minutes before coming out of their hiding places.

Stephanie was first, waving a hand in front of her nose as she grimaced. "It stinks in there."

Eric stretched a leg to a lower branch, ready to shimmy from his perch.

"Hey sweetheart," came a voice from behind. Stephanie shifted and gasped.

A fifth man surfaced out of the brush. A wicked smile played on his lips. Advancing toward her, he looked her up and down. "You're a pretty thing." He snatched her wrist and tugged. "Come wit' me. We're gonna 'ave lots of fun."

"No, we're not." Stephanie planted her feet, struggling to escape the man's grasp.

The ogre laughed, yanked her close, and placed his nose close to hers. "I'm glad you like it rough, sweetie, cuz I do too."

Clutching a chest high limb, Eric edged across the branch, careful not to look down. He took tiny sidesteps. The branch creaked. Pausing, he quietly inhaled and inched three more steps over the thinning limb.

The branch groaned. A loud crack echoed. Eric felt as if he were suspended in mid-air for half a second. He hit the ground full force. He blacked out on impact. Moments passed and he woke up, sprawled over the broken log.

It and Eric missed Stephanie who sat next to him, her eyes were round, and her mouth was opened wide. The solid end of the branch struck her new buddy. He'd been shoved into the dirt, and he lay face down. He wasn't moving.

Stephanie didn't seem to care he was knocked out. She swung a foot and kicked at her would-be abductor's head. "Sorry bastard. Don't you ever put your hands on me again."

Eric slowly climbed to his feet, fighting not to moan. He brushed at the bark and soil embedded in his skin. "Easy, Steph. We got 'em."

"And I got you."

Eric gradually turned around. A gun barrel was pointed at his forehead. An evil smile stood behind the weapon. "Y' got a choice. Let the lady go wit' me or die."

"Pretty sure the choice's already made."

A wicked laugh followed. "You're a smart one."

Dried leaves crackled from behind. The latest guest swung around, aiming his pistol. Eric quickly scooped up the gun lying on the ground, next to the unconscious man, and whacked the guy on the head.

He teetered to one side. Darla popped out of her hiding place. He leaned her way, about to collapse. She shoved him in the opposite direction. He toppled over the embankment and splashed into the murky swamp. He screamed at the top of his lungs as he fought the mud and gunk to try to escape.

Darla ran to Eric. "Sorry. I couldn't get to my pistol."

He dusted his palms. "You took care of business. S'all that matters." He glanced around. "Let's get out of here."

Stephanie gestured toward the other side of the island. "We're not going to finish our trip?"

A loud boom reverberated overhead. Tree blinds obstructed their view, but an obvious storm brewed.

"I vote we return to Tluq Cay, regroup, and try again tomorrow." Darla scanned the forest. "Dodging those guys is scary but fighting rough water during a thunderstorm will be worse."

Stephanie turned so her back faced them.

"Steph." Eric patted her shoulder. "Our chances improve if we come in the morning. The island isn't as active during the early hours."

She reluctantly nodded.

They trekked across the trail in silence, their weapons prepared for battle if they came upon more encounters. Thankfully, they neared their original site sans more incidents.

Eric stretched his neck as they closed in on their original spot. He expected Auster to be gone or hiding, waiting for him. Except he wasn't. Auster still lay on the ground. Eric squinted. His brain began to scream as his heart hurdled inside his chest.

A cluster of slugs punctured Auster's cranium, and the hits weren't clean. Blood oozed from various apertures.

He stretched out an arm to avert the women's advancement, although he couldn't shield them from the grisly sight.

Stephanie released a soft cry and backstepped. Darla moved to stand beside him. "Someone wanted to make sure he was good and dead."

Eric wiped away a sudden burst of sweat dripping off his brow. "I gotta thank whoever did this for putting the image in my head. This isn't something you can unsee."

Darla grabbed his arm and pointed. His gaze followed her finger. His lurching insides froze. A pistol lay near Auster's bloodied temple. Eric's pistol.

"This is bad." No longer intimated by the shot-up

corpse, he walked to Auster and orbited his body. "Very bad." He picked up his piece.

Darla's head shook. "Not a great idea."

"You gotta better one? What happens if the police discover *my* gun next to a murder victim? One you reported tried to execute me?"

"They can't investigate this island. It's not their territory."

"The way things have gone, that'll change." He tucked the hardware into his constricting waistband. "Authorities may not do shit to help us, but you can bet your ass, they'll fry me if they find my gun lying next to a murdered local, territory or not. They won't even bother to investigate. They'll lock me away and lose the key."

The sky growled, reminding them of the inclement weather's approach. Dark clouds rolled in at warped speed. If they didn't hustle, they'd be drenched and stranded.

Darla inspected the sky. "We'll argue later. We have to move to get ahead of the storm."

Neither he nor Stephanie objected. They dashed toward the water and to their parked jet skis.

Darla calculated the squally ocean. "Eric, you drive Stephanie's jet ski since you're more experienced."

He strolled to the damaged vehicle and performed a visual examination before mounting without question. Now was not the appropriate time to implement a smartass quip.

He took the key from Stephanie and waited until she was settled behind him. He revved the engine, and then zoomed into the sea next to Darla.

Waves rocked and tossed their jet skis in the air.

Thunder grumbled, and cracks of lightning blasted above.

An additional noise intermixed with the thunder. Engines.

Eric checked behind. "Shit. Company."

"The unwelcomed kind." Darla pushed the throttle.

Four grizzly looking men were on jet skis. Each held various forms of artilleries. Loud pops erupted. Bullets began to zoom over their heads.

Eric and Darla attempted to return fire. Turning toward the rear to aim and shoot plus driving on treacherous waters was near impossible.

"Haul ass to that rock formation." Darla gunned her motor. "It's full of small spaces, and we can take cover until they leave."

"What if they follow us?" Eric took another quick look at their assailants. "We'll be trapped."

"I doubt they'll stay in the water much longer. That's a mean thunderstorm. They won't survive the surges."

"What about us? How are we gonna survive?"

"One problem at a time, please."

They accelerated and drove toward the structure. Waves slapped into their rides as they pushed the vehicles across towering whitecaps.

Darla found a narrow, smooth sheet of water heading toward the rock. Eric swerved to follow. A sudden, strong gust shoved a huge amount of sea in their path. He veered away. Leaning to the left, Darla strained to turn. Upsurges wedged underneath and tossed her and the watercraft into the air.

An explosion of bullets erupted. She detached from the vehicle, screeching as she plummeted into the deep.

A piercing splat followed as her jet ski crashed into the ocean. Laughter spewed amid the deafening booms. The men spun around and headed toward the island.

Eric slowed to a stop. He waited for Darla to emerge. Except she didn't.

Rumbles and crashes surrounded him, but he didn't hear them. His pounding heartbeat drowned out all other sounds. He stared at the spot where she'd vanished.

"Where is she?"

Eric winced. With all the turmoil, he'd forgotten Stephanie sat behind him. "Dunno, Steph." He hit the jet ski's throttle. "But I'm gonna find her."

Chapter 15

Eric ignored the inclement weather, and gunned the motor, heading to the overturned vehicle. Combing the perimeters, he cruised across the bumpy upsurges, hopeful to spot Darla's bobbing, wavy locks beyond the ocean's plane.

Only he didn't find a sign she'd ever been in the vicinity.

Ignoring the sickness whirling in his gut, he attacked the aggressive swells, strong arming his ride just to make minimal progress. Finally, he neared the upset Sea Doo. Using extreme caution, Eric moved a thumb off the throttle, and allowed his craft to slide to a halt.

Stephanie wobbled behind him and stood on the footrest, clutching his shoulders. Her nails dug into his bare skin. A wisp of her breath blew across his neck as she gasped.

Eric flinched as his own heart hitched. He did a double take to make sure he saw the same. A spray of blood was scattered across the Sea Doo's fiberglass bottom. Darla's blood. He leaned across and flipped the jet ski upright.

"She's okay, right?" Stephanie lowered, squirming to sit onto her perch. "You don't think she's..."

A massive lump formed and lodged in his throat. He refused to believe the worst. "No. She's here, somewhere, and I *will* find her."

Only Darla was on limited time, and he had to locate her fast. Clearing his thoughts, he swung a leg over and stood on the side, prepared to track down the love of his life. Knees slightly bent; his arms were straight over his head as he breathed in.

"Hey," came a high shriek across the briny water. "I'm here. Over here."

Eric and Stephanie twisted toward the shouts. Relief swept over him. Darla stood on a low, flat rock formation, waving her arms.

"I'm gonna use her jet ski. You can handle this one, right?"

Stephanie nodded.

Not wasting a second, Eric leaped into the water, remounted, powered up the vehicle, and zoomed Darla's way. Adrenaline spewed throughout his body. Vaulting waves hurled him into the air, landing with teeth rattling force when striking the water.

"Careful," Darla warned as he cautiously approached the narrowed solid structure. "Those breakers will ram you into these pillars and mess you up."

"I'm watching, luv." He concentrated on gaining admittance as he bordered next to the dense layers.

Once he engineered the jet ski into the tight gap, and was secure enough to reach her, he elevated to his feet. Gathering Darla into his arms, he swung her off the surface. Wrapping her arms around his neck, she tossed back her head and giggled as the jet ski fiercely swayed, almost toppling sideways. They plunged to the seat, Eric depositing Darla crossways in his lap.

Their gazes connected as her laughter faded.

"I'm glad you found me." Her southern twang sounded husky. "I was afraid I'd be stuck out here during the storm. Heavy wind and blowing rain could've washed me away."

He smoothed the drenched curls off her forehead and inspected her gash as blood seeped down her cheek. "You re-injured your head."

She touched the wound and winced.

"You gotta get stitches this time."

"It's probably not as bad as it seems."

"Let a doctor decide." His hand slid to her shoulder and across her spine. He tugged her to him, and sniffed, savoring her sweet scent. "You scared me when I couldn't find you," he mumbled into her hair.

She pulled away and flashed an uncertain smile. "I was a little frightened myself. Dodging bullets was bad, and the swim over here wasn't much fun either."

He stared into her eyes. Her pupils darkened as she returned his look. His heart gave a firm thud as a river of saliva teemed the interiors of his mouth. Slight, heated breath wafted across his skin.

Tightening his embrace, he dipped his head and urgently brought his mouth down and pressed hard. Her lips parted, allowing his tongue to slip inside and intermingle with hers.

Her body quivered against his as she eagerly responded to the pressures of his insistent mouth. The kiss deepened. His head slanted the opposite way, relishing in a carnal reintroduction.

An engine putted nearby. They leaped apart. Disappointed, Eric half-turned.

Stephanie urged her water vehicle next to theirs, wearing a smug grin. "Don't let me interrupt."

Eric flashed a quick grin at Darla. "Continue later?"

She surveyed the turbulent storm clouds moving in. "I'm not seeing we have much choice." Her leg flung over the middle as she settled in the front.

Eric lengthened an arm past Darla, unhooking the life vest fastened to the handlebars. "We didn't have time earlier but put this on."

"What about you?"

"Guess I'll hang onto you."

She glanced over her shoulder and beamed. "You better hold on tight."

He shifted closer, strengthening his hold. "Not a problem, luv."

They fought the angry whitecaps the entire voyage. Surfs were high and choppy while the grumbles careened above. Yet, the thunderstorms delayed their fury until well after the trio parked.

Once they landed at their home base, they split. Stephanie dragged a protesting Darla to the infirmary to let a doctor inspect her head wound, while Eric headed back to his room. He wanted to organize his thoughts before speaking to police.

Also, he meant to find out why Finn rearranged his exit plan. Like Darla and Steph, he agreed Finn acted stranger than normal. Him not catching a flight home might be suspicious, yet Eric didn't quite buy Finn was the person behind the attempts on his life. But he'd been wrong before.

Wearily, he treaded to his bungalow, his tired body insisting on rest. Only other obligations mandated his attention first. Although he did anticipate a minimal amount of self-indulgence before attending to his tasks.

A long, hot shower and change into dry clothes were first on his agenda.

Treading across the sidewalk to his hut, he seized the doorknob and turned.

"Shit."

Finn had engaged the lock, and Eric's keycard and ID were still in his room, which left him no way to enter.

Eric rapped on the door.

Nothing. No surprise. Finn's normal sleep time happened during the daylight hours, and he was a deep sleeper. Bomb explosions wouldn't wake him.

He fisted his palm and pounded. "Finn?" More thumps followed. "Cm'on Finn."

Still no answer.

"Open up or I'll ring your mum, and tell her the gas pedal didn't really stick, but you were drunk when you drove your car straight through her garage and crashed into the swimming pool."

The knob twisted. Each notch snapped with a distinct click. The doorway creaked. A worried Finn peeked through a small crack. "Y're s'pose to take that to your grave, man."

Eric shoved the door open and stomped inside. "Apparently, I did."

A skeptical Finn eyeballed Eric. "Right, you're supposed to be dead. What's up with that?"

"You're in show business. You should understand how rumors work."

Finn's confused gaze followed Eric as he moved farther into the room.

"Swear, I'm not a ghost." Eric scanned the crammed space. The women weren't exaggerating.

210

Stacks of boxes were everywhere. "What's all this stuff?"

Darting in and out of the tall mounds, he finally found what he was looking for at the far end of the room. An open box. He elevated to peek inside.

Finn looped past him and smashed the lid shut. Eric leaped backwards. "Damn, Finn, y' nearly squished my nose." He tapped the side of the box. "So what's the big secret?"

Finn closed the lid tight. "Um, a new project. Nothing interesting."

He wasn't going to tell Eric what he was up to without a lot of prodding, and at the moment, Eric was too drained to care.

He maneuvered around the remaining cartons toward his bedroom. He paused at the doorway and whipped back to Finn. "Weren't you supposed to go home?"

"Changed my plans." Finn gestured at Eric's circulation-hindering pants as an obvious redirection. "Those are cool. Where did you find them?"

"Want 'em? They're yours."

"Awesome. I can wear them at my next golden oldie's concert. Ladies will go crazy."

"They're super tight. Y' gotta go commando. I suggest you dry clean 'em, first."

Inside his bedroom, Eric extracted his weapon from his waistband, placing it in the nightstand drawer. He scurried to the bathroom, undressed, and stepped under a hot spray. Thirty minutes later he emerged from the shower.

He walked into the bedroom to dress. The bed beckoned. Housekeeping draped back the covers, revealing fresh sheets. Four fluffy pillows were assembled by the headboard.

He adjusted the towel around his waist, struggling to ignore the temptation. How long had it been since he slept in a real bed? If only he had time. Except he must speak to the authorities and alert them of recent events.

One more glimpse at the inviting comfort, and he uttered, "Fuck it," and then dove into the covers. Within moments, he fell into a peaceful doze.

****

"Shoulda stayed asleep." Eric shook and rattled the rusty, iron bars. "I got rights you know. I demand to talk to my lawyer," he bellowed into a dark, tapered hallway for the hundredth time. "Now." Once again, his ultimatums were met with a deafening quiet.

Furious, he paced the grimy floor of his ten-foot jail cell. His latest living quarters.

He breathed in, still not grasping how this whole nightmare materialized. After he awakened, he carried out his plan to speak to law enforcement, aware their jurisdiction outside this island was nil. Regardless, he preferred to update them and have the incidents documented. He might've fudged a bit by omitting his finding his gun by Auster's body.

Instead of the usual semi-half interest they displayed in the past, they were attentive—a huge improvement—until they slapped a pair of handcuffs on his wrists. They dragged him kicking and yelling across the building. Then he was hurled into this dim, dank, and foul-smelling piece of crap cell.

Beat after standing so long, he ambled to his so-called bed, which was nothing more than a piece of covered plywood suspended from the wall. It reminded him of a badly constructed diaper changing table in a public restroom. The length was approximately as long.

He sat on the plank and bounced. He feared the extra weight would cause it to smash to the ground. The hinges strained, but the slat held. He stretched across the top and angrily stared at the ancient, stained ceiling.

Cops denied his request to make a phone call. How would he let Darla know about his *tiny* glitch.

A jangle clattered from the rear. A bar sliding reverberated. Another poor schmuck was being cast into this hellhole, but at least he'd have a neighbor.

"Okay, you're free to go," declared a voice in broken English.

Ah…a lucky prisoner was about to depart, which stunned him. He thought he was the only one locked up.

He cranked his neck to see. Eric's cell was open. A guard loitered outside. His stance displayed annoyance.

Eric vaulted off the bed and sped through the exit. The guard led him to the front of the building, and onto the main office.

Darla waited inside. A ringlet of hair was intertwined with her finger. Like a magnet, she turned to face him as he entered. A band aid covered her wound on her forehead. Corners of her lips lifted as their eyes locked.

His heart gave an abandoned flutter as he smiled in return. Forgetting the past few hours, he allowed the memory of their kiss to linger.

A movement ahead of Darla caught his attention. His elation vanished. Morgan Wilmington stood on Darla's far side.

She didn't seem aware of Eric's scowl. She rushed to him. Hands on his shoulders, she drew him near and whispered, "Let's get you away from here."

"We're just gonna walk out?"

"Yes we are." Darla looped her arm through his and guided him toward the exit.

He checked behind. "They won't say we're tryin' to escape and shoot us, will they?"

"No guarantees. Just move and don't look back."

They hurried past Morgan, who remained inside, speaking to an officer.

Outside police headquarters, Eric skidded to a halt, waylaying Darla. He turned her to face him and brushed his lips against hers. "What did the doctor say about your head?"

"It isn't the worst he'd seen, but he did have to put in five stitches."

"Hmmm. What'd I tell you?"

"Gloat later." She took his arm again and urged him into the street away from the police station. "We need to vacate ASAP."

They continued their hurried stroll. "How'd you know they locked me up?"

"Morgan was at the Tequila Sunset bar across the street. He saw you go in. He also noticed you didn't come out. Fortunately, he knows how the island system can work with tourists. He called Stephanie, who told me. I came right over."

"With him."

"He met me at the station."

Darla checked behind, and Eric's gaze followed. Morgan jogged to catch them. Once he'd joined them, they hustled across the walkway, and stepped onto the street, trekking wordlessly to their resort.

After traveling several blocks, Eric broke the

silence. "How much was bail?"

Darla and Morgan exchanged a glance. Their expressions didn't offer any assurance. The sum was probably astronomical.

"Morgan didn't exactly post bail."

"They just let me leave?"

"No. He had to bargain to get you released."

"Bargain? You're saying," Eric reversed to confront Morgan. "You…what?"

"Bribed them."

"You're fucking kidding me." He whirled around and stomped away. He'd have to sell a kidney to repay this asshole.

Darla marched to him, grabbed his arm, and gave it a shake. "Buying them off was the only way they'd let you go." Her tone softened. "Eric, they accused you of stealing Blaine's ransom, killing Auster, and faking your death. They also know your gun was used to kill Auster."

"The fucking island isn't even in their jurisdiction so how would they know that?"

"I don't know." She glanced at Morgan. "But they could've kept you, you know, like forever."

"Or make you stand in front of a firing squad," Morgan put in.

Eric froze, grappling to wrap his brain around one more potential catastrophe. Maybe Finn was right. Evil walked these streets. He mentally marked Tluq Cay off his list of future vacation spots.

"You're safe now." Darla took his hand and tugged. "But local cops invent the rules as they go. You might consider heading home tonight."

He disengaged from her, jammed his hands into his

pockets, and shrugged, unsure what more fear the island could inflict. "We're searching the island tomorrow."

Morgan raised a brow. "You're going back to the island?"

"Eric might have discovered where the pirates are holding Blaine. We're checking in the morning."

"You're planning to save him without paying the ransom?"

"We don't have a choice. We haven't been able to raise the funds, and we still owe you a ton of cash." Darla's gaze skated to Eric. "Don't delay leaving. I can figure it out. I can find Blaine."

"Alone," Eric deadpanned. "Or will you bring along Steph and Finn?"

"Stephanie can be some help. Now, Finn?" She wrinkled her nose. "I'm sure we can make use of his talents."

"Forget it. I'm staying till I'm certain Blaine's alive."

Darla appeared on the verge of protesting but reconsidered. Eric smiled inwardly. She knew him well enough to know he wouldn't change his mind.

****

They entered the resort's patio. Guests began to assemble for the evening's scheduled party and firework show.

"I need to check on my guys, Dar, I'll see you in a while." Morgan veered away. "Eric."

"He'll see you in a while?" Eric whirled to face Darla. "What's that about? Did you have to promise him something to pay off the cops?"

"I didn't promise him anything. You know I don't work that way." Anger shook in her voice. "He's made numerus trips to this archipelago, and *he* knew bribery was the only way to get you out of jail. He offered to put up the funds, and I accepted because we don't have the money." A finger poked his chest. "You didn't bother to thank either of us for saving your sorry butt."

A long pause stretched.

"That guy sure knows how to play you."

"Play me? You're insinuating he's instigated all this, this insanity?"

"No, but he's sure fast to swoop in and fix your problems."

She countered with an indignant scowl.

"Fine." Eric snatched her hand and led her to where Wilmington and his team congregated. "Wilmington."

Morgan nodded and ambled to them.

"Just wanted to say thanks. I appreciate you helping me. When this is over, we can work out a payment plan."

"You're welcome." Morgan smirked. "I'm happy to help Darla's friends."

"Whoa, wait...Darla and me, friends?" Tamping down his instant fury, Eric chuckled. "Darla and I are a lot of things, but one thing we'll never be is friends." Before giving Morgan a chance to reply, Eric quickly orbited away. "Happy?" he hissed at Darla as he swept past her.

She hurried to catch him. "That parting *friend* remark wasn't necessary."

"I agree. Why would he ever believe we're friends? But we discussed this already."

"Not what I mean, and you know it. You sounded childish, and you were rude."

"And he wasn't?"

"That's not the point."

"What is the point?"

"The point is, we've yet to establish anything couple-wise. You don't get to act like we're together when it's convenient."

Eric's expression feigned innocence. "You certainly acted like we were together earlier today. Or did I misinterpret your meaning?"

"You know what? Never mind." She spun away. "Morgan." She flashed a smile as he looked up. "I'm ready for that drink now."

Without giving Eric a glance, she hurried to Morgan and took his arm. They strolled to a nearby table.

Eric planted his fists onto his hips. "Are you fucking serious?" Morgan held a chair out for Darla. "And now she's sitting." No longer able to stomach the scene, he turned away. "Can't everyone see he's manipulating her?" he yelled at Stephanie, who'd joined him.

Stephanie aimed her index finger and thumped his chest. "You're the one he's manipulating."

"What? No he isn't. I see right through his little game."

"Yes, he is, and no you don't. Darla's been trying to repair your relationship since you two reconnected. But as usual, you won't fully commit. Then you want to act like she belongs to you? She isn't yours. Not until you're ready to make a total commitment."

A shoulder raised. He nodded in Darla's direction. "She's doin' all right without me."

"No, she's not. Forgive her. She's been by your

side since the day you met. If she hasn't proved her love by now, then you're hopeless. Quit whining, let go of your anger, and go get her."

Eric dropped into a chair. "I just ticked her off five thousand different ways."

"Stop worrying about her mood and make it clear you want her. And to avoid future misunderstandings you need to seal the deal this time."

Chapter 16

"I never expected you to fall for a Neanderthal."

Darla averted her attention from her drink. "What?"

"Him." Morgan slung a chin Eric's way. "Look at him. He's a caveman. He's glaring over here like he wants to grab you by the hair and drag you back to his cave."

Darla glanced toward Eric. He stood on the far side of the patio, chatting with Finn.

She'd rather not discuss Eric, but she insisted on correcting Morgan's assumptions. "Eric's and my relationship isn't any of your business, but to avoid any future misconceptions, allow me to clarify. Eric's never once disrespected me. He's always taken care of me. He values my decisions, and he asks for my opinion too. He's angry, yet he hasn't called me names nor dissed me privately or publicly, which he could've since he has instant access to every media outlet. He's an emotional man. Once he gives his heart away, it belongs to that person, infinitely. He overreacted because I devastated him."

"Fair enough." Morgan paused. "Let me ask you a question, then. Your suggesting we have a drink in front of him. Did you intentionally throw me in his face to piss him off? Is that how you treat a man who cherishes you? Seriously, Dar, if he's not a cave man, then you crushed him."

She cringed at his calling her out. She quickly backtracked. "I'm not perfect, particularly when I'm mad." She hesitated to carefully choose her next words. "I regret I brought you into our fight. I shouldn't have."

"You're upset too. You wanted to annoy him because you're still in love with him."

"Yes, I love him very much."

The spark of optimism in Morgan's eyes dimmed. "I don't have a chance, do I?"

Darla observed Morgan sympathetically. He'd been so generous with his bank account and gone out of his way to lend his knowledge instead of ignoring the situation, which showed a lot of growth on his part. He did apologize for the past, and he seemed sincere. She envisioned a possible friendship later, but he would never recapture her heart.

But then again, perhaps this was karma working its magic.

"You broke me when you left and married another woman, especially in such a callous way. Yet, I healed extremely fast once Eric entered my life. He and I split three months ago. The ache is as painful today as it was the day it happened. That says a lot. I'll never get over him. He's a part of me. He's in my soul."

The remaining hopefulness in his expression diminished. "Your feelings for me can't compare to how you feel about him."

She didn't respond. She didn't need to. Chatter surrounding them amplified as a band onstage played a lively tune. "Must be the fame," Morgan finally uttered above the noise.

Darla straightened in her chair. Heat surged and

coated her face. "Excuse me?"

"Fame. It draws women."

"You believe I love Eric because he's famous?"

"Not you, necessarily." Morgan chuckled. "I didn't explain the details of my divorce, did I?"

"I assumed your selected matrimonial time expired. You received your trust fund, so you bailed."

"Nowhere close. I didn't want my marriage to end."

"She left you, then?"

He nodded. "She's had a crush on Tommy Betters since she was a teenager."

"The actor?"

"The same. They've been friends for years. Her feelings were never returned, and nothing ever happened between them. She ran into him at a regatta one weekend while I was here working. She never spoke to me again. Just Fed Exed me the divorce papers."

"How horrible."

"Friends told me sparks flew on that trip. Supposedly they've been inseparable since."

"You cared about her?"

"I grew to." He raised a shoulder. "I mean, she wasn't you…"

"I'm sorry, Morgan."

"Not your fault." He gazed into her eyes. "I guess this is it, huh?"

"I do wish you the best." She scooted her chair back. "I'm grateful for all you've done. I'm not sure how we'll ever repay you."

"I'll forgive the entire debt if you give me another chance."

Darla sat speechless. She couldn't consider his suggestion, but they owed him so much money. What a relief it would be to not be obligated to him.

"It wouldn't be fair. We already know how it would turn out."

"Thought I'd give it a shot. Remember, I'm making an offer he won't."

"What's that?"

"A wedding band and forever."

Darla opened her mouth to reply, only she didn't have a clue what to say.

The band's vocalist saved her. "Hey, hey folks. We have an incredible treat tonight. Spiraling Up and Raging Impulse guitarist, Eric Boyd, and Raging Impulse's lead singer, Finn O'Conner are here. Eric wrote a brand-new song, and they're gonna perform it just for you." An uproar erupted over the crowd. "Let's hear it for the guys." He gestured to the left. "Eric and Finn."

Darla forgot about Morgan and his offer. She twisted around in her seat. Finn trailed by Eric strolled onstage. Eric carried his favorite acoustic.

Continuing to the microphone, Eric spoke. "I began writing these lyrics months ago, but circumstances had me go brain dead b'fore I finished. This trip unclogged my creative channels, and I've completed the song. Track's called, Broken Man. Hope you like it." He sat on a high stool and perched his guitar on a knee. A haunting intro drifted into the night air.

Finn began to croon. The melody wasn't Eric's usual romantic ballad or an angry anthem, or even the cutesy jingle he occasionally penned. His lines touched the soul, speaking of a man who had been torn in two with no chance of repairing his heart.

Darla fought to hold in her sobs. He admitted her leaving had hurt him, but this song truly conveyed his spiraling emotions.

Applause and cheers exploded after the final strain faded.

Darla raised her glass to retrieve her napkin and wiped her eyes.

Morgan stood and tossed a few bills onto the table. "A huge diamond and a ton of money will never compete with that, will it?"

"Thank you for the drink," she commented. But he'd already walked away.

Tears continued to threat as she rushed to meet Eric. Forgetting their disagreement, she snatched his free hand and squeezed. "Your song's beautiful."

"Thanks, luv." He disengaged and carefully placed his instrument in its case. "I hoped you'd get it."

She dabbed at the wetness flowing down her cheeks. "So much, I'm crying."

"Awe, stop. You know I'm no good with waterworks."

"Your fault."

"Are you and," he dipped his head toward Morgan, who huddled with his work team, "done with your drink?"

"Yes, we're finished. For good. I made it clear he and I won't happen." She flashed a sad smile. "Even if we can't fix us."

"I'm thinking maybe we can give us another shot." He grinned and took her elbow. "I want to show you something."

Guiding her away from the party, he led her to a

narrow, uphill path. After taking a sharp curve, they walked downward, crossing a flattened plane.

Darla gasped as she took in the sight. They stood in a circle of lush greenery, which sat in a valley of mountains, backlit by dusk skies. Torches flickered, illuminating the scenery.

A glimmering, aqua pond sat in the center. A thin fog shimmered off the water. In a far angle, a small waterfall poured off protruding granite and splattered into the pool.

Stone benches had been inconspicuously positioned for sitting. Folded, fluffy towels rested on top.

Darla twirled in awe. "Where are we?"

"Natural hot springs. Water's mineral-rich and has healing powers."

"Is this part of the resort?"

"It is. But you gotta have connections to get a reservation." He indicated toward a corner. A small table decorated with lit candles waited. "Dinner's included in the package."

"This is breathtaking. Some lucky couple will have a lovely night."

Silence briefly ensued. "We're the lucky couple. I reserved it."

"When?"

"Six months ago. B'fore my scheduling was fucked up, and b'fore we split." A suddenly unsure Eric waved at the table again. "Dinner's in an hour…if you want to stay."

"Of course, I'll stay. I can't believe you did this. It's amazing. So romantic." She looked at an uneasy Eric. "Don't take this the wrong way, but it's not really…you."

Eric cleared his throat. "Actually, I planned to ask you to marry me. Here, tonight."

Darla's heartbeat escalated. Eric intended to propose? He alluded to proposing numerous times the past few days, but he acted like he hadn't been ready to take the step.

She swallowed to keep the quiver out of her voice. "Is that why you were so upset when I wanted to move in?"

He didn't respond.

"I'm sorry I spoiled your surprise. But in my defense, I didn't know your plans."

"Your suggestion came out of left field and knocked me on m' ass. I didn't know what to say. I researched to discover the perfect spot to ask you to be my wife. I shopped to find you the ideal ring…" He shrugged. "In hindsight, it would've been best to let you move in, and gone ahead and asked you, but…I'm sorry, luv."

The small bit of lingering resentment disappeared. Their gazes linked. Eric moved toward her.

She held up a palm. "Wait a minute, you bought a ring?"

"I was gonna ask you to marry me, I figured I needed one. Bad idea?"

"No, it was a wonderful idea." Her arms spread wide. "This is all so wonderful."

"But? Questions are running through your head. I can almost see 'em."

"I'm confused why you didn't cancel tonight." Her arms released and her hands slapped her thighs. "I'm more baffled as to why you brought me here, now.

We're not a couple, are we?"

"Your call."

"This one has to be mutual. Can you deal with your anger, forgive me, and go forward?"

"I can. I have. I'm done." Eric stepped closer. His palms rested on her shoulders. "Can you forgive me?"

"Most definitely."

He gathered her into his arms and dipped his head, placing his lips on hers. The kiss was soft, sweet, and swift, then he pulled away. "I can't be near you too long. My willpower's shaky." He flashed a guilty grin. "Not sure if we're ready to go that far."

"I do need a few minutes to process this."

"The springs are therapeutic, and we could use some therapy after our week. How 'bout a swim before dinner?"

"Sounds fantastic."

He offered her a hand. "Cabanas are this way." He escorted her to a bathhouse behind the waterfall and pointed to the right. "Swimsuits are inside."

Darla strolled into the ladies side. She dropped into the one chair, needing time to take in what Eric had revealed. Except time wasn't available. He was waiting.

She stood and hurriedly siphoned through an array of swimsuits, until she found one she liked. Quickly changing, she seized a bathrobe lying on a counter, and draped it around her shoulders.

Eric was already in the water, soaking. She walked to the pool and skimmed a toe across the surface. "How is it?"

"Heaven," he lay back and floated on his spine.

Darla wandered to a set of stairs. Dropping the cover-up, she plunged into the pool, and leisurely swam to him.

"Watch your stitches."

"My head is dry."

A piercing whistle followed by a soft pop echoed above.

Darla gazed at the sky. "Morgan's fireworks display."

"I usually enjoy fireworks, but this being Wilmington's company kinda taints it."

"Just forget who's doing it and watch."

Colorful explosives highlighted the atmosphere. Eric inched closer. Darla relocated in front of him. His arms wrapped around her waist, and tightened, bringing her nearer. She relaxed into his chest.

"I love you, Darla."

She turned to him. "I love you, too, Eric."

A corner of his mouth lifted. "Maybe we're readier to physically reconnect than we first believed."

"Maybe…"

He lowered his head and claimed her mouth.

A clatter from the upper deck intruded. They released each other and bounced apart. Two resort employees had appeared and attended to their meal.

Eric released a frustrated sigh. "Dinner's served."

They waded through the pool and mounted the short set of stairs. Donning their robes, they strolled to the table. Waiters discreetly stood off to the side, prepared to assist whenever needed.

Darla effortlessly sliced a piece of her filet mignon. "This is delicious."

Eric placed his utensil down. "I have a confession."

She nervously met his blue gaze. "Should I be worried?"

"Not sure." He paused. "This spa package comes with a room...a bedroom."

"For the whole night?"

"It's booked until nine in the morning."

She laid down her fork. "I'm full."

He patted his mouth with his napkin, then pitched it across his half-eaten food. "Me too."

Hand in hand, he led her past the pond toward a small building behind the cabana to a pair of opened French doors.

Darla stopped in the doorway. "We need to talk."

Eric loudly exhaled.

"I want you to go home tomorrow. You need to leave as soon as we finish our search. This island isn't safe, specifically for you."

"You worry too much."

"Eric. I mean it. Leave Tluq Cay. I thought I lost you once, and I can't bear the idea of losing you again. Promise me you'll go back to California. Regardless if we rescue Blaine."

"I promise, luv." He narrowed the space between them. "I promise."

Chapter 17

"Thank you." Darla threw herself into Eric's arms and looked into his eyes. "I don't want you to go, but if heading home saves your life, then I'm for it."

"I'll go like I promised, but it's under protest. I don't want to leave you on this island alone."

"I'll be fine once you're safe. I'm scared something bad will happen to you if you stay."

He backed away. "Never heard you admit to bein' afraid of anything."

"We all have fears, and I'm having a major panic attack. It worsens every day you're on this island."

"My job's to watch over you. If I'm not here, who'll take care of you?"

"Exactly. If you're shot facing a firing squad or if another goon beats you until you're dead, you won't be around to look after me, will you?"

He moved nearer. His fingers combed through her tousled curls. "Not to make light of this conversation, but can we save it for later? All this grim talk's interrupted what's about to be the greatest makeup sex ever."

She coyly smiled. "Our discussion can wait."

He flashed a naughty grin. "We've got a lot of catching up to do." Glinting blue eyes traveled up and down, taking in her body. "I'm past ready to start."

A giggle escaped. "I think you have already."

"Not yet." His hands covered her breasts and gently squeezed. "Now we're underway."

He let go of her and wrapped his arms under her rear. Hoisting her up, he hugged her close, and whisked her past ajar, double French doors, carrying her to a canopied bed. He gently laid her on the mattress.

He hovered over her, lowering to his elbows. His mouth claimed hers. His kiss was long, hard, and deep. Breaking contact, he untied her robe and slid it over her shoulders. Then he turned her on her side and unhooked the upper half of her swimsuit. The top fell away.

Rolling her onto her spine, he gazed at her and smiled as his thumbs grazed her aching peaks.

A weak groan escaped.

He cupped her mounds with his palms and lowered. His tongue traced down her throat's slender column while he stroked and molded her breasts. He tweaked her nipples between his fingertips till touching no longer satisfied.

His head dipped farther downward. Hot breath floated over her skin as a trail of soft kisses caressed her ripened flesh. Greedily, he seized possession of the nub and nibbled with his teeth.

Darla squirmed underneath him as an onslaught of raw yearnings devoured her senses.

Lips attached to her breast, his hand moved toward her bikini waistband. He invaded the underside, skating to her middle, and inserted two fingers.

Pleasure surged. Darla jerked, silently begging for a release as his strokes harmonized with his grazing tongue. Eric abruptly raised and wiggled the remainder of her damp bikini off. He propped onto his knees, gripped her legs, and opened them.

Fingers once again crept between her inner thighs. Slowly, but deliberately, his pressured strokes breached her legs farther apart.

He lowered and skimmed tiny kisses across her golden skin. He paused at her center, encompassing heated suppleness between his lips.

He didn't move. Then his tongue slowly dipped and swirled inside of her.

Clutching the comforter, Darla's soft hisses merged into whimpers. The miniscule movements triggered a mounting vibration. Riptides of spinning pulsations spiraled downward.

Unrestrained cries rippled from her throat. Intense eruptions detonated and carried her to a dazzling utopia.

He broke away. She preferred him not to stop, but tonight wasn't just about her. She took a moment to reclaim her faculties.

Exhibiting a come-hither grin, she undid his robe, and took it off. She glided a fingertip around the band of his swim trunks.

An eyebrow arched as she nodded.

Darla yanked his wet suit down. Positioning his hands on either side of the mattress, he tilted over her. She skimmed his backbone. Her nails brushed up and down before resting her palms on his chiseled chest. Nuzzling the familiar sprinkle of dark hair, she swept her tongue across one of his tautened nipples, savoring his tangy flavor.

"Feels wonderful," he murmured as she explored each ripple of firm muscle. His head plunged on her shoulder, his gasping breaths warm and moist.

She raked a hand through his coarse hair, then circled around his solid length, giving him a featherlike, but insistent squeeze. Force exuded from his rigid penis, the skin stretched over the shaft, the apex smooth, and near explosion. She pumped, her thumb rotating in skillful rings.

"Enough." His voice was husky and laced thick with need. He levered above her. His hot, throbbing erection rubbed her thigh as he elevated. Her spine arced to massage her center against his stiffness. With a formidable thrust, he pushed himself inside her, evoking currents of delight to spark.

He rotated his hips at a repetitive leisurely pace. Blood hummed in her veins. "It's been so long." Darla exhaled, thrilled he was on his way to satisfying her.

"Way too long," Eric panted, his tone revealing the recognizable wildness brewing underneath his gentleness.

Her mouth opened below his, soaking up his drugging nectar. Tongues united, danced, and curled. Their hips engaged in an erotic rhythm as she relentlessly moved in time, matching his gliding juts. Passionate tides assaulted her. The mellow drive transformed into untamed, reckless, and impatient. Each stroke brought her nearer to shattering climatic conclusion.

On the brink of orgasm, he decreased his tempo, prolonging her enjoyment.

"Eric," she murmured in a ragged breath. "Please, now…"

She didn't need to make the request twice. A hand slipped under her butt, holding her still as he targeted a series of swift thrusts into her. Warmth shattered below her abdomen. Pulsating waves expanded into a frenzy of exquisite sensations, ending with a profound shudder.

Once she was finished, he buried himself into her deep and groaned in blissful agony, illustrating his long, powerful final instants. He collapsed on top of her and stayed until he could move. Then he resettled beside her. They lay tangled together, their soft breathing the only sound.

He dropped a peck on her forehead. "Glad you're back, luv."

They drifted off to sleep. It seemed like they dozed a few moments when a whoosh of air awakened Darla. She slightly elevated and squinted at the sunrise beaming through the unsealed doors.

She shook Eric. "Hey. Wake up."

Ignoring her, he stuffed his head under his pillow and grumbled. "Five minutes."

"We're short on time. We have to hurry so you can catch a plane after our search."

Reluctantly, he tossed the pillow aside and sluggishly rose. He glanced at the clock then gazed at her and smiled. "We still got forty minutes b'fore check out."

Darla extended her neck. "We sure do."

He eased her back onto the mattress. "I don't plan on wasting a spare second."

Minutes before the allotted time, Eric and Darla left their sanctuary. Hand in hand, they strolled in content silence.

"We're meeting at the boat rental place in an hour, right?" Eric asked when they reached her bungalow.

"That's the plan. Will you text Stephanie and remind her?"

"Doubt if she needs a reminder, but yeah. I'll

message Finn, too."

"You're including Finn?"

"I gotta keep him close so I can watch him. If we're wrong about him, he can be an extra pair of hands and set of eyes. If we're right…"

"Your call." She stepped in and slid her hands up his chest. "You're still leaving this afternoon, right? Regardless if we find Blaine."

He rolled his eyes. "I'll make arrangements before we head out."

"I don't want you to go, Eric, but we need you off the police's radar. They've zeroed in on you, and I have a bad feeling they won't let up until they arrest you or worse."

"I thought Wilmington paid them off."

"Yesterday. They're extortionists. Who's to say the whole process won't start over, today?"

"Comforting."

"It isn't, and we can't afford to shovel tons of cash in their direction, especially when we're in dire need of funds for other reasons."

"Fine," he grudgingly agreed. "I'll leave."

"Thank you. I don't think I could bare your dying again."

"You won't, luv."

"Don't forget your gun."

"Don't worry." Eric grinned. "Don't suppose I gotta persuade you to bring yours?"

"I'm carrying two." She paused. "And I might do a mini search when we're on the island and see if I can discover where Auster hid my sig and my phone. I feel naked without them."

Eric's mouth curved, and his eyes twinkled.

"There's very good reason why you feel naked. Has nothin' to do with missing guns."

****

Eric texted Stephanie regarding their plans and just in case he didn't run into him, he sent Finn a message with the locations and time to meet. He meant to get to the bottom of whatever Finn was up to, but that may have to wait until later.

Stephanie immediately replied, but Finn didn't. Neither's response surprised him. Eric doubted either slept a wink last night. Stephanie was probably anxious, and ready to find Blaine, and Finn's regular bedtime resided around seven in the morning. He'd need to adjust today. He would go with them, and Eric intended on scrutinizing his every move.

Rounding a bend, he headed toward his bungalow. An odd sound echoed in the wind. He stopped. Voices. They seemed to be coming from his hut's direction.

He slowed to a stop and peeked around the corner of a neighbor's home.

"Shit," he uttered.

Two men in uniform waited outside his doorway. They pounded on the door, apparently not the first time by the intensity of their knock.

Eric backed into the stucco wall behind him and listened.

"What is it?"

Eric sidled closer and braved another glimpse. Finn stood at the threshold, clad only in pajama bottoms. His hair was messy, and his jaws sported a light shadow.

"We must speak with Eric Boyd immediately," one of the men said in broken English. "Get him, at once."

236

Chapter 18

"Eric's not here," Finn informed the officers.

The policemen looked at each other. Their features displayed their doubts. "When do you expect him to return?"

"He texted me a while ago. Said he's on his way."

The men exchanged glances again. This time both smiled. "Excellent. Can we come in and wait? It is important we speak to Mr. Boyd as soon as he arrives."

Finn moved from the entrance. "Sure, why not?"

"You visited headquarters in regard to Mr. Boyd, correct," one of the men inquired.

"Yeah," Finn confirmed. "Hey. You guys want coffee or—" The chat faded as the door closed.

"Son of a bitch." Shaken, Eric left his hiding spot and hurried away in the opposite direction. His mind reeled as he backtracked to Darla's cabin.

Why did the police want to speak with him—again. And why did Finn talk to the them about him earlier? Was he behind these bizarre events? Was his aim to get Eric thrown in jail? Or killed?

He arrived at Darla's hut without incident and thumped on the door. She responded within seconds of his knock. "Aren't we supposed to meet at the boat rental place?"

Eric fought the urge to push his way inside. "Can I come in?"

She stepped out of his way.

He rushed through the doorway. "Shut the door." Scampering to a window, he peered past the drape to make sure he didn't miss anyone tailing him.

Darla twisted the deadbolt and spun toward him. "What happened?"

"Two cops were at the bungalow when I arrived."

"What did they want?"

"What do you think they wanted? Me." Once he was sure no one followed him, he dropped the curtain. "Finn told them I wasn't home."

"Thank goodness."

"Not so much. He also told them I was on my way, then the sorry ass invited them in to wait for me."

"Oh my." Darla motioned at the sofa. "Sit and relax. You're safe here." She headed out of the room. "I'll bring you some coffee."

Eric lowered to the couch and glanced outside again.

Darla returned moments later holding a steaming cup and handed it to him. "Apparently, our suspicions about Finn are accurate. But his motives really baffle me."

"Who knows what goes on in his head? It's Finn."

"No, it's crazy, Eric."

"Crazy? You realize who we're talking about?"

"There are a lot of negativities to be said about Finn, but he isn't vindictive. Nor does he possess the patience to plan such an elaborate plot."

"He isn't working alone, remember? Finn's broke. Being without means, especially once you've lived a cushy, high life, will make you do peculiar stuff to get that lifestyle back."

"That's true." She waited. "Sorry, but we need to put this conversation on hold. We have to go, soon. You didn't get a chance to shower. We have a few minutes before we meet Steph. Do you want to borrow my shower and rinse off?"

Eric grinned. He set his coffee cup on a nearby table and rose, ready to forget this entire situation and move on to something more interesting. He seized her hand and tugged. "Only if you join me."

"I've showered already."

He directed her toward the bathroom. "I see you missed a spot or two."

****

A half an hour later, Eric and Darla walked hand in hand to the charter location.

An anxious Stephanie paced in front of the entrance. "What took you so long?"

"We're only a couple of minutes late, Steph."

Realization registered across Stephanie's face. "Never mind." She paused. "Don't get me wrong, I'm thrilled you two kissed and made up, but please can you put your reunion on hold until Blaine's home?"

"Consider us on a break." Darla smiled. "Hopefully, we'll locate Blaine, and he'll be in your arms by the end of the day."

Eric searched the area as they strolled into the building. "I thought you said Blaine's dad was coming, too?"

"He was. But Blaine's mom and my parents are flying in. He decided to stay and meet them instead."

Eric frowned. "Sounded like he really wanted to go with us when I talked to him earlier." He examined Stephanie's face. She may as well have written the word guilty across her forehead. "What'd you do to Blaine's dad, Steph?"

She huffed. "He *suggested*, or rather told me to go be with my parents. Apparently, I'm too emotional, and I may inadvertently hurt a rescue attempt instead of helping it."

"But you're here and he's not. Where is he?"

"Probably still in the bathroom." She grinned sheepishly. "I might've jammed the lock after he went inside."

"You trapped him in the loo?" Eric chuckled. "Not gonna put you in good with the in-laws."

"We can hash it out after we find Blaine."

They walked to the counter and chatted with the agent. On his recommendation, they chartered a smaller Catamaran, one tourists frequently used. If anyone unsavory spotted them, they would presume they were sightseers cruising the islands and hopefully leave them alone.

An attendant led them to their vessel. They boarded quickly, donned life jackets, eager to sail before trouble found them again.

Darla had the most boating experience and manned the helm. She pressed a button and the engine fired effortlessly. Slowly, she steered them out of the slip.

"Wait. Eric. Darla." They whirled toward the dock. Finn ran through the yard, waving his hands. "Don't leave."

Darla sent Eric a silent what should we do, look. He lengthened his neck and scanned the perimeter. Finn appeared to be alone. "Let 'em on. But if I find out he's tryin' to get me killed or arrested, I'm tossing his ass overboard and leavin' 'im to the sharks."

Darla reversed and held the boat near the slip's edge. Finn scrambled onboard.

He stared at Eric. His expression exposed his hurt feelings. "Why are you goin' without me?"

Eric pitched a life preserver at him. "I went by the bungalow this morning to check on you. You were busy entertaining."

Finn one handedly caught the vest and pierced the lifejacket's armhole with a fist. "You mean the cops?"

Stephanie frowned at Darla, who shook her head. "Long story. I'll explain later."

"Yeah, I mean the cops. You blabbed I was on my way home, then you let them inside. What'd you do? Serve 'em tea and bake 'em a cake while they waited to ambush me?"

"Didn't you get my text?"

Eric stiffened. "What text?"

"I sent you several messages warning you not to come back."

Eric dug into his pocket and removed his cell. The icon indicated three messages were sent by Finn, each advised him to stay away.

"No, I didn't see 'em." He stuffed his cell into his pants, though he wasn't convinced Finn was on his side. "I overheard you'd previously contacted them about me, too. What was that about?"

"You were supposed to 'ave died. I was trying to find out if the story was real. Didn't want Darla or your mum and dad to hear it over the news if it was true."

Darla reduced the boat's speed and turned to Finn. "When were you alerted of Eric's death?"

His chin raised to examine the sky. "The day after he disappeared."

"Strange," Darla said to Eric. "That was twenty-four hours before the fire."

Eric glanced at Finn. "Maybe you're mistaken?"

"Possible, I guess. No, I'm sure it was the day after. I scheduled a flight home. I cancelled b'cause you were dead. I went to the police, but no one would tell me anything. They said there was an ongoing inquiry."

"Ugh," Darla grunted. "They told me they couldn't investigate because the crime didn't occur in their jurisdiction. But it does suggest you should've been killed earlier than you allegedly were."

"Great. This whole fucking situation smells worse than sour milk." Eric sat back in his seat and eyed Finn. "Are you sure your cop friends didn't follow you?"

"They're still at the bungalow." Finn's lips curved into a sly grin. "I excused m'self, telling 'em I needed to check on something, then I snuck out the backdoor."

"Nice." Eric rolled his eyes. "You're gonna end up standing next to me in front of a firing squad."

"That'd make major headlines, wouldn't it?"

Miles of ocean stretched in front of them as Darla guided the vessel toward the island. The seas were calmer than normal, which Eric took as a positive, although he was hesitant to declare any circumstance encouraging. Double negatives shadowed every optimistic turn.

They advanced toward land, and Darla guided the vessel to the unexplored side. The boat hit something solid and jumped. Eric peered over the side. "Looks like a sand bar."

Darla quickly navigated the bow away from their target. "The water is too shallow to get close. I'll damage the hull if I push it, and we'll be stuck. I have to go back to the other side, and we'll just hike over."

She skillfully maneuvered the vessel away from the danger and steered them into a dock on the other side of the island.

The group took off their lifejackets. Eric exited, jumping onto the landing, then he held out his arms to assist Darla and Stephanie.

Finn followed them off board. His usual pale skin had transformed to a greenish color. "Man, the pitching made me queasy."

Eric released a sarcastic cackle. "That ride was easy compared to the others we've taken."

"I shouldn't have eaten such a big meal. Talked the cops into buying me breakfast."

"Of course you did."

"Let's get moving. Our time's short." Darla swung her backpack onto her shoulders and took the lead. "Jungle's this way."

"This isn't the same path we took before." Stephanie nervously searched the wooded area. "Is this route shorter?"

"I'm not certain of the exact distance. We've never covered the same course," Eric told her. "Which isn't a bad thing. We want to avoid the path we took last time in case those nasty guys with guns are waiting for us."

Soundlessly, they traipsed into the forest's untamed maze. Island winds eerily rustled the trees above. Their movements were sluggish, but once they cleared the brush, the path uncluttered, and the trip became easier. They rambled across the woodlands, then tracked across a tapered cut road heading into a smaller mountain range.

The road converted into an unsteady terrain, and

the elevation increased as they scaled the slopes. Stifling sun beat down as heat radiated off opaque rock. Muggy air clung to their skin, dampening their clothes until they were drenched in perspiration. Their progress slackened to a near standstill.

Finn wiped his forehead with his sleeve. "The heat's 'bout to melt me into a puddle of nothin'."

Darla swung her backpack off her shoulders. "I make a motion we take a break." She unzipped the top and began to dole out tepid bottles of water.

"I second." Stephanie took her bottle and sank to sit on a nearby rock.

Eric parked near the base of the mountain and inspected the primitive artery preceding upward as he guzzled his drink. "The other side of the island's maybe a mile off."

Finn moaned.

"The humidity isn't helping us. It's gonna get worse as we go farther in. We'll need to watch out for each other, health-wise."

"Hey, Eric." Finn leaned closer and lowered his voice. "Why are we doin' this?"

"Doin' what, Finn?"

"This hike from hell."

"We think Blaine is being held near the back of the island. We're gonna rescue him. But I already explained this to you."

"No, you didn't. And Blaine isn't on the backside."

"Yes, I did, and if he's not there, where is he?"

Finn pointed up the mountain. "In a cave on a mountain."

"Where did you come up with that idea?"

"I didn't come up with anything. The kidnappers

told me."

"Like in a dream?"

"No. After I paid the ransom."

"When you paid the what?"

"The ransom money."

"Altitude gettin' to you, Finn?" A wrinkle formed between Eric's brows. "You're flat broke, remember?"

"I was, but I'm not now. I created a project and got enough donations to pay off the kidnappers."

"Not following. Back up and explain."

"Those boxes in our bungalow? They're full of T-shirts."

"Pirates want cash, Finn, not shirts."

"I started the Save Blaine Campaign."

"Still confused. Go further back."

Finn rolled his eyes and moaned like Eric should understand. "I set up an online fundraiser, called the Save Blaine Campaign. I bought shirts wholesale for five bucks apiece, and printed Blaine's picture on the front. Whoever donated the equivalent of twenty-five American dollars or more, receives a T-shirt. Fans went wild. They want to help. Cash is flowing in from all over the world."

"You're serious?"

"Yeah. I paid the pirates last night."

Eric stared at Finn for what seemed like forever. He did appear rational, and he acted sincere. "That's fucking genius, Finn."

"I even got enough to repay Wilmington. And I compensated myself. Ten percent."

"Ten percent?"

"My idea. I did the work. I deserve compensation."

"How hard is it to sit behind a computer and type?"

"Harder than you imagine."

Eric took a minute to digest this information. Questions tumbled around in his brain. "Why didn't you tell us about your project sooner? We did ask what was in the boxes."

"Honestly? I figured you'd look at me like I was nuts and blow me off like always. I wanted to prove I could do it before I said anything."

A brief silence ensued.

"You're right, Finn. And I'm sorry. Your plan is brilliant, and I'm relieved we won't be in debt to the whole world the rest of our lives." Eric stopped. "Did you actually meet these pirates?"

"No. They gave me a drop off address. But they confirmed they had the money, then told me where I could pick up Blaine."

"In a cave. On a mountain."

Finn fished into his pocket, brought out a piece of paper, and unfolded it. "I found this under my door b'fore the cops came."

Eric took the page. A map. He studied the bearings. and glanced up at the mountain where they rested. "If I'm reading this right, we're here. This is the mountain." He gazed upward and squinted. "And there's the cave on the side."

"What are you two whispering about," Darla interrupted.

"Finn has done research on pirate kidnappings." Eric shot Finn a stern look and shook his head. "He believes Blaine might be in a cave." He pointed. "Like that one."

The women squinted at the tiny hole puncturing the mountain's rim.

Darla returned to Eric. Her expression appeared perplexed. "You want to check?"

"It can't hurt."

"Except it'll cost us time we don't have. If he's not in a cave, then we'll have to continue our search."

Eric considered his response before speaking. "Maybe we should split. Two climb and two hike to the other side of the island. That way we'll cover all bases."

He didn't like fibbing to Darla, especially since she realized he wasn't being truthful, and he'd pay for his discretion later. But in case Finn was being deceptive, he'd only harm Eric, and the women would be safe.

"Sounds like a solid plan." Darla watched him closely. "Who should go up and who should continue on?"

"Finn and I'll climb. You and Steph can search the other side of the island."

Darla crawled to her feet. "We'll meet here when we're done. Hopefully, one of us will have Blaine." She walked to Eric and slid off her sunglasses. She blinked at the bright sun, inspecting the horizontal strait. "Awfully steep. The slab is smooth, probably metamorphic."

His brows drew together.

"Means heat, pressure, or both changed the mass." She smiled, aiming a thumb at her chest. "Geologist."

"Thanks for the lesson."

"You have another lesson coming after this is over." She stared into his eyes. "One about not keeping secrets from your girlfriend."

"I'm aware."

"You'll explain once this is over."

He swiped a kiss across her lips and headed toward

the trail. "Later, luv."

"Eric."

He turned back to her.

"Come back alive and in one piece. Not a negotiation."

"Understood."

He and Finn began their climb. In the beginning, the passageway didn't appear treacherous, but the incline became more extreme as they advanced. The walkway developed into a natural stone staircase, only stairs didn't make their hike simpler. Instead their ascension was sharper and more challenging. Portions of the vertical winding rubble was dangerous and difficult to mount.

Each new trial emitted a groan from Finn. "I'm sweating bullets, and my feet're 'bout to fall off."

"Same here. Just focus on rescuing Blaine."

"I am." Finn slithered to a halt and rested against the side. Eric did the same. "Why didn't you tell Darla and Steph about the map?"

"Because they would insist on coming along. I'm guessing if we do find Blaine, he won't be alone."

"You mean pirates will be with him?"

"Possibly. And they may not be too friendly."

"They have their money."

"They're pirates, Finn. They're not exactly the honest upstanding type."

"You think they may double cross us?"

"Or they could ambush us."

"Might've been safer stayin' with the cops."

"I'm curious about something." Eric paused. "This T-shirt venture. You had no money to get it off the ground. Where'd you find the capital to purchase your inventory?"

"Credit card."

"You have a credit card?" A memory suddenly hit him. "You mean *my* credit card? The one you borrowed?"

"I used it for a good cause."

Mentally calculating, Eric staggered like a drunk as he restarted his climb. "Holy fuck, Finn, you had to've maxed out my credit limit."

"For Blaine."

"We'll discuss your business tactics and you paying yourself ten percent when this is over."

After two hours of scaling, they closed in on the cave's mouth. Carefully, Eric crept past the borders, while Finn hung back.

"See anything?" Finn whispered.

"Just dark."

"It's safe to enter."

Eric glimpsed over his shoulder.

"Gut feeling."

"Hope your gut's right."

He slithered around the perimeter and stopped. Finn followed and stood next to him. "Wow, what a difference. Feels like we're in a refrigerator."

They rested and allowed their eyes to adjust to the dimness. The interiors weren't as dark as first believed. Slivers of light beamed past minor cavities and revealed a divided channel.

Finn pointed in each direction. "Which way?"

"You're the one with the gut feelings, you tell me."

He tilted his head, aiming his nose high in the air. He squeezed his eyes shut and inhaled. "To the right."

Curving rightward, they trekked down a long

passage. Dagger-like stalagmites hung from the ceiling, and low-hanging stalactites sliced the ground on either side. Their footpath dissolved into a massive opening, sporting a six-meter ledge. At the threshold was a straight drop into an obscure blackness. A narrow foot width ridge was the only link to the other side.

Finn gazed into the black hole. "I might've misjudged."

"Can't be perfect every time. Let's try door number two." Eric spun to leave.

Finn snatched his arm. "My intuition wasn't wrong." He signaled across the thin formation.

Eric pivoted. His chest constricted, and his heart collided painfully into his ribcage as he viewed the dreaded scene across the way.

Attached to a boulder, bounded, and gagged on the other side, hung a lifeless Blaine.

Chapter 19

Eric stared past the natural sandstone arch. Kidnappers had a blindfolded Blaine somehow pinned to the wall. A thick sliver of tape covered his mouth, and ropes entwined his wrists and ankles. His chin touched his chest like he was asleep or...

"He isn't movin'."

"I see that." Finn squinted. "He's alive, right?"

"Dunno." Eric stood near the brink of the cavity and extended his torso across. He performed a mini fist pump. "Yesss. Fingers on his left hand wiggled."

Finn strolled up and leaned in. An elbow speared into Eric's spine.

Eric stumbled forward, teetering toward the canyon's edge, centimeters from plummeting into the black hole. His heart battered against his sore ribcage. Balancing on tiptoe, his arms flailed to oppose gravity's sturdy pull.

"Finn," he yelled, relieved his vocal cords functioned.

Finn flinched, but his attention didn't stray away from Blaine. Another moment passed.

"Finn," Eric desperately pleaded.

Finn spun toward him. A gasped escaped. Snatching a belt loop, he swung Eric backward a second prior to a fateful tumble. The momentum lifted Eric's feet off the ground. Gravity pulled him downward. He crashed onto the floor and landed on his spine. Arms spread out to his sides, he lay motionless on the cold, stone surface.

Finn stood over him with his hands on his hips. "You gotta be more careful, man. Y' almost went over."

Eric rose in a jerky, sluggish motion until he was sitting. "Yeah, *I* gotta be careful."

Suspicion escalated. Was the poke an accident or coincidence? Up until this point, Finn appeared to be truthful, although how could he be sure? He couldn't. Eric let his guard down, but that wouldn't be happening again.

Slowly, he crawled to his feet.

Finn's attention had returned to Blaine, whose hands wildly flapped. "Is he trying to tell us something?"

"Probably hello and good-bye."

"Good-bye?"

Eric waved at the extension within the gorge. "Chances are we'll plunge to our death trying to get across. He's saying so long."

"Then maybe only one of us should go."

"Why one?"

"If we both fall, nobody'll rescue Blaine."

"Darla and Steph are smart women. They'll figure it out."

"Blaine's in bad shape. Might be too late. If you don't make it across, I can go down and bring in professionals." He paused and cleared his throat. "Which we might oughta do anyway."

"Let me remind you, any expert in the vicinity is tied to the law, and the law intends to throw my ass in jail. Or worse."

"Darla's ex's acquainted with the right people. He might have better luck if we ask 'im to help."

"No way. He's an asshole. I'd rather distance our association."

"He seems like a stand-up guy. Plus he's always supported us financially."

"So he can reunite with his former girlfriend."

"He's not the only ex wanting to reunite with her." Finn cackled. "And from where I'm sitting, you're winnin'."

Eric's jaw tensed. While he was thrilled about him and Darla reconciling, he wasn't ready to share details, particularly with Finn.

Besides, they had to keep their focus and figure out how to release Blaine. "It's gonna take both of us to get him down. We can attempt to cross one at a time if it makes you feel better, but we each have to go."

"I had lots of ear infections as a kid. My equilibrium's always off. I'll drop like the Times Square ball on New Year's after the first step."

"Then you'll need to stay on double alert. To save time and keep from arguing, I'll lead, but you're coming, too." He marched to the rim. "Let's get this over with."

His attention was drawn to the terrifying abyss below. A shudder passed through him.

Conditions had been hazardous since his plane touched down on the island's runway. He'd been near death daily. Nevertheless, heights made him queasy, and this frightened him more than having a gun pointed at his head. At the moment, better odds were on surviving a bullet.

He forced his gaze forward and took several deep breaths in preparation to walk a high wire without a net. He raised his left leg.

"Don't look down."

Lowering his limb, he sighed and glimpsed over his shoulder. "Thanks Finn. That's sound advice."

"Better yet, shut your eyes."

"Shut my eyes? How the hell will I see?"

"Trust your instincts. Feel your way."

"Be feeling m' way to angels if I listen to you," Eric mumbled, then instructed in a louder voice. "You're distracting me. Don't say another word until I'm across."

His heart pounded as he took a shaky step onto a ledge that wasn't much wider than his shoe. Arms held straight out, he carefully placed one foot in front of the other, heel to toe, swaying slightly with each step. His nerve endings squeezed tighter the farther he paced.

Concentration remained centered on his waiting comrade. He refused another glance downward. If he did, vertigo would kick in, and he'd plunge into obscurity.

Gradually, he closed in on solid ground. Mere meters separated him from safety. He longed to hurry but restrained his urges. Down to three steps, two, and one, then the ball of his foot touched a secure firmness. Eric didn't think about what he just accomplished or bask in his relief. If he spent too much time pondering, he'd probably faint.

Instead, he rushed to Blaine, knelt, and immediately began to unknot the thick twine around his left wrist.

Blaine garbled. Eric stood. Blaine pressed the back

of his head into the rock wall behind.

"Oh yeah. You bet." Eric removed the blindfold and tossed the dirty fabric over the ridge and into the bottomless pit. He snatched the corner of duct tape covering Blaine's mouth and ripped it off.

"Son of a bitch," Blaine shouted. "Could you be a little rougher?"

"Nice to see you, too, mate." Eric laughed, relieved to see Blaine maintained his spirit. "Finn, ya comin'? Be needing a spare pair of hands in a minute."

Finn didn't budge.

"Cm'on, Finn. Shut your eyes and feel your way."

A loud, guttural shriek filled the cave. Eric winced and turned toward Finn.

Finn had backed into the far wall, flattening himself against the rock. He screamed again, simultaneously taking off in a full run.

Eric opened his mouth to stop him, but he was too late. Finn sprinted over the ridge and skidded to a halt. He sauntered to them like it was no big deal.

Eric and Blaine exchanged looks. Eric shrugged and went back to work.

Once untied, the duo hoisted Blaine over the hook, and lowered him, settling him onto his feet. He toppled to the ground. Eric clutched him under an armpit, while Finn held onto the other, helping him stand.

Blaine's complexion reddened. "Haven't used my legs since...not sure how long I've been hanging round here."

"Today is day eleven."

"Can't believe I lasted that long." Once again, he attempted to walk, but grabbed onto Eric, who held him upright. "How'd you find me?"

"Pure accident, and it's a long, horrible story. I'll explain when this is over. Let's get you to your bride."

Blaine's limp body braced. "Stephanie? She's here? Is she upset?"

"She has her moments." Eric grinned. "She's on the island. She'll be fine once she knows you're okay. You ready to see her?"

Blaine beamed and nodded.

"Eric." Finn spoke up. "Blaine can't walk without help. How will the three of us get over that tiny arch?"

Eric scratched his head. "Dunno, but we won't be runnin' across, that's for sure."

"There's an easier route." Blaine aimed a forefinger at an undersized opening no one would detect unless they were aware of its existence. "There's a tunnel. It's safer."

Finn studied the opening. "I vote for safer."

"Safer it is." Eric took a step then froze. "Wait a second. Could we have come in that way instead of doing the tightrope act over the ridge of death?"

"I can't say for certain, but that's the direction the voices came from when my kidnappers checked on me."

Eric glared at Finn. "So much for your intuition. If we'd turned left, we would've walked right up to Blaine."

"My intuition is just fine. I led you to him, didn't I?"

Another argument to save for later. They needed to hurry and leave in case unwelcomed company arrived.

They hoisted Blaine to his feet, did a pinwheel turn, and carried him toward the alternate course.

Inside the tunnel was dark. Twisty curves came out

of nowhere, inducing run-ins with the rock's hard walls. Damp floors made balancing difficult, and the air was brittle and thin, making breathing a strenuous exercise.

"Can we stop a minute?" Finn wheezed.

Eric wanted to escape this island, but he had to admit he was exhausted, too.

He lowered Blaine to his feet. "Five minutes."

They rested in a rare, but dimly lit space. Eric and Blaine stood, using the side as a perch. Finn squatted and lobbed a pebble from one palm to the other.

"How'd they abduct you?" Finn asked Blaine.

"Don't recall. I was knocked unconscious."

Finn shook his head. "Sucks you were kidnapped on your wedding day."

"No joke."

"Did you ever get a look at the pirates?"

"There were no pirates."

Eric shoved off the wall. "No pirates?"

"No. Two guys came to visit me regularly. I think one was my abductor. Huge guy, powerful, strong. He had a strange accent."

"Interesting." Though Eric was confused. Blaine had described Auster. "We were told a band of pirates took you. The hotel manager even showed us their calling card with the ransom demands on the back. We've been communicating with them since you went missing."

"You paid a ransom? With what?"

"Another long story, and I'll tell everyone everything once we're out of here."

"Well, I dunno who you paid, but I can guarantee it wasn't pirates. The other guy, the leader, was American. Pirates wouldn't allow someone from the

U.S. to join their forces, especially in this region."

Eric contemplated. Fragments of the past eleven days reeled through his mind. Some pieces of the puzzle were beginning to fit. "I gotta find Darla." He looped his arm through Blaine's. "Let's move."

"Darla?" Blaine's brows dipped. "Didn't you say to never speak her name in front of you again?"

"Fate's funny."

Finn laughed. "Competition's funnier."

"Finn, I swear—"

A soft rumble reverberated from above. The trio froze. The floor beneath their feet trembled. Snaps and pops splayed as cracks formed and spread through the rock on either side. Bits of rubble pelted their skin.

Finn inspected the boulders overhead. "Earthquake?"

"Dunno what's happenin', but I'd say it isn't good."

The low growl quickly expanded into a roar. An earsplitting eruption thundered above. More rock, larger chunks rained upon them.

Eric gazed upward. "The mountain's collapsing on top of us," he shouted. Without hesitation he and Blaine started down the path. "We gotta go now. Run, Finn, run."

****

"Shouldn't we start?" Stephanie stared at Darla who watched Eric and Finn scale the final link up the mountainside.

"Huh?"

"Shouldn't we leave now? We still have a ways to go."

Darla stood in silence until the men were out of

sight. "We need to follow them."

"But Eric said—"

"Eric's lying."

Stephanie's head snapped around. "He's what?"

"Not telling the truth. I don't know why." She swung her backpack onto her back. A foot lifted and stepped onto the rocky path. "But I aim to find out."

Stephanie pointed to the dot, pinpointing the cave's height and distance. "They're keeping Blaine from me, aren't they?"

"Maybe they want to make sure he's okay before you reunite."

Stephanie seemed to buy her explanation. She followed Darla and hoisted onto the mountain's crest. Gradually, they scrambled up the dense trail. Both concentrated on the climb and didn't engage in much conversation.

"Darla, Stephanie."

The women halted and peered over the rim. Stephanie frowned. "Morgan?"

"Seems so."

"That's weird. Why is he here?"

"Good question." Darla sighed, not quite understanding Morgan's appearance. They were a fourth of the way up, but to avoid any awkward questions, they needed to turn back. "We better go see."

The women spun and hastily headed down. Darla slipped in front of Stephanie once they reached the bottom. "Don't tell him the guys are in the cave," she murmured as she passed.

Morgan approached them. "Aren't you supposed to be looking for Blaine instead of rock climbing?"

"We're using the height to check our bearings."

Darla flicked a curious gaze his way. "What are you doing here?"

"You mentioned you and Eric planned to search for Blaine. Thought I'd join the hunt."

"Oh…that's not necessary." She twirled a ringlet around her finger tight. "I'm sure we've got this."

"The more involved the better, right?" Morgan smiled. "Plus, I have news. I may have located a pirate hideout where Blaine could be stashed. I can show you where."

An anxious Stephanie shifted around Darla. "You know where pirates are holding Blaine?" She rushed to Morgan. "What are we waiting for?"

"Um, Steph," Darla began, but Stephanie ignored her and swiftly disappeared into the brush.

Morgan waved a hand. "Come on, Dar."

Uneasiness crawled up her spine. She didn't want to leave. Blaine was in that cave, and so was Eric and Finn. She planned to discover why his whereabouts was suddenly a loosely kept secret.

But her choices were to go with Morgan and Stephanie, who was already five lengths ahead or expose Eric. Though she didn't understand her reluctance to reveal Eric's whereabouts, she went with her gut feeling. She moved forward, falling into step with Morgan.

"Where is Eric, by the way? I figured he'd be on Blaine's rescue team or at least acting as your personal bodyguard."

She disregarded his flippancy, deeming a correction not worth the effort. "We split up to save time. He and Finn are checking another area."

A low growl began to roll inside the earth. The

ground trembled. Darla halted and gazed at the sand pulsating beneath her sneakers.

"Darla." Morgan took her elbow. "We have to go. It's not safe here."

Stephanie reappeared. "What's that noise? Why is everything shaking?"

A deafening blast erupted. Darla turned toward the sound and gasped. Black fog covered the mountain's peak. Rocks and dirt tumbled down the sides and bits of debris showered over them.

Darla swallowed the gigantic lump in her throat as she stared at the instant mass of destruction. No one could've survived the blast. Eric—she couldn't allow herself to fall apart. They wouldn't survive either if they didn't move.

She swept past Morgan and snatched her friend's hand. "Hurry, Steph."

"But what about…"

"We have to leave."

They darted through the forest dodging one catastrophe after another. Heavy branches from standing trees snapped and cracked, then plummeted to the ground. Weaker trees shimmied and cracked, toppling onto their sides.

Creatures scuttled about, searching to find shelter. Sections of earth parted, forming deep crevasses. Water rapidly filled the fractures.

Darla forced her mind to remain blank. She couldn't allow herself to consider what happened to Eric, Finn, and possibly Blaine.

But what would cause a mountain to detonate? It wasn't a volcano. No gasses were involved. The only way it would have blown up is if someone…she skidded to a halt.

Morgan stopped behind her. She spun to him. Surely not. She had to be wrong. Except who else had the ability and the means to blow up a mountain.

"You," she accused "You did this?" Morgan stood motionless. He didn't respond, but he didn't need to. His veiled expression told her she was right. "But why?"

"Firework shows don't pay enough to maintain my lifestyle."

"Your family's wealthy. Extremely. Why would you need to…?"

"When my wife split, so did my trust fund. My parents put in a clause. To keep money coming in, she and I had to be married for five years. That didn't happen, so my cash flow ceased. The pyrotechnics business is all I have."

She glanced at the mountain. "You knew Eric was in the cave."

"Of course, I knew. I sent Finn a map with directions to find Blaine."

Darla shuddered. She did her best to shove aside the implication because she wanted answers. "Why did you want Eric dead?"

Morgan chuckled. "I hate to admit this, but Eric's a pretty sharp guy. He doesn't immediately trust or blindly accept. He asked questions, and he digs for answers. He doesn't let up. He was especially suspicious of me. Couldn't have him investigating me. He could've ruined everything."

Stephanie leaped between her and Morgan. "You're a pirate? Did you kidnap Blaine, too?"

"Sorry Steph. Business is business. And no, I'm

not a pirate. I just pretend to be."

"Kidnapping is business?"

"I have a lot of employees on my payroll. I pay them well, so they'll continue to work for me."

"I don't get it. Why did you loan us the initial ransom money?"

"So he could steal it, then double and triple the amount. That's how he profits," Darla interjected.

Once again, Morgan didn't reply.

"This was all for nothing." Stephanie attempted to swallow her tears. "You didn't get a dime from us."

Morgan closed the distance between him and the women. "Enough chit chat." He stepped behind Darla and slipped her backpack off her shoulders.

"No…" she snatched the air as he held it above her head.

"No as in no guns, Dar." He hung the strap over a shoulder, saluted, then circled around and headed toward an intact wooded area.

"You're just going to leave us," Stephanie yelled.

Morgan spun and faced them. "I wasn't. But now you know. I can't allow my friends and family to find out."

"But aren't you in love with Darla?"

"He loves money more, Steph. He proved that four years ago." Darla rose to her tippy toes hoping to find an opening. "We have to follow him. He knows the way out of here. And we don't."

The friends viewed the destruction. Landslides tumbled across the jungle, shattering all in its wake. Gray vapors rose and smothered the air. A solid wall of boulders and soil headed straight toward them.

Stephanie gazed at Darla. "We're not going to

make it, are we?"

"As long as we're here, we have a chance."

"Is Blaine here? Eric? Finn?"

Darla bit her bottom lip and shook her head. "I doubt it. Superman couldn't survive that blast." She snatched Stephanie's wrist and tugged. "Come on. The island will be overrun soon. Us dying won't bring them back."

Stephanie allowed Darla to lead her away. Except Darla didn't know where to go. The direction Morgan went was already covered with debris and smoke.

"Darla," came a shout above the tumbling rubble. "Darla, Stephanie, where are you?"

Darla and Stephanie exchanged a surprised look.

"Eric?" Darla blinked away her sudden tears of relief. "Eric. We're over here."

Within seconds, a dust covered Eric fought his way out of a pile of fallen branches and trees. Darla released Stephanie and sprinted to him. He caught her in a quick embrace.

"We gotta go, luv."

"But which way?"

He took her hand and grasped Stephanie's arm. "Stay with me."

The trio sprinted past turmoil and ruins. Darla tried to keep her focus on escaping, but it was difficult to disregard the senseless devastation. Even if humans didn't live in this vicinity, the damage would affect the island's ecosystem many years. Sad. Greed destroyed so much.

"We're almost there." Eric puffed. "The dock is around the corner and a little farther up the shore."

He guided them past the curve and skidded to a

stop. Morgan emerged from the thick haze.

"Shit."

"You must be part cat." Morgan held Darla's pistol in both hands, aiming it at Eric's forehead. "But life number nine is about to come to an end."

Eric backstepped and motioned for Darla and Stephanie to get behind him. "I figured it was you. You've been playing us all along."

Morgan smiled at Darla, who remained by Eric's side. "Didn't I tell you he was too smart for his own good?"

"This is between you and me, Wilmington. You got your payoff, now let the women go."

"Sorry, friend. No can do. They know too much." He edged toward them. The gun barrel still directed at Eric. "I'll let you be the gentleman, though." The trigger eased back. "You can be the first to die."

Without warning, Morgan's feet left the ground. He did a half flip and landed with a forceful thump.

Dusting his hands, Finn stepped around him as he lay still in the dirt. "Time to shut him and his nasty business down."

Darla's gaze seesawed between Eric and Finn. "What just happened?"

Eric kneeled, placing two fingers on Morgan's wrists. "Finn's studied martial arts for years. He's earned many degreed blackbelts and won tons of tournaments. I'd say this is his biggest win yet."

"Wow, Finn. I'm impressed."

"Me too," Eric agreed. "You saved every one of us. We owe you big time."

Finn's chin dropped, but not so far that he covered his smile.

Stephanie bounced on her toes. "Thank you for helping us, Finn, but I need to know something. Did you find Blaine and is he okay?"

"We did." Eric stood and pointed at the boat bobbing in the waves. "And he's waiting for you."

Chapter 20

"I now pronounce you husband and wife." A roar emitted from a tiny crowd surrounding the newlyweds. The preacher beamed at the happy couple. "By all means, Blaine, kiss your bride."

Darla blinked away her tears of joy. Her friends had certainly leaped a lot of high hurdles to reach this moment, but they finally achieved wedded bliss.

Her attention drifted past the smooching twosome. Eric stood at Blaine's side. His hands were rigidly in front of him, but his eyes sparkled when their gazes met.

Once the bride and groom finished their first kiss, guests hurried to offer their congratulations.

Darla stepped off the dais at the same moment as Eric left his spot. They circled the invitees, meeting in the middle.

He grasped her hands in his and gave her a peck on the cheek. "You look beautiful."

Murmuring a demure, "thank you," she felt her skin heat, although she couldn't fathom why.

"Not a lot of people can pull off such a bright blue."

"So not my color, is it?"

He looped an arm through hers, guiding her farther away from the excitement. They strolled arm and arm out of the sanctuary's backdoor.

"Quite a day."

"The ceremony was beautiful." She inhaled and smiled. "Not a single hitch."

The nuptials occurred in a miniature, clapboard, one-hundred-plus year-old church. Lovely, stained glass windows filtered in the afternoon light. A mile-high steeple and a breathtaking mountain range set as the backdrop added to its charm.

"Yeah. They deserved to have everything go right after what they've been through." Eric grinned. "So how have you been? Have you recovered from the worst vacation of the century?"

This was the first time they'd been together in two weeks. Once they returned to the island, Eric and Finn immediately boarded a plane and flew home to California. Darla, Blaine, and Stephanie stayed to speak to authorities.

After, Darla traveled to Stephanie's family home in Montana to assist in arranging an impromptu wedding. Eric had arrived that morning.

"Honestly, I haven't had time. Steph's kept me hopping with wedding tasks."

He brushed a kiss across her forehead. "Poor you."

"Did you take care of your business at home?"

"I did." An evil grin spread across his face. "I made a few phone calls, too."

"You did? To who?"

"Ummm…let's see, the United States Navy."

"The Navy?"

"Yep. Though Morgan says he isn't a pirate, his tactics are in line with how pirates operate. The officer I spoke to agreed. They've begun an investigation. I also contacted a watchdog group who monitors criminal activity overseas and investigates police corruption. They are very interested in the island's unethical practices and are looking into it."

"Wow, you were busy. I'm impressed." Darla kicked off her heels and scooped them off the grass. "Anyone else?"

"The Justice Department. I reported Blaine's kidnapping. I also informed them about the attempts on yours, Steph's, and my life. They'll be in touch, too."

"You covered almost all the bases."

"It's the least I could do since the authorities weren't interested in punishing Wilmington on Tluq Cay."

"He was paying them to look the other way or do his dirty work," she commented with a tone of disgust.

Darla, Blaine, and Stephanie had taken a groggy Morgan to the police. Blaine relayed his experience, receiving an indifferent response. They didn't blink an eye after Darla informed them about the island's destruction or the many attempts on Eric's and the other's lives. Authorities released Morgan before the group's plane left the islands.

"I made a phone call, too," she told him.

"To who?"

She flashed a wide smile. "Morgan's parents."

Eric tossed back his head and laughed. "Are they pleased how their golden boy's earning a living?"

"The Wilmington family aren't opposed to underhandedness when it comes to making additional cash, though they tend to stay within the lines of legalities." She paused. "Only to avoid negative press."

"Mummy and daddy give any hints how they're going to deal with their baby's bad behavior?"

"Nope. And I don't care. I'm just glad it's over, and we're all okay." They stopped walking. Darla dropped her shoes, stepped in front of him, and slid her palms up his chest. "This is such a happy day. Can we not talk about Morgan?"

He wrapped his arms around her waist and brought her closer, murmuring into her soft curls. "We never have to mention his name again."

"Hey, Eric."

He exhaled and slackened his hold. Finn lumbered their way. A tall, slender woman strolled by his side.

"I wanted to ask you about Finn's new friend," Darla whispered. "Who is she, and where did she come from?"

"That's Lola. Finn's new girlfriend. She's a bartender from Tluq Cay. She flew to California with us."

"Wow. He works fast."

"Probably helps they can't communicate. She speaks French, and Finn talks crazy. Perfect match, eh?" A crease formed across his forehead. "Y' know, I'm almost certain I paid for her ticket to fly stateside. I think I bought the outfit she's wearing, too."

"Pretty dress. Why are you buying Finn's date new stuff?"

"I loaned him my credit card in Tluq Cay. He's never returned it, and I'm sure he's using it to impress his lady."

"You're a nice man." She elevated to her tiptoes and gave him a quick kiss. "Give him an option. Either he returns the card, or you'll close the account."

"No choice. I'm closing the account." He rotated to an approaching Finn. "Whatcha need, Finn?"

"You think the minister will marry us?"

"Marry you?" Eric's voice raised. "When?"

"Today. We want to make things official as soon as possible."

"Didn't you just meet?"

"We've known each other almost a month." Finn and Lola exchanged loving glances. "Why wait when it's right?"

"Um, I guess so." Eric pressed his lips to Darla's ear. "Can you take over? I got nothing."

"I'm on it." She stepped forward. "I'm excited you found each other, Finn. You make an attractive pair. I'm sure the pastor would be thrilled to perform your ceremony, but legalities have to be taken care of before you can get married. You know, like a license?"

"Man, I forgot about the whole licensing thing. Lola's gonna be disappointed."

Darla nodded at Lola. She introduced herself, then repeated the conversation in Lola's native language. They chatted briefly, then Darla spoke to Finn. "She's fine with waiting until you meet the legal requirements. I also get the impression she would rather have her own day instead of sharing it with someone else."

"Most women probably feel that way. And she'll have whatever she wants. Thanks, Darla. See ya at the reception." He spun away and led his girlfriend to a waiting limo.

"Does Lola understand what she's agreed to?" Eric asked, once they were out of earshot.

"She gets it."

"I wish her luck. She'll need it."

"Finn deserves love and happiness, too."

"Speaking of love." He took her hand, brought it to

his lips and grazed the top. "I love you."

"And I love you."

"Are we completely done with our fight?"

"We each told our side, apologized, and we've, um…"

A corner of his mouth lifted. "True, but sex's never been a problem for us."

"What exactly are you wanting to know?"

He hesitated. "You still interested in movin' in?"

"You're serious?"

"I only have one stipulation."

"A stipulation?"

His hand dipped into his jacket pocket. He brought out a small, blue box. He opened the lid. "You have to wear this."

Darla gasped. "Eric, it's gorgeous."

He sank to a knee. "Darla Hennessey. Will you do me the honor of becoming my wife?" He cleared his throat. "Notice this proposal comes without a prenup."

"I get the need for a prenup, and I've changed my attitude. I'm not opposed to signing one."

"Great luv, but that's not the question I want an answer to."

"Oh." There was a brief hesitation. "That should be a given."

"I'd like to hear it if you don't mind. Some excitement in your reply would be nice, too."

She threw her arms around his neck, knocking him off balance. "Yes, yes, yes, I'll marry you." They laughed and tumbled to the ground.

"You need to save those yeses for a more private celebration, luv."

"No worries. I've stored up a lot of yeses since

we've been apart."

The blue in his eyes deepened. "Wanna give me a yes now? I'll pretend I left something in my hotel room and our driver can make a quick stop."

"We're supposed to be at our best friend's wedding reception."

"We just got engaged." Eric stood, helping Darla to her feet. He gathered her into his arms and swiped a kiss across her mouth. "They'll understand if we're a little late."

A word about the author...

I'm Debra and I write romantic/suspense novels, with a bit of steam and a lot of fun. Creating stories is my passion. My favorite days are when I can tune out the universe, huddle over my laptop, and let my imagination go wild.

More of my loves. My kids—I am the proud mom of two, Stephen and Hannah. I'm also a proud mother-in-law to Astrid and Ryan. I'm a huge animal lover and am "mom" to a houseful of adopted fur-babies. Animals know that when they show up at my house they have a forever home. And Texas—I'm a lifetime Texan. Born in Waco, I grew up in a small town south of the city. In my early 20s, I left and lived in different areas within the state. Twenty-eight years later, I happily returned home. I hope to have one more move in me. My dream is to live by the ocean, sit on the deck with a glass of wine, and write. More loves: Mexican food, my flower beds, painting, photography, travel, shopping… Oh, yeah, and chocolate. Lots of chocolate.

Bucket List accomplishments. In my 40s, I did something I'd always wanted to do: returned to school to further my education. I received my bachelor's degree in 2011. My day job is working in the education system, teaching special needs children.

Writing. I received my first publishing contract with The Wild Rose Press in 2013, and my initial release debuted in September the same year. I'm an active member of the Central Texas Romance Writers of America Chapter, and I serve as secretary of the group.

Contact me at: debrajupe@gmail.com